The Payback

Book 3 in the Clarke Pettis Series

Christine Pattle

Chapter 1

Clarke Pettis wriggled into her dress in the cramped changing room, knocking over her handbag and spilling half its contents onto the floor. She pulled up the zip as far as she could reach before bending down carefully to retrieve everything, trying not to let the pristine white satin brush against the floor.

She quickly stuffed her purse and phone safely back in her bag, followed by a scarf, a pair of gloves, and a used concert ticket from last week. The remaining item, a folded piece of paper, stared at her defiantly, daring her to leave it on the floor and walk away. She picked it up by one corner with two fingers, as if it might burn a hole in her hand, and dropped it into her handbag before changing her mind and pushing it firmly down to the bottom of the bag.

"Is everything ok? Come on out so I can admire you," Clarke's mother, Diana, called through the door.

Clarke composed herself and walked out into the shop.

"Wow! You look stunning," her mother said excitedly. "I've been dying to see the dress all week."

Clarke stared in the full-length mirror. For once, her appearance really pleased her. She wanted an understated wedding dress, something classic and elegant, avoiding at all costs any resemblance to a meringue. The lovely white satin dress that clung to her body and showed off her figure fit the bill perfectly. Best of all, the wide half sleeves covered her well-muscled swimmer's shoulders. She absolutely loved it.

"It needs taking in slightly," she said to the assistant.

"Of course." The assistant checked the fit and pinned a couple of small tucks in the dress. "We'll have it ready for you on Monday."

"The wedding's next Saturday," Diana reminded her, then turned to Clarke. "Why don't we go for a coffee?"

Clarke smiled. Right now, she craved a nice strong cup of coffee.

1

"What's the matter?" her mum asked as they sat in the coffee shop. "You're very quiet today."

"I've got things on my mind, that's all."

"Is it the wedding? You're not having second thoughts, I hope?"

"No, absolutely not. Well, slight nerves, perhaps, but not second thoughts." She loved Paul and no longer doubted that this would be forever.

"That's a relief," her mother said, "since I've already paid for the dress." She laughed. "So, what is it?"

Clarke replied in one word, "Tammy."

"Tammy? What about Tammy?" Diana looked worried.

"Evan wants me to visit her in prison." She'd been having serious misgivings about the idea ever since Evan Davies, her manager at Tebbit & Cranshaw, the firm of forensic accountants who Clarke now worked for, had suggested it. And, in the last two years since Tammy got arrested and then convicted, she'd managed to avoid visiting. "I received a visiting order this morning." At this very moment, it was burning a hole in the bottom of her handbag. She dreaded seeing Tammy again.

"Is that any of Evan's business?" Diana asked.

"Tebbit & Cranshaw has been asked to trace the money Tammy stole from Briar Holman." When she said Tebbit & Cranshaw, she actually meant *herself*. She had been asked as, in this particular case, *she* was the big attraction. The management at Briar Holman knew of Clarke's history with Tammy Doncaster from when they both worked for the company. Clearly, they assumed she stood a better chance of getting the money back than anyone. Clarke was a lot less sure of that premise than they were.

"They assume if I talk to her, she might tell me where she's hidden the money."

"Fat chance of that, from what I've heard of Tammy," her mother said. "It's three million pounds. She won't give that back in a hurry."

"I completely agree. Tammy won't tell me anything. She fed me a pack of lies before, didn't she? Why would she tell the truth now?"

"Evan shouldn't be asking you to do it."

"Evan's not putting any pressure on me." But Clarke fully realised how much he wanted her to do it, which did pile on the pressure. "What should I do? I still feel guilty that I helped get her convicted, and even guiltier about not bothering to visit in two years. She was meant to be my friend."

"Friends don't lie like she did, and they certainly don't attempt to kill you. You can't blame yourself for other people's mistakes."

"I know, but I can't help it."

Clarke worried about how difficult it would be to see Tammy again. She'd never actually visited anyone in prison, and it didn't sound as if it would be a pleasant experience. Surely prison would have changed her, probably not for the best. Clarke wouldn't blame her one bit for being bitter. Tammy killed a man, so she wouldn't get released anytime soon. That must be depressing, contemplating the many years stretching in front of her. Clarke wondered what she would say to her. What did you say to someone you'd put in prison when you wanted to get them on side so that they would tell you where they hid the money they embezzled? There were no words to make that happen.

Right now, the three million pounds Tammy stole probably languished in some private bank account on the other side of the world, waiting for her to be released from prison. She would want the money then. No way would she give it up now.

Tammy had endured a tough start to life. Occasionally, in moments of weakness, Clarke even considered that she might deserve the money to make up for her rubbish childhood. But life didn't work like that. Even if Clarke could half justify Tammy stealing the money, murder was unforgivable. A rough childhood would never provide an adequate excuse. Anyone with Tammy's intelligence understood the difference between right and wrong. She should never have done it.

But Clarke worried that Tammy would blame her for helping to get her convicted. She blamed herself, so of course Tammy would hold her responsible. It would be too harrowing to visit Tammy in prison. She really didn't want to go.

"I still need to finalise the seating plans for the wedding," Clarke said, eager to change the subject. "People keep forgetting to RSVP or they do it right at the last minute, not to mention the number of guests who suddenly decide they're on a special diet. They have no idea how difficult it is organising a wedding when you've got a full-time job."

"Darling, let me help you. You only have to ask," Diana said.

"I might take you up on that. It's getting stressful. And all I need now is this Tammy business on top of it!" Clarke sighed loudly.

"You don't have to visit her if you don't want to. Prison visiting isn't in your job description."

Clarke agreed with her mother. As a forensic accountant, visiting criminals wasn't in Clarke's remit at all. Tracing the money was, and if visiting Tammy proved the only way to get close to learning where she'd hidden it, how could she refuse? If Tammy dropped her only the tiniest little clue, perhaps she'd be able to unravel the complicated trail and locate the missing money.

And if Tammy let her guard down even for a second, she might give away that tiny clue Clarke needed. She laughed out loud.

"What's up?" Diana asked.

"Nothing." Tammy was so intelligent. What were the chances of Clarke actually outwitting her? Nil, and yet she managed to do it before. It hadn't been easy, but she did it. Under stress, which Tammy would be in prison, people made mistakes. With luck, Clarke might find that something. But it would need more than one visit to stand any hope of success, and the prospect of even one visit, let alone several, overwhelmed her. Did she even want to start the process if she may not be able to finish it and visit as many times as necessary to get the job done?

"I forgot to tell you," Diana said, "Auntie Fenella's coming to the wedding. I know she said she couldn't, but she's managed to get some time off. She's flying in from Australia. And as she is paying for the venue and the catering, you'll have to change the seating plan to fit her in."

Clarke nodded. "Yes, of course. We can shuffle things around a bit. It's not as if I've worked out the seating plan yet, anyway." Yet another job she needed to do. Organising a wedding was endless. She understood perfectly now why rich people hired wedding planners.

Auntie Fenella was Mum's sister and by far her favourite auntie. Childless herself, she treated her and Rob, Clarke's younger brother, as her own children. So naturally, when Clarke announced her engagement, Fenella volunteered to pay towards the wedding. Clarke never realised how expensive weddings could be, so she was enormously grateful to Auntie Fenella for paying for the reception. Mum bought the dress, and her brother was buying the cake. That ticked off all the important things. They agreed to economise slightly on other stuff, although Paul promised her a fabulous honeymoon trip. He stubbornly refused to give away the destination, but she secretly hoped for somewhere exotic. Wherever it turned out to be, it would be nice to spend so much time alone with Paul without his job getting in the way. She looked forward to being Mrs Waterford.

"What date is Auntie Fenella arriving?" It would be nice to catch up with her before the wedding, as Clarke and Paul would leave for their honeymoon first thing the following day. She didn't imagine she'd get time to talk properly at the reception.

"Oh, she's coming a couple of days before the wedding. I'll try to arrange for you both to meet her when she gets here. You can all come over for dinner."

"That would be great." Clarke couldn't wait to introduce her to Paul.

"I'll organise it," Diana said. "Anyway, perhaps you should visit Tammy. It might give you some closure. And then you can stop torturing yourself for putting her there."

"It might bring back a lot of horrible memories." Clarke would rather forget the entire experience.

"I don't honestly think it's going to make any difference to how much you remember, whether you visit or not. You haven't forgotten any of it, have you?"

"No."

"So, you may as well get some closure. You did the right thing. Now you need to stop worrying about it because none of this is your fault. It's perfect timing. Go before the wedding and get some closure on it. Then you can start your new life with Paul."

"You're probably right." Clarke decided to talk it over with Paul. He'd met Tammy, and he knew exactly what Clarke went through because he'd worked on the case. But her mother was wrong about getting closure. She would never shake off the awful memories of Tammy imprisoning her in a derelict flat and nearly killing her.

If she planned to take a trip down memory lane, perhaps she should visit their old colleagues at Briar Holman first. She hadn't been anywhere near their offices since she'd left her job there. Memories of Tammy kept her away. She wondered if any other of her old colleagues were affected in the same way, or if any of them ever visited Tammy. Somehow, she doubted either of these things.

She most needed to speak to Douglas Doncaster, Tammy's ex-husband. Predictably, he divorced Tammy as soon as she got convicted, but Clarke didn't blame him. Tammy had already left Douglas a few months before she got arrested, so divorce was always on the cards.

Douglas wasn't the most approachable of people, making Clarke even less keen to speak to him, but he may be able to point her in the right direction regarding where Tammy might have hidden the money. He may possess some tiny piece of information in the back of his mind that he didn't consider important, which might be a crucial part of the puzzle. And, although Clarke would bet that Douglas hadn't visited Tammy, he may have heard something. His solicitor must have visited her regarding the divorce. So, perhaps Douglas could tell her how Tammy was coping with prison and what to expect.

Yes, she should go back to Briar Holman. If she wanted closure, however impossible that might be, she needed to get closure on everything. It would be nice to see her old colleagues, Andrew and Ken, assuming they still worked for the company.

Clarke wondered how often the prison would allow her to visit, because her mum was right, it would be best to get it over with, and if she was only allocated one visit a fortnight that wouldn't give nearly enough time to extract any information from Tammy. It would take a long time to gain her confidence, for her to trust Clarke enough to tell her anything.

The whole idea was crazy, especially with Tammy being the biggest liar going. She fabricated stories and twisted the truth and would never reveal anything unless Clarke tricked her into it, which would be a difficult thing to do.

Chapter 2

Clarke walked up to the prison entrance, clutching her visiting order. She wasn't sure how she'd let Evan finally talk her into doing this. She already wished she hadn't come. What if Tammy didn't want to see her? Or what if she got nasty? Clarke would hardly blame her for that. After all, Clarke's testimony in court convicted Tammy. She suppressed the notion, trying not to blame herself. It was Tammy's fault. It was Tammy who stole the money, Tammy who murdered Bradley Acres. Tammy had only herself to blame. But, however much Clarke told herself all that, it didn't make her feel any less guilty.

A queue of visitors waited to go in.

"Who are you here for?" the blond woman standing in front of her asked.

"I'm visiting a friend." Clarke willed the queue to move faster so she didn't have to talk to the other visitors.

"I'm seeing my sister. She's in here for GBH, silly cow. My name's Rebecca. Call me Bex."

"Hi, Bex, nice to meet you." Clarke hesitated, unsure whether to give her name to this stranger. Bex smiled at her expectantly. She was only being friendly. Despite wanting to fade anonymously into the background, it would be rude of her not to answer. "I'm Clarke."

"Like Superman, Clark Kent?"

"No," Clarke said, not feeling very much like Superman. "There's an E on the end."

"Well, Clarke with an E on the end, you don't seem very happy," Bex said.

Clarke shrugged. "I don't really want to be here. I shouldn't have come."

"Hell, nobody *wants* to be here. I'm sure your friend will be pleased to see you. They always are. They never get enough contact with the outside world. That's why I keep forcing myself to come.

Linda's my sister. How can I not come? How can I leave her here and ignore her, however stupid she's been?"

Clarke smiled at Bex, who was obviously a much better person than her. Clarke contemplated running out on Tammy, even now. How awful must life be for Tammy? Perhaps her visit would help. "How long have you been coming here?" she asked Bex.

"Linda's been banged up for three years. If she behaves herself, she might get out early. But who knows what she's going to do then. She can't stay with me. My hubby would kill me." Bex scowled. "So, what did your friend do? Why is she in here?"

Clarke paused. She supposed it wouldn't do any harm to tell her. "She stole some money and murdered someone." Simply saying it out loud made her feel less guilty about the whole situation. It made it seem perfectly reasonable for Tammy to be locked up. Again, she reminded herself that Tammy was the guilty one, not her. All she was guilty of was finding out the truth.

"That's bad," Bex said. "I guess she'll be in for a long time. You'll be visiting a lot."

Clarke hoped not. "I'm only coming this time to test the water. She may not even want to see me again after today." Was that her biggest fear, that her old friend might actually send her away and tell her never to come back? Evan, her boss at Tebbit & Cranshaw, would be disappointed if she didn't get some answers to enable them to locate the missing money. She felt bad about that, too, using Tammy to further her career. She didn't come here today with any saintly aspirations of helping Tammy.

She wondered if Tammy got many visitors. Definitely not Douglas. What about Tammy's many friends? Perhaps some of them came, although when life became tough, you quickly found out who your real friends were. Clarke expected most of Tammy's friends would have disappeared instantly. Some of Clarke's so-called friends vanished pretty quickly after her accident, back when she served in the fire brigade. No one was sure then if she'd even walk again.

At least her best friend still remained true. Thank God for Gina. She became a tower of strength after the accident, especially when Paul walked out on her, unable to cope with things. That must be about six years ago. Clarke shook herself, trying to get rid of the bad memories. She loved Paul and was about to marry him. He'd grown up a lot since that dreadful time, and she didn't need any painful reminders of his past mistakes.

The queue shuffled further along as they let a few people at the front go inside. Clarke wondered how long this might take, as it threatened to rain at any moment. Yet again, she wished she hadn't come, but she was here now, so she may as well get on with it. If she didn't like it, she'd leave.

The queue dwindled faster than Clarke expected. They must suddenly have got more officers inside to process the visitors.

"I'm in," Bex said cheerfully. "See you later."

Clarke watched as, beyond the barrier, a prison officer patted down Bex and took her bag. Was prison visiting going to be that bad? They treated the visitors as if they were guilty, no better than criminals themselves. Probably some of them were. Clarke most definitely wasn't a criminal, but they would undoubtedly make her feel like one when her turn came to go in.

"Ok, you next." The prison officer opened up the barrier for Clarke to walk through. "Give us your bag."

Clarke handed it over reluctantly. The officer searched it and put it in a locker, returning to pat her down, checking for weapons or contraband being smuggled in. Why hadn't she brought anything for Tammy? She should have got her some cigarettes. Tammy didn't smoke, unless she'd taken it up since she'd been inside, but Clarke recalled watching TV programmes where prisoners used cigarettes as currency to swap for other things. Ironic that Tammy was three million pounds better off at the moment. And yet she probably couldn't even afford to buy a couple of little treats in prison. It served her right, Clarke reminded herself yet again. That's what she deserved.

As if she didn't already feel like a criminal herself, they took Clarke's photo and let the sniffer dog check her out. At last, she walked through a metal detector, then into the main part of the prison. The door slammed shut behind her. She shuddered, a deep fear of incarceration probably brought on by her final experience with Tammy. The entire building oozed despair, and the giant sense of foreboding about the visit threatened to overcome her. For a moment, she closed her eyes and took a deep breath in a futile attempt to calm herself. She'd left it too late to back out now.

Another prison officer showed a group of them into a room filled with tables. Prisoners in orange tabards sat at each table. There must have been about twenty of them. Mostly their visitors were already sitting opposite them, some of them having two or three visitors each. Four prison officers, one with a dog, patrolled among the tables, trying to spot signs of trouble. Clarke hoped there wouldn't be any.

Clarke surveyed the room, searching for Tammy. Her heart bashed out a rhythm that would have befit a drummer in a rock band. What terrified her so much about the prospect of meeting Tammy? Was it simply guilt? For a moment, she recalled those dark few days she spent with Tammy, imprisoned in that derelict flat.

Tammy had been violent. She fought with Clarke more than once and gave her some serious cuts and bruises. She'd been lucky not to have far worse injuries. She was lucky not to be dead.

Initially, she didn't recognise Tammy. Clarke drew a breath, horrified at Tammy's appearance. What happened to that glamorous, bright woman whom she used to work with? Tammy wore no makeup, making her dark skin seem almost pale. Her once glorious hair was twisted into short, greasy dreadlocks, and she'd lost a lot of weight. But the eyes were the worst. As Clarke got closer, she realised Tammy's eyes were blank.

Clarke tried to hide her shock. This woman was a shell of the person Clarke used to know. If Clarke felt guilty before she came here, it was nothing to what she experienced now, realising she had single-handedly destroyed Tammy. Why didn't she leave things alone when she still had the chance? Perhaps then Bradley Acres wouldn't have been murdered. That scenario had haunted her constantly over the last two years. Would Tammy be living it up in the Caribbean now with all the money if Clarke hadn't interfered? Would that really have done any harm? Clarke deleted the notion from her mind, admonishing herself for even thinking such nonsense. Tammy broke the law. She shouldn't be allowed to get away with it. Clarke wasn't responsible for that. For a second, she closed her eyes. In her head, her mum insisted it wasn't her fault. She took a deep breath and smiled.

"Hello, Tammy." Her voice came out raspy, as if she'd lost all powers of speech.

"What are you laughing at? And what are you even doing here? Why did you come?"

"I wanted to see you." The rapid-fire questions had caught Clarke off guard. She didn't know what else to say.

"Huh!" Tammy said, standing up. "After all this time? Why didn't you come when I first asked you? Did you get my letters?"

A prison officer immediately came over. "Sit down, Doncaster. Don't you go giving any trouble."

Tammy smiled briefly before turning it into a scowl. "Officer Hunter, when do I ever give you any trouble?" She sat down.

"Just don't," Officer Hunter said. She wiped her hand across her forehead.

Clarke was concerned about Tammy making the prison officer uncomfortable. Beads of sweat on her shaved head glinted under the harsh strip-lighting. Although she appeared to be a similar size to Tammy, well-matched in both height and weight, Clarke worried whether Officer Hunter would be able to protect her if Tammy got nasty. She reassured herself. There were three other officers and a dog in the room. Tammy wouldn't be able to do anything here.

Instinctively, Clarke curled her bad leg under the chair, hoping to keep it well out of the way in case Tammy got any ideas about attacking her and kicking it. Her old injury made her ankle her most vulnerable spot, and she didn't intend to risk aggravating it. Tammy could still do a lot of damage before any of the prison officers reached her. It would only take a couple of seconds. And why wouldn't she? After all, she killed Bradley Acres, who didn't do anything to deserve it. What would Tammy do to her, given the chance to get close enough? Had her anger been festering all this time she'd been in prison? Clarke tried to imagine how much Tammy must hate her now.

"So, did you get my letters?" Tammy repeated the question, louder and more adamantly this time.

"Yes," Clarke said, instantly wishing she'd lied and said she never received the letters after all. "I got some of them. I didn't read them all." Officer Hunter had moved away now, leaving Clarke vulnerable.

"Then you should have come before now."

Clarke guessed it would be a bad idea to tell Tammy she hadn't been able to face visiting her. "I didn't think you'd really want to see me. I wondered if you only wanted me to come so you could be horrible and blame me for everything."

"Too bloody right," Tammy said. "You could have got me out of that flat and let me go. I wanted you to rot in hell."

Clarke shook her head. If Tammy seriously believed that, she was delusional. It had been impossible to get her out, even if she'd wanted to. She'd been lucky to get herself out alive. And Tammy had conveniently forgotten who imprisoned who in the first place.

"I'm sorry." Clarke turned away to avoid meeting Tammy's eyes. Across the room, Bex looked up and smiled at her. Clarke tried to smile back.

"Right," Tammy snorted. "At least you're here now, but don't imagine we're friends. We're not."

"No."

"I suppose any visitor's better than no one. Tell me something nice. Are you still at Briar Holman? What's happening there?"

"I don't know," Clarke said. "I left. It wasn't the same without you. I got another job." Clarke didn't intend to tell Tammy where she worked now, in case she tracked her down. And she certainly didn't want Tammy to find out about her new career as a forensic accountant, specialising in investigating fraudulent activities. That would go down like a ton of bricks, and Tammy would get suspicious of her if she eventually plucked up enough courage to start questioning her about the money she'd stolen.

"Well, bully for you." Tammy spat out the words angrily. "Wish I could make a career change now."

"I haven't been back to Briar Holman since..."

"So, you've not seen Doug?" Tammy asked.

Clarke shook her head. She never really got on with Douglas Doncaster. As the assistant chief executive at Briar Holman, his path didn't cross much with hers. "I'm sorry you got divorced,"

"I'm not. Doug's a twat."

"I'm still sorry," Clarke said.

Officer Hunter stared pointedly in their direction. She pretended not to notice, relieved that someone was keeping an eye on Tammy.

"So, tell me something nice," Tammy said. "Something nice about the outside world. What am I missing?"

Clarke glanced up, reassured to spot a CCTV camera high up on the wall in front of her. She racked her brains, but her mind blanked.

Surely, Tammy read newspapers in prison. She must have some idea of world events. "It's raining," she said. She couldn't think of what else to say, not without giving away any personal details.

"I can see that. We do have some windows in here." She thumped her fist on the table. The prison officer looked over at them again but didn't move. "Aren't you doing anything nice? How's your love life?"

"I don't have one." No way would she admit to her impending wedding. She didn't want to give Tammy any chance to trash that plan. For a moment, Clarke wondered how she would ever manage to extract any useful information from Tammy, especially without being prepared to give anything back. She didn't want Tammy to find out anything about her.

"If you aren't going to tell me anything interesting, what's the point of coming?"

"What about you?" Clarke asked, knowing she needed to salvage the situation before Tammy completely clammed up. "Do you get any visitors? I'm sure I can't be the only one to come." Which of her dozens of friends were still in touch?

"Huh," Tammy said. "It's funny how so-called friends disappear at the slightest sign of trouble. That includes you too, Clarke, in case you're wondering."

"I'm sorry, but it was different for me, under the circumstances." A few minutes ago, Tammy had insisted they weren't friends. Why would Tammy expect her to visit after everything that happened? She didn't even understand herself why she came. Did she have to spell out to Tammy that she had nearly killed her in that block of flats? No doubt Tammy would twist that to be Clarke's fault. For all of Tammy's shortcomings, Clarke would never criticise her story-telling ability.

"If you must know, Katie and Ned visit regularly. But they have to travel from Dorset, and they can't leave the farm for long, so they don't come as often as they'd like." Tammy got to her feet again.

"Officer Hunter!" she called across the room.

The prison officer immediately walked towards them. "Are you causing trouble again, Doncaster?"

Tammy scowled at her. "I want to go back to my cell," she announced. "And *she* needs to leave." She pointed angrily at Clarke.

"Tammy, I'm sorry."

"What's the problem?" Another officer came over. "You'd better not be causing trouble again, Doncaster."

"Take me back to my cell," Tammy said petulantly.

"Well, you can't. You'll have to sit there until visiting's over. Then you can go back with the others."

"I can take her," Officer Hunter said, "if you can manage without me for a few minutes. She'll be more trouble than she's worth if we make her stay here."

Officer Hunter led Tammy towards the exit. Clarke watched her go, wondering if she should make her own way out or wait for someone to escort her. She doubted she'd be able to negotiate the prison's tight security measures on her own.

Tammy turned as she left the room. "Get a life, Clarke," she said loudly.

Clarke stood up but remained frozen to the spot, looking around for someone who might show her out. She hadn't expected the visit to go perfectly, but this had been a disaster.

Chapter 3

Clarke walked for nearly ten minutes to return to her car, in the nearest parking space she'd been able to find on a side road about half a mile away. Even though Ranleigh Marsh prison was situated in the middle of nowhere, there was no car park for visitors, and double yellow lines were painted on all the surrounding roads, making it impossible to park anywhere near the building, maybe for a good security reason, but the restrictions certainly didn't make it easy for visitors. She shut the car door and locked it as soon as she got inside, immediately taking out her phone and dialling Paul. She'd feel better once she'd spoken to him. He would help her make sense of things and calm her down. Paul, a detective sergeant, knew the whole story about Tammy. He'd helped put her in Ranleigh Marsh.

Clarke waited for the phone to ring. Simply hearing Paul's voice would be nice right now. Two rings. The phone cut to voicemail. Clarke hung up and burst into tears.

Clarke sobbed for several minutes. She didn't often cry, but the tension and emotion that had been building up all day flooded out of her now in great wrenching sobs.

Once the tears dried up, Clarke blew her nose loudly and checked herself in the rear-view mirror. What a mess. Her eyes were red from crying and the wind had tangled up her hair like a bird's nest. She found a comb in her handbag and teased the knots out of her hair but couldn't do much about her eyes.

Right now, she longed to be home with Paul. Perhaps she should have left him a voicemail. But what would she have said? She'd already told him she would visit Tammy this afternoon, and he hadn't been happy with her decision. It would concern him more if he picked up on her distress but wasn't able to leave work until later. They could talk this evening.

Without warning, the emotion of the visit overcame her again. Another stream of tears flowed down her cheeks. Why ever did she come here? Tammy wasn't worth it. If she could turn the clock back, even a couple of hours, she absolutely would.

The entire experience had been horrible, more horrible even than she'd imagined. Tammy clearly hated her. She wished she'd never come. Prison was turning Tammy into a person she didn't recognise and, even though she fully deserved her punishment, it distressed Clarke to witness its effects. Tammy was once so vibrant and happy. The contrast only served to highlight the massive difference in her now. Clarke rested her head on the steering wheel and sobbed some more.

After a few minutes, she wiped her eyes. Why did she promise Evan she would visit Tammy? He would expect her to come again and again until she gained Tammy's trust and persuaded her to divulge where the money was hidden. She hadn't done a very good job of that so far. She even failed at making polite conversation, so how would she ever wheedle out Tammy's biggest, most precious secret?

Her thoughts turned to Bex, who visited her sister every fortnight, without fail. Clarke wondered how Bex coped with it. Maybe it was different for family. Tomorrow, she would tell Evan she wouldn't come again. He would have to find Tammy's stolen money some other way.

How difficult would it be to trace Katie and Ned in Dorset? If they were close enough friends to visit Tammy, they might know something. Tammy may have confided in them. Perhaps they would lead her to the money. She vaguely remembered they lived on a farm somewhere near Blandford. Surely, she would be able to track them down fairly easily. Not that they would tell Clarke anything, but she would kick herself if she didn't try.

She would try to contact Tammy's old friends in Tredington through Facebook. It might help. Anything would be better than having to visit that awful prison a second time, not that Tammy wanted to see her again, anyway.

Clarke sat back, attempting to compose herself. She'd stay here a little longer until she felt ready to drive home. Her fingers flicked to the radio, turning it on. Anything would be better than this silence. It might distract her enough to take her mind off the awful place she'd just visited.

Maggie French looked at her watch. Almost time to start shoving the visitors out. Sometimes it was worse than herding cats, but most of them did as she asked. Where the hell did Sadie Hunter get to? She needed her to help take the prisoners back to their cells. Sadie had probably gone to the loo. She'd be back soon. Otherwise, they would have to manage without her.

Maggie stuck her head round the door to the office where Val Cottam sat and asked her to help watch the remaining prisoners while she escorted Linda back to her cell. She was always trouble, so she took her separately before they dealt with the visitors. "Come on, Linda, time to go. Visit's over." Maggie would need to watch herself, mindful of Linda's legendary temper. She resisted the temptation to handcuff her. She wasn't supposed to do that without good reason. Mind you, she could soon invent one. But perhaps this time she'd stick to the rules. Hopefully, Linda's visitor might have softened her up so she wouldn't give any trouble. Linda's sister, Rebecca, was a regular. Maggie wondered why the sister continued to waste her time on a lowlife like Linda.

Linda dragged herself along at the slowest pace possible. Maggie gave her a shove on the shoulder to chivvy her up. She wanted to go home on time today, and if Sadie didn't come back soon, she'd be late finishing.

"Come on, hurry up. I haven't got all day."

"Yeah, ok, Officer French, I'm coming as fast as I can. Can't I say goodbye first?"

"No time for that. You should have said it before."

Linda poked her tongue out at Maggie. "See ya, Bex," she said to her sister.

"In a fortnight," Rebecca said.

Maggie grabbed Linda's arm and steered her towards the door. "My colleague will show you out in a minute," she said to Rebecca.

"No hurry, love. I'll sit here a bit."

Still no sign of Sadie. Maggie wondered if she had a problem with whichever scumbag prisoner she last took back to the cells. As soon as she remembered it was Tammy Doncaster, it became obvious why she was taking so long. Nothing with Tammy ever proved straightforward. She would undoubtedly have manufactured some drama to delay Sadie and wind her up.

Linda shared a cell with Tammy Doncaster at the far end of the south wing. When they got there, Maggie found no sign of either Doncaster or Sadie. She wondered what might have happened to them. Probably in the governor's office for Tammy to get a dressing down, if her past behaviour was anything to go by.

On her way back, she detoured to the staff toilets. She opened the door and called Sadie's name. No answer.

Mindful of the time, Maggie returned to the visiting room. "Any sign of Sadie?"

"No," Val said. "She's probably in the loo."

"I already checked. She's not there," Maggie said. She hoped Sadie was all right. The visitors were being escorted out. They'd take the inmates back to the cells, then she would search for Sadie, provided it didn't take too long. Maggie had promised to be home early today, as she and her husband were going to meet up with some friends in Brackford later. "I'll find her when we've sorted this lot out."

"Ok," Val started to round up the remaining visitors.

Maggie badgered them to hurry up. "Come on, you lot. All visitors, out now." It didn't pay to stand any nonsense. Sometimes visitors were all right. Oftentimes they were bigger criminals than the women they visited. You couldn't always tell. So, she treated everyone in here the same, inmates and visitors.

Val returned quickly as soon as she'd signed out the straggling relatives.

"Ok, let's get these scumbags back to the cells." Maggie barked out orders to the prisoners. She needed them to behave today, or she would be late for her evening out.

"Can't we stay here?" one of the prisoners said.

"No, you bloody can't. You need to return to your cell. And consider yourself lucky you're allowed to have any visitors at all." She wasn't allowed to threaten the prisoners, but she could find a reason to take away their visiting rights in an instant if they gave her any trouble. The latent threat still didn't always stop bad behaviour.

"I suppose you want a holiday in the Maldives as well," Val said.

"That'd be right nice."

"Tough luck. All you're getting is a holiday here at his majesty's pleasure. And if you don't behave and come back to the cells quietly, you'll be enjoying room service in here for a lot longer."

"Ok, keep your hair on, missus."

Maggie shook her head. A bit of respect would be nice. Not much chance of that from this bunch of slags.

It didn't take too long to return the prisoners to their cells.

"I'll find Sadie," Maggie said, planning to start with the staff room, to check if any of the other officers had seen her. She hoped they wouldn't need to search every cell, or she'd never get home on time. She needed to locate Sadie quickly. More importantly, she was desperate for a pee.

Maggie pushed the door of the staff toilets open and strode towards the two cubicles. She shoved at the door of the nearest one.

It moved a few inches, then caught against something solid. Damn. Someone should have stuck an out-of-order sign on the door. She ran into the adjoining cubicle, unable to hold it in any longer. As she sat on the toilet, she wondered what she would wear tonight. Something pretty. Something as far removed from a prison officer's uniform as possible. Probably that nice pink dress she'd bought last week.

Glancing at the floor while she pulled her trousers up, she nearly fell back in shock. Bloody hell! A hand stuck out from under the partition between the two cubicles. She yanked up her zip and barged out of the cubicle, kneeling on the floor outside the door of the adjacent toilet. It was impossible to see much under the partition. Reluctantly, she lay down with her head on the filthy floor. She'd be washing her hair as soon as she got home, for sure.

She got a better view now, and the sight made her gasp in horror. "Oh no! No!" Sadie lay sprawled on the floor inside the cubicle.

"Sadie. Can you hear me?" No response. Had she collapsed inside the cubicle? She tried again to open the door, but Sadie lay against it, preventing it from opening more than a couple of inches. Quickly, Maggie popped back into the adjoining cubicle and put the toilet seat down to stand on. She just managed to peek over the top of the partition wall.

"Oh, my good God!" Sadie lay on the floor, almost naked. Blood congealed around her throat, with a large red puddle on the floor. Maggie was pretty sure Sadie was dead.

She took some deep breaths, trying to compose herself, then pressed the alarm button on her radio before racing out into the corridor.

"Hey," she shouted as she spotted Val at the end of the corridor. She ran towards her. "It's Sadie Hunter. Get help. Full lockdown. And we need the police and an ambulance fast. And tell the governor." They needed to instigate the full emergency procedure for this.

"What's happened?"

"It looks like she's been knifed. Hurry."

Maggie rushed back into the toilets. If Sadie was still alive, she needed to help her before it became too late. Maybe she could reach her. If she lay down in the other cubicle, she might be able to pull her away from the door and gain access.

The alarm sounded, the emergency siren battering her ears. The noise would blast out for ages. The cells would all be automatically locked, as well as the main entrance gates and all the internal doors. She hoped that wouldn't slow down getting the paramedics in here. Whatever was going on out there, someone had better show up to help her soon.

She grovelled on the floor, crawling forward in an effort to squeeze into the small space between the toilet and the partition wall. She should have gone on that diet. With a bit of a wriggle, she managed to reach under Sadie's armpit. She tugged at her and Sadie slid a few inches towards her. That might be enough.

As she got up, Maggie banged her head on the side of the toilet. She returned to try the door again, but it still proved hopeless. Someone slimmer than her might be able to squeeze through the gap. She opened the outer door onto the corridor. Thank God, Janice, the prison governor, approached with two fellow officers in tow.

"What's going on?" Janice called.

"Governor, it's Sadie Hunter. She's been attacked. Quick, Val, come with me. I need somebody small." She grabbed Val, practically dragging her into the toilets. "Can you squeeze through the gap?" Maggie pointed to the door. "You'll need to be careful, but maybe you can help Sadie. Be prepared, though. It's not pretty." She didn't want to say out loud yet that Sadie might be dead. For the first time, she wondered who was responsible for this.

"I'll try."

Val already looked a bit green, giving Maggie second thoughts about making her do this. "Just check if she's still alive. If she's not, come straight back out."

"We've locked down the whole prison," Janice said. "The other officers are making sure everyone's safely back in their cells, and they're doing a head count."

"Did you call an ambulance and the police?" Maggie didn't think they would need an ambulance. It looked way too late for that.

"On their way," Janice said. "What's happening, Val?"

"I think she's dead, Governor." Val's voice wavered pathetically.

Maggie instantly regretted asking her to go into the cubicle.

"Then get out immediately," Janice said. "It's a crime scene."

Val squeezed out through the gap in the doorway. "Her throat has been slit. There's blood everywhere. It's horrible."

Some of Sadie's blood had transferred to Val's clothes. Maggie hoped Val wouldn't start panicking when she noticed. "Are you ok? Do you want to get a glass of water and sit down?"

Val nodded. Maggie wondered how long Val would last in this job. You needed to be tough to survive. There were some pretty rotten women in here. You needed to be able to cope with anything. Val's sensitivity would be her downfall.

"Why don't you go and wait for the police at the main entrance," Janice said. "Bring them here as soon as they arrive. We'll wait here and guard the scene."

"Yes, Governor."

"You are sure she's dead, aren't you?"

"Yes, Governor," Val whispered just before she threw up.

Chapter 4

Clarke stopped crying. It seemed like she'd been sitting in her car for ages. Seeing Tammy after all this time, and in that state too, brought out a lot of well-buried emotions. They'd bubbled up to the surface and erupted in a flood of tears as soon as she shut the car door. She needed to get over this. Her mother was right. Somehow, she needed to throw off her guilt about Tammy and stop blaming herself.

She started up the engine and turned the car around on the quiet side road where she'd parked. What a pity she would have to drive back past the prison to get home, but she would turn her head away and ignore the building as she drove past. Everything would be fine.

She tried to forget about Tammy. The trouble was, as soon as she decided she wouldn't think of Tammy, of course Tammy became the only person in her head.

It proved impossible to avoid seeing the prison, not without the risk of crashing the car. Police cars were parked outside the entrance and a very loud alarm sounded. The police hadn't been there when she left. Whatever was happening inside, she'd had a lucky escape. Was it a riot or worse? What a relief not to be caught up in the middle of that. Silently, she thanked Tammy for ending the visit early, then she renewed her resolve not to visit her again, however much Evan begged.

In front of her, a low-flying police helicopter skimmed the tops of the huge oak trees lining the road, pulling her focus away from the sombre prison building. Something bad was happening, but she didn't want to find out what. As she headed out of the area, she speeded up. The faster she left the vicinity, the better. She simply wanted to get home.

Detective Sergeant Paul Waterford stood at the prison entrance with Detective Constable Barry Medway, waiting to be let in. He was well acquainted with many of Ranleigh Marsh's inmates, having personally put a lot of them inside, so that guaranteed they wouldn't be pleased to see him.

They hadn't divulged the identity of the murder victim. Hopefully, one of the prisoners. He had a long list of ones he wouldn't be sorry to see dead.

The security guard recognised Paul. He showed his ID anyway. He would still have to go through all the same security procedures as everybody else entering the prison.

"Officer Cottam will show you where to go," the guard said, pointing at a young prison officer waiting by the door.

"I'm Val. Follow me." She led him down a corridor Paul didn't recognise.

This wasn't the route he normally took into the prison.

"We have to go the long way round," Val explained. "Once the emergency lockdown gets activated, access to some parts of the building becomes much trickier."

"What happened?" Paul asked.

"It's one of my colleagues, Sadie Hunter. She's been murdered. It looks like someone cut her throat, and she was half-undressed." Val's voice wobbled, and she struggled to get the final words out.

"I'm sorry," Paul said. "Are you ok?" She displayed all the signs of shock.

"Not really. Maggie found the body." Tears ran down Val's cheeks and she wiped at them with the back of her hand. "She made me go in to check if Sadie was still alive. It was horrible." Val used her security pass to open another door and let Paul through.

"Any idea who might have done it?" Paul asked.

She shook her head. "Spoilt for choice here. The place is full of murdering types." Val stopped outside the ladies' toilets and knocked on the door.

The door opened immediately. Janice Whaley, the prison governor at Ranleigh Marsh, stood in the doorway.

"Good to see you, Janice." Paul stepped forward. "Is the victim in here?"

"Yes. Come in."

Paul pulled on his crime scene gear: plastic overalls, overshoes, and latex gloves. He didn't want to contaminate the scene any more than necessary, although, by the looks of things, they might as well have been holding a party in there as another prison officer appeared behind Janice. Janice introduced her as Maggie French.

"What happened?" Paul asked. He would need to talk to Maggie if she found the body.

Janice held the door open for Paul and Barry. "We don't really know. Sadie was helping with visiting hour. Next thing anyone knew, she'd gone missing, then Maggie found her in here."

"Any idea who did it?"

Janice laughed. "We've got a building full of women with previous form. Take your pick."

Paul wondered if she'd been talking to Val as both women had said pretty much the same things. "Could it have been one of the visitors?"

"That's unlikely," Janice said. "They've all been accounted for and escorted out. I don't believe it was an officer either. None of my team would do that."

"So, it might be an inmate," Paul said. He would keep an open mind on that. "When did you last see Sadie?"

"She was only missing for about twenty minutes," Maggie said.

"So, who had access to this part of the building during those twenty minutes? Can you make me a list? Prisoners and officers. Everybody."

"All the staff has access," Maggie said, "but I'm sure it wouldn't be any of them."

"Doesn't matter. Put them on the list anyway," Paul insisted. "What about the prisoners?"

"Sadie left the visiting room to take Tammy Doncaster back to her cell."

"Tammy Doncaster? Did you say Tammy Doncaster?" Paul asked. If Tammy was involved, it was bad news. Immediately, he worried about Clarke.

"Yes. Nasty piece of work, sulky cow."

"Go and get her. I want to question her now." Paul snapped out the order. Tammy might have been the last person to see Sadie alive.

How did Tammy get tangled up in this? Of all the people... Did she kill Sadie? It wouldn't be the first person she'd murdered. Paul suddenly got a dreadful foreboding about this case. If it was Tammy, the level of violence had escalated. And why would she do it in here, when she would obviously get caught?

"Did Sadie ever fall out with Tammy? Did she upset her?"

"Everybody upsets Tammy. She doesn't like anybody. Sadie got on with her better than most."

"I'll fetch Doncaster," Maggie said.

"Take her to my office," said Janice. "Radio me when you get there and I'll bring DS Waterford along."

"Yes, ma'am."

Another prison officer showed Erica, the scene of crime officer, into the ladies' toilets, which were now becoming crowded.

"I'm pleased you're here," Paul said.

"What have we got?" Erica was keen to get down to business as usual.

"She's in the cubicle." Paul pointed to the one on the right. "It's tricky to get at. Do you want me to remove the door?"

"It might make it easier," Erica said. "Either that or I have to go on a serious crash diet in the next five minutes."

Paul assessed the door hinges, which were conveniently on the outside of the cubicle, making it a simple job to lift the door off. He clasped his fingers around the edges of the door and heaved upwards. It shifted about half a centimetre. He'd have to get underneath it. Crouching down, he put both hands under the bottom of the door, rested his shoulder against it, and pulled. Boy, it was stiff. Obviously, it hadn't been taken off its hinges since first being fitted. The door was pretty firmly stuck.

"Do you need some help, Sarge?" Barry gave the door a kick with his boot, which loosened it a little.

One more big heave from underneath and the door suddenly jerked upwards by several inches. Paul almost fell backwards as the door tilted towards him, but he managed to upright himself as Barry assisted to support the door's weight to stabilise it. Paul carried the door out of the way, leaning it against the wall.

"That wasn't so difficult," he said, lying through his teeth.

"Not a pretty sight, is it?" said Erica. The pool of blood on the floor was starting to congeal. "Who took her clothes off?"

"She might have been changing," Paul suggested.

"Into what?" Erica shook her head slowly. "There's no sign of any clothes, so presumably whoever killed her took the clothes. They at least possessed enough decency to leave her undies on."

Paul wondered what had happened to Sadie's uniform. They would need to do a thorough search for it.

"It looks like something's been shoved in the cistern. It might be her clothes," Erica said.

Paul leaned across the body to lift up the lid of the cistern, jumping back as he got sight of the contents. "Looks like a huge dead rat."

He was glad to be wearing gloves but still was loath to touch the offending item.

He pulled the object out gingerly, holding it with the tips of his fingers as if it might bite him before putting his hand under it to scoop it up. It wasn't alive. Wasn't an animal either, thank God, just a drab brown messed-up thing. Whatever the matted mess started life as originally, dunking it in water hadn't done it any favours. It wasn't Sadie's uniform, that's for sure. He allowed it to drip before putting it into an evidence bag.

"Looks like hair to me," Erica said. "Dreadlocks, I'd say. Find out if anyone in the prison has dreadlocks. They must have come from somewhere."

The prison governor waited in the corridor outside the door.

"Have you got any staff or inmates with dreadlocks?" Paul asked her.

The governor's face looked shocked. "Tammy Doncaster," she said.

This was unexpected news. "Where is Tammy? Wasn't someone supposed to be fetching her?" He'd hoped Tammy wouldn't be involved, but he was afraid she might be up to her neck in this.

"Maggie's gone to fetch her."

"See where she's got to." He longed for this to be a mistake, and that Tammy Doncaster wouldn't be tied up with any of this, especially not today. Clarke was supposed to visit her this afternoon. "Did Tammy have a visitor earlier?" He needed to reassure himself that Clarke was all right.

"Maggie would know that," said Janice. "I've tried to radio her, but she's not answering."

"I really need to question Tammy Doncaster."

"I'll chase up Maggie." Janice marched down the corridor purposefully.

Paul went back into the toilets. "Any initial thoughts?" he asked Erica.

"She hasn't been dead long. Cause of death might be anything. Her throat's been slit, but let's not jump to conclusions until I can confirm if that happened post-mortem, or whether it was the cause of death. There's a fair bit of blood, so it might have been the cause, but don't quote me on that."

Paul resisted a smile. He rarely got any useful information out of Erica so early in the case. She must be particularly happy today.

The clatter of shoes in the corridor signalled Janice returning, with Maggie in tow.

"Bad news," Janice said. "Doncaster is missing. We can't find her anywhere."

"So, she may have done this?" Paul's good mood deserted him as quickly as it had come. He tried to work out the implications. It was complicated. If only it was someone other than Tammy Doncaster.

"Yes, it's possible, but we're sure she's not in the prison."

"Have you got CCTV?"

"Yes, of course," Janice said.

"I need every single camera from the moment Sadie went missing." He would set Barry Medway on the task of trawling through the footage. At least the prison should have plenty of CCTV. That might hold the key to this. But, if they couldn't find Doncaster, if she'd escaped, it would be a disaster. How the hell did she manage that? Paul wondered if Clarke would be in any danger, especially if Tammy killed the prison officer in order to escape, which now seemed likely. As soon as he got out of here, he would check that Clarke was ok. First, he needed to talk to Maggie.

"Did Tammy have a visitor this afternoon?" he asked her.

"Yes, yes. A tall girl."

That would be Clarke, Paul guessed. "What time did she leave?"

"About three thirty. She'd have left pretty much the same time as Sadie took Tammy back to the cells. Tammy ended the visit early and started to kick off, so we removed Tammy and sent the visitor home."

"Show me the route Sadie would have taken with Tammy." He needed to work out what might have happened.

"She wouldn't have come this way. Come back to the visitors' room with me and I'll walk you through it."

Paul followed Maggie, hoping it wouldn't take too long. He longed to check his phone, but all visitors to the prison were made to leave mobile phones with Security. No exceptions. He needed to call Clarke, both to make sure she was ok, and in case she could help. She was, after all, one of the last people to see Tammy before she probably murdered Sadie and before she escaped. And Clarke would have been in the vicinity of the prison when Tammy left.

"They sat at that table." Maggie pointed to a table in the middle of the room. "Then Sadie would have taken Tammy through this door."

Their footsteps echoed loudly in the tiled corridor, meaning Paul had to concentrate on what Maggie was saying.

"And here we need to turn right instead of left. Left goes to the staff toilets, right goes straight back to the wing. Sadie never would have taken her to the staff toilets. It's strictly forbidden for any inmates to use them and they can't even get through that door without a security pass."

"But Sadie would have a pass." Paul wondered where Sadie's staff security pass was now, and if Tammy might have talked Sadie into taking her through the security door to the staff toilets. If she'd faked being really desperate for the loo, Sadie might have given in.

"She wouldn't have let her through," Maggie said.

So, maybe Tammy overpowered Sadie and used her pass key to get through the door, then dragged her all the way up to the staff toilets. Paul tried to visualise the scene. No, that was ridiculous. It was too far to drag a heavy body without anyone noticing. That option would have taken too long. Someone would have come down the corridor in that time. And Sadie wasn't that small either. She appeared to be quite short, as far as he could tell from the twisted way she lay on the floor, but her curvaceous figure would add up to a lot of weight.

"Where's Sadie from?" Paul asked.

"Caribbean," Maggie said vaguely, as if that would pinpoint her exact place of birth.

"Do you remember which island?"

"Saint something or other. Saint Lucia, perhaps. I don't know any others. I can't remember."

Paul resolved to ask Clarke where Tammy came from. They may have bonded over something like that. Perhaps Sadie was more helpful towards Tammy than she should have been because of that.

"So, then what?" Paul ran through the possible scenario in his head. They'd gone to the toilets. Tammy killed Sadie. If she planned to escape, maybe she wanted the prison officer's uniform to help her get out. Did she have the nerve to walk out, bold as brass, wearing a prison officer's uniform? Yes, he realised. Yes, she probably did. But could she really pull that off? He supposed Tammy and Sadie were a similar size and shape. They were both black. But that's where the resemblance ended.

He remembered Tammy had been stunning. He most definitely wouldn't apply that description to Sadie. He recalled Sadie's plain face and shaved head. Suddenly, the dreadlocks in the toilet cistern made sense. Could Tammy have shaved her head quickly enough, and with what? The whole idea was ridiculous. She would never have pulled it off. But why else would she undress Sadie? And where were Tammy's clothes?

And if Tammy slit Sadie's throat to kill her, the uniform would surely be covered in blood and so would Tammy. None of it made sense. Yet, somehow, Tammy murdered Sadie and managed to leave the prison. He simply didn't have a better theory yet. He would have to leave Erica to process the crime scene while he and Barry took the CCTV back to the station. With luck, Erica would come up with a more plausible idea.

Paul returned to speak to the prison governor.

"I've alerted the authorities about the missing prisoner," she told him. "They've got police helicopters searching for Doncaster already. She won't get far. She'd need a lot of help to get away. The prison's miles away from anywhere."

Paul hoped she was right. He needed to check on Clarke before anything happened to her. He hoped Tammy didn't receive her help from Clarke.

Chapter 5

As soon as Paul retrieved his phone and left the prison, he phoned Clarke. His phone showed a missed call from her a couple of hours earlier. That must be about the time she'd finished her visit to Tammy.

"Clarke, are you ok?" Thank God she'd answered on the first ring. After everything that happened at the prison, he was worried sick about her. "Where are you?"

"I'm at home."

"Are you on your own?" His fingers clenched around the phone with worry. Tammy better not be with her.

"Yes, what is this?"

Clarke sounded annoyed, as if he might be accusing her of something. Paul breathed a sigh of relief. Tammy obviously wasn't with her, or she would have reacted differently, although she would have probably denied it either way.

"Nothing," he said. "Keep the door locked and don't go out until I get home."

"Why? What's up? You're scaring me."

"It's ok. I'm probably worrying about nothing." They both lived in Clarke's flat now. Tammy knew the address. "But please, stay inside with the door locked."

"Only if you tell me why."

Paul counted to ten in his head, trying not to snap at Clarke. Sometimes her enquiring mind proved a nuisance rather than an asset.

"Well, why?" Clarke asked again.

Aware of Clarke's relentless persistence, he forced himself to tell her the truth. "Tammy escaped from prison this afternoon."

"No," Clarke gasped. "But I visited her today."

"I know." Paul still struggled to work out the connection and whether Tammy chose the day of Clarke's visit deliberately. "It happened immediately after you left." He decided it was best not to mention the murder yet in case he alarmed Clarke when she was at home on her own. He would be home particularly late tonight.

Paul put his phone back in his pocket, relieved that Tammy wasn't holding Clarke hostage somewhere or forcing her to drive her out of the area. He wondered if that might have been her original plan, the reason she chose the day of Clarke's visit to escape. What would Tammy do when that plan went wrong? Who would she turn to? He didn't trust her one bit not to go after Clarke, given the chance. It was vital to find her. Fast.

Outside the prison, a full police search was in progress. Uniformed officers and police vehicles were being dispatched in all directions. Above them, the police search helicopter circled the area. Police tape cordoned off the main entrance of the prison, mainly to hold back the small contingent of press that had already got wind of the situation.

Paul spotted DCI Jonathan Price striding towards him.

"What happened? How in hell did Doncaster escape?" DCI Price scowled.

"I have a theory, sir, but it's all guesswork at this stage." Paul shuffled nervously. He hated guesswork. It had an annoying propensity to be wrong and make him seem like an idiot. He really didn't want to tell the DCI about his idea, not yet.

"Well?"

Paul glanced sideways at Barry. Clearly, he wasn't about to offer any help. "What if Tammy murdered the prison officer, Sadie Hunter, took her uniform, shaved her head so she would resemble

Sadie, and walked out, using Sadie's security pass and wearing her uniform?" Now that he'd said it out loud, it sounded ridiculous.

DCI Price obviously thought so too. "That sounds completely implausible," he said. "For a start, security would recognise her when she handed in her keys." All the prison officers had to sign out and hand in their security pass and keys every day when they left the prison.

"There's a new guy on security. He only started two days ago. I doubt he could tell the difference if Tammy and Sadie Hunter looked vaguely similar."

The DCI frowned. "Well, let's see what the evidence tells us. Is Erica on the job?"

"Yes, sir." Paul hid his annoyance that the DCI didn't believe him. He wished he'd kept his stupid theory to himself.

"Anyway, I'm going to be the senior investigating officer on this case."

Paul tried not to show his surprise. "Yes, sir."

"DI Swales has been taken to hospital and, as you are aware, DI Foulds is still on holiday, trekking round the Brazilian jungle, or something like that. There's no one else available. Seeing as you're familiar with Tammy Doncaster, you're going to have to do a lot of the work on this case."

"Yes, sir," Paul said, torn between pure fear of having a much bigger role in a murder investigation than he'd had to date, and euphoria that the DCI was presenting him with an amazing career-boosting opportunity. Except the odds of him pulling it off were so high as to be off the scale. Right now, he was terrified of screwing up. "Will DI Swales be off for long?" Paul got on well with Harry Swales. He hoped the DI would make a rapid recovery.

"Let's hope not. In the meantime, I'll be keeping a very close eye on things, but I've got a lot on my plate right now, especially with being so short-staffed. I expect you to keep me fully up to date on this," DCI Price said.

"Of course, sir."

"Where are you going now?"

"We're headed off to break the news to the victim's husband, sir," Paul said. "I need to get going. Rachel's going to act as family liaison officer. I don't want her arriving before me."

The DCI nodded. "Make sure you keep me informed."

Paul pushed through the gathering crowd to where his car was parked, Barry following right behind him. Within a couple of minutes, they were headed away from Ranleigh Marsh to see Archie Hunter.

The Hunters lived locally. Paul checked his watch. Gone six already, so Archie should be at home.

Sadie and Archie Hunter's house turned out to be a pretty little semi-detached with a well-tended garden, not what he expected at all. Paul knocked loudly.

A tall black man opened the door almost immediately.

"Archie Hunter?" Paul asked.

"Who's asking?"

"Detective Sergeant Paul Waterford, and Detective Constable Barry Medway." They both showed their IDs. "Can we come in?"

"I'm busy."

The man obviously distrusted the police. Paul didn't want to break the bad news to Archie on the doorstep. "It's about your wife, Sadie," Paul said. "Best if we talk inside. Please, can we come in?"

"Is she ok?" Archie asked.

"Can we come in?"

THE PAYBACK

Archie stood aside for Paul and Barry to come past and shut the door behind them. "Living room's straight ahead." He followed them in and slumped onto the sofa.

He didn't offer them a seat. Paul sat down opposite him, without waiting to be asked.

"I'm afraid I've got very bad news," Paul said.

"Has Sadie been in an accident? I'm always telling her she drives too fast."

"No, not an accident. I'm afraid it's much worse than that." Paul always hated breaking news like this to the next of kin. Tact and sympathy didn't come naturally to him. "Sadie was murdered this afternoon."

"Murdered? No. That's impossible. I spoke to her at lunchtime."

"I'm sorry for your loss." Those trite words, which he had said dozens of times to people such as Archie, would do nothing to comfort him at a time like this, but words were all he could offer.

"What happened?" Archie asked.

"We're still investigating, but we're pretty certain it was one of the prisoners." Paul didn't want to divulge too much information at this stage. In any case, it would be much too soon to hit the husband with the full, gory details of Sadie's murder. He would find out soon enough. But not today.

Archie gazed into space.

"Barry, can you make a cup of tea," Paul said quietly.

Archie pointed towards the kitchen, opening his mouth to speak. No sound came forth. He continued to shake his head.

"Can we call anyone for you, a friend or a relative?"

Archie found his voice at last. "There's my brother." He searched in his pocket for his phone, dialled the number, and passed the phone to Paul. "Can you explain to him, please? I don't know what to say."

Paul took the phone.

Archie's brother, Winston, seemed as shocked as Archie. He promised to come over in about half an hour.

Barry brought in the tea, putting the mugs down on a small glass table next to the sofa.

Archie seemed buoyed by the news that his brother was coming over. He took a sip of his tea, then promptly set it down again.

"What about Sadie's colleagues?" he asked. "Surely someone should have helped her. Why didn't anyone help her?"

"I don't know," Paul said, "but I'm sure we'll get answers to all of those questions very soon."

Archie put his head in his hands. "My poor Sadie."

Paul gave him a minute. "I'm afraid we will have to ask you a few questions," he said.

"Yes, of course. If it helps get the bitch who did this. Do you know who it was? Somebody must have seen it."

Paul didn't want to admit yet that they had a suspect. He ignored the question. "How long did Sadie work at Ranleigh Marsh prison?"

"About three years, but this last year she hated it. Was it Tammy who did it?"

"Why do you say that?" Paul wondered if some sort of connection existed between Sadie and Tammy. Nothing else made sense.

"It must have been Tammy. She made Sadie's life hell."

"How did she do that?" Barry asked.

"Sadie was getting more stressed every day. She wanted to leave."

"Did Sadie say that?" Paul wished he could tell Archie Hunter something that would make him feel better. Anything. For once, he really felt for the victim's husband. Usually, he eyed up the husband as a potential suspect, but, in this case, Archie couldn't possibly have murdered his wife, as she had been safely locked within Ranleigh Marsh prison. Or, not so safely, Paul reminded himself.

"She would never have told me. But she didn't have to. It was obvious."

"How?" Barry wrote it all down, scribbling furiously into his notebook.

"We've been married for over twenty years. I know her." Archie started shaking his head frantically again. "This is all my fault. If I hadn't lost my job, I would have let her give up the prison job. She could have done something with a smaller salary. But we rely on her salary to support us both."

"How long have you been unemployed?" Paul asked.

"I haven't been able to find a job for nearly a year. It's a lot of pressure on Sadie." Archie started to cry. "She shouldn't even have been there. I should have let her give up that job. She hated it so much."

Paul noted that some of the time he still referred to Sadie in the present tense. He wondered when Winston Hunter would show up, or the family liaison officer. They couldn't leave Archie on his own, not like this. "Did Sadie tell you why she hated it?"

"It was that Tammy. She made Sadie's life hell."

"What did Tammy do?" Paul needed to know why Archie pointed the finger so definitely at Tammy for his wife's murder.

"It was Tammy. I knew it. I'll bloody kill her if I get my hands on her."

Paul wished Archie could get his hands on Tammy. There were no sightings of her yet. Best he didn't tell Archie that.

"So, do you remember any particular incidents between Tammy and your wife?" Paul believed Archie's gut feeling. After all, he'd had experience with Tammy himself. But he needed specifics.

"Only every single bloody day. That woman made life hell for poor Sadie."

"That's awful," Paul said. He thought of Clarke. He'd be devastated if he lost Clarke as Archie had lost Sadie. He would try his best to get justice for Archie, for Sadie.

"Sadie wasn't a pushover. She was quite tough. I guess Tammy must have been tougher."

Paul nodded.

"I never met her," Archie said. "Sadie always described her as a real piece of work. She threatened Sadie so many times to make her take stuff in. I don't know how she managed it. Prison security is really tight, but she must have found a way to bypass it. I told her to tell the governor she was frightened, but she worried she would get fired, and without her job, we would lose the house. She loved this house." Archie attempted a smile, but it didn't get past the sadness in his eyes.

"It's a beautiful house," Barry said.

"What sort of stuff did Tammy make Sadie take in?" Paul wanted to keep the conversation on track.

"I don't know the half of it. She wouldn't tell me everything, but she started off with small treats, like chocolate and a shampoo bottle full of rum. And then she took in a mobile phone."

Paul wondered how Sadie could have smuggled a phone past the security searches and X-ray machine that the staff was made to go through daily. Did she have an accomplice working in Security? "What about razor blades?" he asked.

Archie shook his head vaguely. "She'd have been a fool to do that. Was that what killed her?"

Paul ignored the question. It would be tragic if Sadie had provided the weapon for her own murder. "Did she ever say why Tammy disliked her?"

"No. Tammy was a bully, but if she assumed Sadie was weak, I don't understand why. Sadie was a strong person. That's why I'm sure Tammy had some kind of hold over Sadie. She threatened her."

"What was the nature of the threats? Did Tammy threaten to hurt Sadie, or did she threaten her family?"

"Both. Sadie doesn't have much family, but her mum lives in an old folks' home. Tammy threatened to hurt her. Oh God, I suppose I'll have to break the news to her. How am I going to do that?"

"How did Tammy find out about Sadie's mother?" Paul wondered if Sadie had been indiscreet about snippets of her private life. It wouldn't be the first time this had happened to a prison officer.

"I don't know. But anyway, she found out, and she milked it for all it was worth. Tammy discovered which care home she lived in, said her friends on the outside would do her in, and Sadie believed her. She couldn't risk ignoring her in case it was all true. And once she gave in and did what Tammy wanted once, she was trapped. Tammy simply blackmailed her into carrying on.

"I should have gone to the prison governor. I should have told her Sadie wouldn't do anything wrong. I should have found a damned job by now. Why didn't I try harder? I was good at my job." Tears dripped down Archie's cheeks. He wiped his face with a dirty handkerchief.

"What do you do?" Paul asked.

"I'm a teacher. I used to be a teacher," Archie corrected himself.

Paul's initial assumption that Tammy may have targeted Sadie because her husband did a job that may be of use to her was clearly unfounded. "Do you have anything that would serve as evidence of Tammy blackmailing your wife? Did Tammy ever write her any notes that she brought home? Anything in writing, or any messages on her phone?"

"No. Sadie would never give out her personal phone number to a prisoner. Never. The prison officers don't even tell the prisoners their full names. It's always Officer Hunter." Archie got up and started pacing around the room. "She had problems before with prisoners trying to get too close or intimidate her, so she was careful to keep them at arm's length. That's why I can't understand how Tammy managed to get to her. It's not like Sadie at all."

"If you remember anything, please call me anytime." Paul got up to leave. Barry immediately followed his lead.

"Where's Sadie now?" Archie asked. "Can I see her?"

"We'll arrange that tomorrow," Paul said. "I'm afraid there will have to be an autopsy. We'll take you to visit her as soon as it's possible." He hoped the coroner would do the autopsy quickly. "We've allocated a family liaison officer to you," Paul said, "to make sure you're ok and keep you informed on what's going on."

"You mean to come and spy on me?" Archie said angrily. "Well, I didn't do it, did I? Because I couldn't possibly have got into the prison. So, there's no need for your family whatsit."

"You're not a suspect," Paul reassured him, relieved not to have to question a grieving relative on their whereabouts at the time of the murder. "The family liaison officer will update you on any developments. And if you remember any relevant information, she'll be here for you to talk it through. It really can help."

Archie didn't seem to have completely warmed to the idea, but Rachel excelled at her job. She'd work her magic and get accepted as part of the family in no time. She'd have to. He wanted someone here, in case Tammy showed up.

Paul really didn't want to have to tell Archie that Tammy had escaped, but he guessed he would have to. "We haven't released this information to the public yet, so I would appreciate it if you would keep it to yourself for the moment."

"What information?"

"Tammy escaped from prison this afternoon."

"What? How the hell did that happen?"

Paul understood Archie's anger. He'd been asking himself the same question for the last couple of hours. "We're looking into that," he said, "but it's best that you have the family liaison officer here, in case Tammy knows where you live. In case she comes here."

"If she comes here, I won't need a flipping family liaison officer, and it'll be Tammy who needs the protection, not me. She comes anywhere near me I swear I'll kill her."

"It's best not to make threats like that, sir," Paul said.

"You know what I mean." Archie clenched his fists.

"Anyway, if we have an FLO here, they can arrest her if she shows up. It's really best that we have somebody here. You might remember something significant. If you do, you must tell them. It might help us find Tammy."

"I guess that will be all right," he said, sounding resigned to the prospect. "As long as she keeps out of my way."

"The FLO will be here shortly. We'll wait until she comes. And of course she'll try to keep out of your way and give you some space, but she'll be here if you need her." Paul sat down again. They needed to go, but Archie was in too much of a state to risk leaving him on his own, especially now that he knew his wife's killer was no longer in prison.

The doorbell rang. "Do you want me to get that?" Paul jumped up.

"Ok." Archie nodded, sinking back into his chair as if his short show of anger had exhausted him.

Paul had hoped it would be Rachel, but Winston, Archie's brother, stood on the doorstep.

"What's going on?" he demanded.

"I'm Detective Sergeant Paul Waterford. We spoke on the phone."

"So, what's going on?"

"I'm afraid Sadie's been murdered. This afternoon, at the prison."

Winston slammed his hand into the wall in anger. "She should never have taken that job. It's no career for a woman, working with a bunch of criminals. She didn't even enjoy it."

"Did she say anything to you about why she disliked it?"

"It's one of the women in there, one of the prisoners."

"Did she say who?" Paul didn't need to ask, but further confirmation always helped.

"I don't know, but she's a nasty bully for sure, although I'm surprised she managed to bully Sadie. But Sadie had a soft spot underneath all her toughness, and if you got her at the right moment, she would do anything for you. How can she be dead? She doesn't deserve that."

"Archie needs a lot of support. He's really struggling to come to terms with this," Paul said, seeing tears welling in Winston's eyes, and hoped deflecting his attention towards Archie's needs would help. "Look after him."

"Of course I will. I've got my bag in the car so I can stay over." Winston straightened up and blinked back the tears that hadn't quite come.

"We're sending a family liaison officer. She should be here at any moment. She needs to stay here. It's part of our investigation process. Please, if either of you remember anything that may be of any significance at all, even the tiniest little thing, please will you tell her? It might be really important."

"Yeah, of course. I want this killer punished as much as you do."

Paul had only just shut the front door when the doorbell rang again.

Rachel had arrived.

"Archie's the husband. His brother, Winston, is here too. Archie's still partly in denial," Paul said, summarising the situation quickly. "Did someone bring you up to speed on the case?"

"Yes," she said. "And I worked on the Tammy Doncaster case when she first got convicted, so I'm already familiar with the background information."

"That's great." Paul smiled at her. "If Tammy shows up here, don't take any chances. She may be armed, and we already know she's dangerous. Call for backup before you do anything."

"Yes, Sarge. We will get her, won't we?"

"If it takes me forever, I will find that woman," Paul promised. "She needs to pay for what she's done." He didn't add that he needed her locked up as quickly as possible because he was worried sick that she might hurt Clarke. He doubted that Tammy would come anywhere near Sadie's husband, but he was pretty sure, if she got the chance, she would go after Clarke. And he couldn't let that happen, no matter what it took.

Chapter 6

Clarke had been waiting forever for Paul to come home. When Paul moved to the Murder Investigation Team, she quickly got used to him working impossibly long hours, but this was different. His phone call earlier, when he'd told her about Tammy escaping from prison, set Clarke on edge. Old memories, painful ones of what Tammy did to her, had haunted her all evening, especially since it got dark. Being here on her own didn't help. After the prison visit this afternoon, which ended with Tammy bristling with hate for her and practically throwing her out, the news of her escape worried Clarke immensely. Would Tammy be stupid enough to show up here? She would certainly be sufficiently arrogant.

She was about to give up on Paul and go to bed when she heard his key in the door. She hurried into the hallway to greet him.

"What happened? Did you find Tammy?" Immediately, she saw on his face that something was wrong.

"Not yet." He gave her a hug.

"The prison visit was awful," Clarke said. She hadn't intended to tell Paul exactly how badly the visit went, but it would be difficult to hide from him the effect it had on her. "Prison's changed Tammy. She looks terrible. I found it impossibly difficult seeing her like that. She's not like the old Tammy at all." *And she hates me for it.* Clarke bit her lip, unsure why she didn't want to admit that to Paul.

Paul sat on the sofa next to her.

"I've got more bad news."

Clarke wondered what could be worse.

Paul put his arm around her. "I got called to a murder in the prison."

"Not Tammy?" Clarke gasped, immediately picturing the worst. Was that why Paul said she hadn't been caught? Did somebody kill her? Even though she hated visiting Tammy and never wanted to go again, she didn't want her dead. It surprised her how much she still cared.

Paul shook his head. "No, not Tammy. It was one of the prison officers."

Clarke breathed a sigh of relief, then tensed again, realising it meant Tammy was still on the loose.

Paul continued. "We're not sure yet what happened, but the body was discovered in the staff toilets."

"Did one of the staff kill her?"

"We don't know for sure. But that's unlikely."

"Well, thank God Tammy didn't get murdered."

"You still care about her?" Paul raised an eyebrow in surprise.

"Yes," Clarke said quietly. "I do."

"Even after the way she treated you? All those lies she told? That woman nearly killed you."

"Don't remind me. I probably should bear a grudge and hate her, but I don't." *Why don't I hate Tammy? Tammy certainly seemed to have no trouble hating me.*

Paul gave her a perplexed look. He didn't understand.

"I spent three years sitting next to her every day at work," Clarke explained. "We had some good times. It wasn't all bad. In fact, none of it was bad. We were great friends, right until the end." Clarke wondered if *friends* was the right word to describe her relationship with Tammy. Friends didn't lie to you. Friends didn't try to kill you. She needed to reset Tammy's status in her memory.

"The thing is," Paul said, taking hold of Clarke's hand.

Clarke worried now that something else bad was coming. What was he not telling her?

"The thing is," he repeated, "we're pretty sure Tammy killed the prison officer."

"Tammy? Why? How? Surely that's not possible." Clarke noticed she still wanted to believe the best of Tammy, despite all the evidence pointing to her murderous capabilities. "You said the body was in the staff toilet. Tammy wouldn't have access to that, would she?"

"We don't have any of the answers yet. It will take time to work out exactly how she did it. I have a theory, and I'm pretty certain the murderer is Tammy."

"What happens now? I suppose she'll go to trial again if you find enough evidence."

"It's not that simple," Paul said. "We have to find her first."

"But you will find her, won't you?" Clarke shuddered, wondering if Tammy had been loitering nearby when she walked back to her car after visiting.

"We hope so."

Clarke took a moment to process the news fully, racking her brain for where Tammy might have gone.

"You'd better tell me everything that happened during your visit."

She considered for a moment. "I'm not sure if Tammy was even pleased I went. You remember those letters she wrote to me last year asking to see me. She berated me for not coming then. I shouldn't have ignored the letters. I should have visited when she asked."

"No, you shouldn't," Paul said. "You weren't ready. It would have upset you too much."

Clarke wondered if she'd been ready today. It still upset her.

"I'm not even sure you should have gone today," Paul voiced Clarke's thoughts. "You know my opinion on that. You shouldn't have given in to Evan. He should never have put you in that position."

"Well, I did and I'm glad I saw her, but she still blames me for putting her there." It wasn't Evan's fault. Evan Davies, her manager, gave her plenty of chances to say no, without any pressure. It was her decision in the end, her that provided the only pressure. And, ultimately, she decided it might help to further her career. She didn't regret that.

"That's what worries me," Paul said. "She's out there somewhere, and she blames you. We don't know what she might do. You need to be really careful."

"She knows where I live."

Paul nodded. "Perhaps you should stay with your parents until the wedding or until we find Tammy."

"I'm not sure." Her parents lived a lot further from the office, which would make life really inconvenient. All her clothes were in her own flat and all the stuff for organising the wedding as well. It would make everything so much more difficult.

"Please, Clarke." Paul gave her a hug.

"I'll sleep on it and decide in the morning. It's too late to ring Mum now, anyway."

"Ok, but I don't want you taking any chances. You know what Tammy's capable of. That's two people she's killed now. I don't want her to make it a third."

"Then you must find her." Clarke folded her arms defiantly, but inside, she didn't feel so brave.

"Do you have any idea where she might have gone?"

"I'm not sure. Would she have gone back to Tredington? She knows the area well," Clarke replied.

"She grew up in Hackney, didn't she?" Paul asked. "Would she go back there?"

"Tammy didn't like Hackney much. That's the last place she'd want to be." Tammy had preferred to forget her Hackney connections. She had rarely mentioned the place to Clarke in all the time she knew her.

"So, where else?" Paul kicked off his shoes and put his feet up on the sofa.

"She said her friends from Dorset came to see her in prison. Would she go there?"

"I'll check out who visited her, from the prison records."

"They've got a farm. A big farm would be full of places to hide. And don't forget she's got all that money, so she can afford to buy her way out of the country."

"I haven't forgotten that," Paul said. "But you and Evan are trying to trace the money, aren't you?"

"Yes." Clarke realised their chances of locating the stolen money had diminished dramatically now. Evan clearly counted on Clarke to wheedle some information out of Tammy.

"You concentrate on that. I'll concentrate on searching for her."

"If we find the money, we'll find Tammy." Clarke was sure of that, but what hope did they have of finding the stolen money now?

Paul smiled. "Between us, we'll have her banged to rights in no time."

Clarke certainly hoped so, but she didn't share Paul's optimism. Already she felt a little less safe, knowing Tammy was at large. She wished she hadn't gone to see her this afternoon. Now she would be the first person on Tammy's mind, so she might come here, expecting Clarke to help her, or more likely she'd be out to get her revenge. Either way, Clarke didn't relish the prospect.

Paul snuggled up to her. "Everything will be ok, but you really should stay with your parents for a couple of weeks. You'll be much safer."

Clarke nodded. "I'll think about it."

"Did anything else happen during the visit? Did Tammy say anything else?"

"She talked a lot about how awful life was in prison. And she looks so dreadful now. Her hair's gone to dreadlocks. She always used to look fantastic and spent so much time every day getting her hair perfect." Dreadlocks! That wasn't the Tammy she remembered.

"And that's another thing," Paul said.

Clarke cringed. If Paul came out with just one more *other thing*, she would scream. There was a limit to how much she could handle in a single day.

"Tammy doesn't have dreadlocks now," Paul said.

"What?"

"It looks like she shaved off her hair."

"Why?" Clarke asked. "Why would she do that?" That sounded most unlike the Tammy she knew.

"The prison officer Tammy killed vaguely resembled her, except the officer's head was shaved. Tammy would look so totally different with no hair, she might be mistaken for the officer."

"So?" Clarke didn't understand what Paul was getting at.

"So, we're guessing Tammy stole her uniform. From a distance, they would probably appear similar enough to most people that no one would question her. She took all the keys and passes, so it would have been possible to walk out, particularly as they had a couple of new people join their security team this week. They wouldn't have recognised anyone that well."

"What makes you think Tammy shaved off her hair?" Clarke struggled to imagine her doing that. Tammy used to worship her hair. She must be really desperate to do something so drastic with it.

"We found the dreadlocks hidden in the toilet cistern." Paul looked more serious. "We didn't find the razor anywhere. She might still have it with her. You need to be careful."

Paul was frightening her now. The prospect of Tammy on the loose with a weapon made her shudder. Would Tammy show up in the middle of the night and do her in? Thankfully, Paul lived with her now except, of course, for the long hours and occasional night shifts—all those times when he was working on a big case.

"Surely, you can trace her movements on CCTV," Clarke said. "There are cameras everywhere these days."

"We're working on it. You've been to the prison. Ranleigh Marsh is in the middle of nowhere. Even where you get back to the built-up areas, there are plenty of gaps not covered by CCTV. It would be easy for Tammy to disappear. The difficult thing for her will be getting access to her money and transport out of the area. That's when she'll have to rely on other people. And that's when she may get caught. Don't worry, I'm sure we'll find her soon."

"I hope so." Clarke knew from experience it was easy to underestimate Tammy. She hoped Paul wouldn't make that mistake.

"Did you discuss your job during your visit? Does she know where you work?"

"I'm not stupid. I told her I left Briar Holman, so I don't suppose she'll go back there. But I made sure not to tell her where I work now."

"That's good," Paul said.

Clarke snuggled into him. This was her safe place. But she couldn't cuddle up to Paul during the many hours he was working. At least she'd be at work all day tomorrow, but coming home to an empty flat suddenly seemed a less good idea. Maybe she would stay with her parents for a few days or with Rob. Her brother lived much closer to the office. She'd arrange something tomorrow.

Chapter 7

As soon as Paul arrived at the station in the morning, DCI Price called him into his office.

"The press is doing its usual scaremongering." He threw a folded-up newspaper at Paul.

Paul caught it deftly. The front-page headline caught his eye. *Killer On The Loose.* An old picture of Tammy, when she'd still been glamourous, accompanied the article.

"Let's hope this doesn't cause a panic," the DCI said.

Paul skimmed through the first couple of paragraphs. They'd certainly sensationalised the story. He'd noticed several journalists outside the prison after Tammy's escape. The alarms and the police helicopter made it an impossible task to keep the situation under wraps. "Who did they talk to?" His initial guess was Archie Hunter. He felt guilty for telling him too much about Tammy's escape. Yes, he felt very guilty about that, but he didn't intend to throw himself under the bus for Tammy Doncaster.

"Archie Hunter." The DCI snatched the paper back. "He's given an interview about his wife and how *horrible Tammy* made her life hell."

Paul said nothing, waiting for the accusation, but none came. Maybe he'd got away with it. Any one of the prison officers might have told the press about Sadie.

"We'll have to set up a special phone line now," DCI Price said. "People have already started calling in with sightings. I can guarantee ninety-nine percent of the callers will be crackpots. They won't even recognise Tammy, not from that photo. She looks nothing like that now."

"Should we release a recent photo, sir, in case the other one percent volunteer something useful?"

"Trouble is, no one has a recent photo, not now that she's shaved her hair off. Well done on that theory, by the way. It looks like you were right."

Paul beamed. The DCI didn't often dish out praise. He renewed his determination to impress him on this case before they brought in someone more senior to take over.

"What's the plan for today?"

"Barry's trawling through the CCTV. I'm going back to the prison. Tammy may have told someone in Ranleigh Marsh what she's got planned."

The DCI nodded. "Keep me in the loop," he said. "The moment you get any developments."

Clarke arrived at the office early in the morning. Immediately after she sat at her desk, her mobile rang.

She extricated the phone from her handbag just before it diverted to voicemail.

The number flashed up as *unknown*. "Hello." Probably someone trying to sell her something. She'd soon get rid of them.

Nobody spoke.

"Hello," she repeated.

"Clarke?"

"Who is that?" Clarke swore it sounded like Tammy. "Hello."

The caller hung up.

It definitely sounded like Tammy. Almost definitely. She was ninety-nine percent certain. Clarke hadn't changed her mobile number in years. Would Tammy have remembered it? She was brilliant with numbers—that's why she had been so good at her job. But why phone her? And why didn't she say anything?

If she'd been trying to freak her out, she was succeeding.

THE PAYBACK 57

Clarke drove into the Briar Holman car park. As she did so, memories of the time she used to work here flooded back. They were a mixture of happy memories and extreme sadness, the latter entirely connected to Tammy. Coming here was bound to be difficult. She would have to toughen up before it turned into too much of an ordeal.

She didn't recognise the receptionist. "I'm here to see Andrew Hardwicke," Clarke said.

Earlier, she arranged by phone to meet with Andrew. As soon as she mentioned the missing money, he practically fell over himself to help, although she guessed he wouldn't have fitted her in for a purely social call. She would need to talk to Douglas Doncaster too and dreaded that conversation so much that she couldn't bring herself to arrange a meeting in advance. Perhaps Andrew would organise it for her. Would Douglas be annoyed that she hadn't approached him first? But she couldn't face asking, certain he wouldn't want to talk about Tammy.

Andrew showed up quickly. "Clarke, good to see you." He held out his hand for her to shake. "I arranged a meeting room so we can talk in private."

"Thank you." That sounded much better than walking into a huge open-plan office where everyone would recognise her and want to talk to her, probably about Tammy. She may have to do that, anyway. Best get it all over with at once so she wouldn't have to return. Already she found it upsetting, and she'd only just set foot in the door.

"Have you made any progress with finding the money?" Andrew shut the door of the meeting room behind her and gestured for her to sit down.

"It's a slow process," she said. "I assume you heard the news about Tammy."

"The breakout? Yes. That's going to make it more difficult to track down the money, isn't it?"

Clarke nodded, reluctant to put it into words, unsure exactly how much Evan had promised him, although Andrew must realise that Tammy's escape changed everything. Andrew appeared much more worried than she'd expected. Perhaps it was his idea to engage her services. He may have a lot more invested in this, career-wise, than she realised.

A knock at the door interrupted them. Ken Langton carried two steaming mugs. He placed them in front of her and Andrew.

"I know how much you like coffee," Andrew said, "so I took the liberty of asking Ken to make some."

"Thank you. Very much appreciated." Clarke smiled. Andrew would never have done that when she worked here. Perhaps, in her current job, he saw her as more of an equal.

"How are you?" Clarke addressed Ken. "It's good to see you." She'd never been that close to Ken, but seeing a familiar face put her at ease. Especially Ken, as he wasn't in any way threatening. No doubt he was still chugging along in the same rut as he'd always been, doing as little work as possible.

"We miss you," he said, with only the tiniest hint of sincerity. "You should come back."

"Clarke's got a new exciting career now," Andrew interrupted. "She doesn't want her old job back."

"Who's doing Tammy's job now?" Clarke asked. She wondered if it might be relevant, if Tammy would be annoyed by it.

"Why? Do you want it?" Ken asked.

"I'm happy where I am. I just wondered."

"We got someone in soon after you left," Andrew said. "He turned out to be quite good."

"Yes, he's great," Ken said.

"Haven't you got work to do?" Andrew stared pointedly at Ken, who took a few moments to get the hint and leave them.

"I don't suppose anyone from the company ever visited Tammy in prison?" She already knew the answer, but she wanted to see Andrew's reaction.

"Not that I'm aware. I certainly didn't. What would I say to her?" he asked. "After what she did."

Clarke privately thought that Tammy would have sent him packing long before he got a chance to say anything at all. She wondered who had replaced Bradley Acres, but she refrained from asking, not wanting to hear the answer. Yet another new face in the office. What must it be like for him or her, stepping into a dead man's job? She felt sorry for them. They would undoubtedly have found out in their first week here.

"I really should talk to Douglas Doncaster," Clarke said.

Andrew's face lit up. "That will be tricky."

Clarke suspected Andrew was about to be the bearer of bad news. He always enjoyed that sort of thing.

"Douglas has gone. He got marched out by security earlier this morning." Andrew struggled to contain his excitement at being the one to inform Clarke of the latest drama. "The official communication said he resigned, but we're pretty sure the board forced him out. It was right after Tammy's escape hit the news."

Clarke wasn't surprised. The board of Briar Holman gave him a hard time when Tammy first got arrested and then again after the trial. They wanted to get rid of him then. Tammy's escape and the prison officer's murder obviously proved to be the final straw.

"I can't say I blame them," Andrew said.

"No, I suppose not." It was a blow not being able to talk to Douglas, however much she dreaded doing so. Clarke wondered if Paul had contacted him yet. He would be an obvious person to talk to, even though he and Tammy were divorced, and he didn't want anything more to do with her. Clarke empathised with that. Douglas

Doncaster was another person trying to get his life back on course after Tammy had tainted it.

"Will Tammy show up here?" Andrew asked. "It would be too risky for her, wouldn't it?"

Clarke wondered how logically Tammy was thinking. The emotional side of her might lead her to seek out Doug. For what? To get back together? Or for revenge? Clarke would bet on the latter.

"With Douglas gone, it's unlikely," Clarke said. "But if Tammy does come here, the new receptionist won't recognise her."

"Good point," Andrew said. "I'll make sure she gets her photo, just in case."

"A photo won't be of much use now. Apparently, Tammy shaved off all her hair. She would look completely different."

"She looked completely different most days when she worked here," Andrew said. "When she altered her hair, sometimes I didn't even recognise her. I had to do a double take in case she was a new employee."

Clarke laughed. She knew exactly what he meant.

"Anyway, how is the new career going?"

"It's good. I'm enjoying it."

"Quite the investigator now, aren't you? You always were persistent with that sort of stuff. Most people give up if they can't get an instant answer, but you keep digging away until you find what you want. I'd say you're in the right job."

"Yes. It feels like it," Clarke said, pleased to get such a glowing reference from Andrew, who rarely said a good word about anybody. "I enjoy it." Going to different offices and meeting new people interested her too, although she'd had a few difficult experiences with that, particularly the contract at Carjon Pharma, when one of their employees was murdered when she worked there. Clarke finished her coffee, pleased that Ken had remembered exactly how she liked it. She smiled. All those years of training him how to make it properly had paid off, although he had rarely made drinks for anyone but himself when she'd worked here.

If she couldn't speak to Douglas Doncaster, she was wasting her time at Briar Holman. Now that she'd caught up with Andrew and Ken, she didn't feel up to facing the whole office. She would sneak out quietly and hope nobody else spotted her.

"I should be going," she said. "But you need to watch out for Tammy. I don't think she'll try to come into the office." Tammy would never want to risk being trapped inside the building. "But she might hang around near the car park. And once she learns that Douglas has left, she'll probably stay away."

"Yes, maybe I should talk to the CEO. He can put out a press release about Douglas resigning. If the tabloids pick it up and relate it to Tammy's escape, I'm sure she'll hear of it sooner or later."

Clarke wondered what Douglas would say to that. She felt sure he wouldn't want his 'resignation' to become common knowledge. But if it protected the other employees at Briar Holman, they probably should issue a press release.

Andrew stood up. "You know the way out, don't you?"

"I'm sure I can remember." Clarke got up and put on her coat.

She walked out to the car, wondering what to do next. Tammy's disappearing act left them with no easy way of tracing the money. She supposed she might be able to track down some of Tammy's old friends. Perhaps they would help her.

Chapter 8

DC Barry Medway was fed up. He always got the rubbish jobs, and this time he was trawling through hundreds of hours of CCTV from the area around Ranleigh Marsh prison. Bor-ing!

He struggled to concentrate. Eager to finish, he fast-forwarded through some of the video. With any luck, he'd spot Tammy Doncaster sooner rather than later, because he couldn't face going through the whole damn lot.

When his phone rang, it provided a welcome distraction.

"Hi." Barry left the CCTV running. He could watch it well enough while he talked.

"You coming out tonight, mate?" his friend Shaun asked.

"I doubt it." Barry was pretty sure he'd be stuck in here watching CCTV until late tonight. He glanced at the pile beside him. Hell, he'd probably be watching CCTV for the rest of his life.

Murders were always the same. They ruined your social life. But that was the job, and he loved it. He longed to do more of the exciting stuff and less of this tedious screen-watching. All he saw on the screen were empty roads. This was a waste of his time. He should be out searching instead.

"If you do fancy it," Shaun said, "we're going to The Ball and Chain pub in Havebury."

"I'll try to come along later, but we've got a lot on at work." He wouldn't try too hard. The Ball and Chain was a dump. Worse than that, it was full of criminals. He wouldn't be popular if he showed up. At least one of the pub's customers would be certain to recognise him.

He forced himself to focus on the screen while still listening to Shaun. It was vital to find Tammy before she killed again. He knew Paul worried that Tammy Doncaster might hurt his fiancée. She and Tammy had history together. Clarke even visited Tammy on the same day that she escaped. Surely that was too much of a coincidence. Barry kept his mouth shut, though. No way would he dare to suggest that his sergeant's girlfriend might have helped Tammy Doncaster to abscond.

Something flashed up on the screen, but he was too busy listening to Shaun prattle on about who was going to the pub this evening. He was sure he'd seen something that he should have given more attention.

"Listen, I've got to go, Shaun. I'll try to make it this evening, but don't wait for me."

"No probs, mate."

Barry wound the CCTV back a few minutes and stared at the screen.

Empty, empty, empty, empty, empty. And then, suddenly, a woman walked across the screen before disappearing equally quickly. Was it Tammy Doncaster? It might be. He rewound the video, pausing it as she stared directly into the camera. Her face was blurred, and was that blond hair real or a wig? He printed a copy. Paul would need to see this. He'd arrested Tammy originally. Perhaps he would recognise her.

The odd thing was, she seemed to be headed *towards* the marshes, not away from them, as they were expecting. Was it possible she would hide out somewhere in Ranleigh Marshes? They should be out searching for her. At last, he would get some action now. Barry snatched the copy off the printer and hurried to find Paul.

"Sarge." Barry caught up with Paul in the corridor just as he left DCI Price's office. He flapped the CCTV printout at him. "I've found something, Sarge."

Paul took the picture.

"It looks a bit like her, doesn't it, Sarge?"

Paul examined the photo. He didn't really recognise her from the blurred image, but he spotted enough similarities to conclude it must be Tammy. "Can you get the face enhanced? Make the image a bit clearer."

"I'll ask the techs."

"It must be her," Paul said. "Look at her clothes. Dark trousers and jumper. No coat, in this cold weather." A bitterly cold November wind had set in over the last few days. No one would go outside in these temperatures without a coat, not unless they were out for a run, and the woman in the photo wasn't dressed for running.

"Yes, you're right," Barry said.

"Well done."

"Will we search the marshes, Sarge?"

Paul shook his head. "She'd never survive outside for this long. Tammy's a real townie, and the marshes are wild and wet. No, she'll most likely have been picked up along that road somewhere. Can you check for any other CCTV further along that road? See if you can find any sign of her leaving in a car."

"Yes, Sarge." Barry's shoulders slumped.

Paul sympathised with him. Trawling through CCTV was everyone's least favourite job. "How much more CCTV do you have to check?"

"Two more tapes, Sarge."

"Finish that, then you can come with me to interview Tammy's cellmate after lunch."

Immediately, Barry's face brightened. "Thanks, Sarge."

Clarke opened up Facebook on her phone. It would be the easiest way for her to track down Tammy's old friends. Tammy used to be very active on Facebook and Instagram, fancied herself as the next big influencer.

She found Tammy's Facebook home page and checked her list of friends. There weren't many. Clarke remembered she used to have well over a thousand. A lot of people must have unfriended her. That seemed a bit mean, though perfectly understandable. Who wanted to be associated with a murderer? Besides, Facebook friends weren't like real friends. How many real friends did Tammy have?

She read the last post Tammy posted on Facebook. She'd been to a restaurant with two other girls, Josie and Keira. Both of them remained on Tammy's friends list. Were they still in contact with her, or did it simply not occur to them to unfriend her? Clarke checked out both of their profiles. Josie's profile didn't say much. It didn't give any clues about the woman herself or where to find her.

Keira was completely different. Clarke quickly discovered her employer's name and that she lived and worked locally in Brackford.

She needed to make a proper plan, or she would screw up her only chance to connect with them. The obvious approach would be to visit Keira at the bank where she worked. With luck, she would catch her when she went for her lunch break.

The only option to contact Josie was through Messenger. She started typing: *Hi, Josie. We've never met. I'm an old friend of Tammy.*

Should she mention Tammy's name so soon, or would that make Josie stop reading and ignore the message? This was going to be difficult. She considered for a minute and typed in some more: *You may have heard in the news that Tammy escaped yesterday.*

I wondered if you have any idea where she may be. I'm worried she might search for some of her old friends. If you can help, please let me know. I'd be really grateful. Kindest regards, Clarke.

She hesitated for a long time before hitting the send button. Would Josie even reply, and how soon? It occurred to her as soon as she'd sent the message that Josie may tell Keira about it, a potential disaster if it put Keira on her guard and made her refuse to talk to Clarke.

It was nearly lunchtime. If she hurried, she would get to Keira's workplace in twenty minutes.

Keira worked in a bank in Brackford. Clarke wasn't sure exactly what job she did. If she was a cashier, she'd probably wear a name badge, so identifying her would be easy, but what if she did a different job? She stared at Keira's photo on Facebook, trying to commit it to memory. Hopefully, she'd recognise her when she saw her.

Clarke arrived at the bank during their busiest time and joined the queue for the cashiers. It would be pot luck which one of the three cashiers served her. The one on the far end looked promising. From this distance, she vaguely resembled the photo. When Clarke got closer to her, she would check her name badge and confirm it.

Reaching the top of the queue, Clarke was annoyed when somebody finished with the cashier closest to her, instead of the one she wanted to see. Quickly, she turned to the person behind her in the line.

"Do you want to go next?" she asked him. "I need to dig some paperwork out of my handbag first." She opened her bag and rummaged in it, pretending to search for something.

"Thanks." The man behind her happily took her place. Thankfully, the cashier at the far end became free next. Clarke moved fast.

"I want to open an account," she said, scanning the cashier's blouse for a nametag. She smiled as she saw *Keira* printed on the white plastic tag. Bingo.

"You'll have to go to the Customer Service Desk," Keira said, pointing to Clarke's right.

Clarke wondered what time Keira would take her lunch break. She checked her watch as if in a rush, then left the bank. Hopefully, Keira would be too busy with her next customer to spot her leaving.

Outside the bank, Clarke loitered, wondering what to do next. What if Keira didn't even come out at lunchtime? What if she'd brought a sandwich from home, intending to sit in the staff room to eat it? Well, she would soon find out. She leant against the wall and waited, keeping her eyes on the door all the time. After ten minutes, she was already bored. Her phone pinged. She pulled it out of her handbag, remembering to keep glancing at the door of the bank.

Josie's reply to Clarke's message came sooner than expected. She hoped she hadn't texted Keira to warn her. Clarke needed to talk to Keira today, because, for sure, Josie would contact her later. She'd be willing to bet on that.

Clarke opened up Messenger to read Josie's message. Damn, it wasn't good. *I don't want anything to do with that woman. I don't have any contact with her, so I've no idea where she might be. If she comes near me, I'll give her a piece of my mind. Please don't contact me again.*

Well, that told her pretty definitely. Clarke hoped she would get some useful information from Keira, because she didn't have any other leads to go on. She gazed longingly at the bank's front door, willing Keira to walk through it.

People entered and left the bank constantly. Lunchtime was particularly busy. The cashiers would probably take turns to eat lunch, or perhaps take their break after the busy period. She might be stuck here for a couple of hours at this rate.

Suddenly, Clarke perked up. Keira left the bank and was already crossing the road. Clarke followed her, jogging to catch up.

Keira disappeared into a café across the road from the bank.

"Excuse me," Clarke said when she caught up with Keira in the queue. "I need your help." A faint glimmer of recognition crossed Keira's face, but she clearly didn't remember her enough to place her.

"What's the problem?" Keira looked concerned and suspicious all at once.

"It's about Tammy Doncaster. I know you used to be friends with her." Clarke spoke fast, wanting to finish before Keira got the chance to leave. "I understand you probably don't want anything to do with her now, but did you hear she escaped from prison?"

"She what?"

"She escaped yesterday. I'm worried she might try to find me or some of her other old friends."

"So, what do you want?" Keira asked.

"Let me buy some lunch," Clarke offered. "Then we can have a chat. You might have some idea where she may be hiding or where she might go next? Anything would be useful."

"Are you police?" Keira asked.

"No, but the company I work for has been contracted to find the money Tammy stole." Clarke took a Tebbit & Cranshaw business card from her bag and placed it on the table in front of Keira. Hopefully, that would be official enough to persuade Keira to help her.

"Ok," she said, "I'll help if I can, but I don't have long."

Keira picked a sandwich, and Clarke grabbed one for herself. The waitress offered to bring their coffees to the table.

"How long have you known Tammy?" Clarke asked.

"Not long. Three or four years, I guess. We used to hang out a lot. Just goes to show, I'm not a good judge of character." She laughed bitterly. "But Tammy was fun, and she always got invited to the best parties. We went to loads of restaurants and clubs too. She introduced me to lots of people. My social life hasn't been the same since."

"Are there any places she particularly loved?" Clarke asked. "Not necessarily clubs or restaurants, but the sort of places she might be able to hide in for a while. Any people she might have trusted?"

Keira considered for a moment while she took a mouthful of her prawn sandwich. "Tammy spent a lot of time in Tredington."

Clarke waited for Keira to continue, hoping she might tell her something she didn't already know.

"She used to live there for a while, after she left her husband. I've still got the address of her flat." Keira tapped at her phone and pulled up some information. She pushed the screen towards Clarke, who copied it down. Was this the address she'd been hunting for when she'd tried to track down Tammy after she went missing from Briar Holman? Things were different back then. She'd been naïve. At least now she realised what she was dealing with. She would never trust Tammy again.

"She wouldn't be hiding in the flat. I'm sure it got sold. But the flats back onto the park and the new nature reserve. That's full of places to camp out."

Clarke knew the park. The council was bequeathed a huge amount of land next to it to create a nature reserve. A large herd of deer inhabited the vast acreage. If they crossed a couple of deserted roads, they could roam for miles, well away from the town. Tammy would never be an outdoor girl, but she was a survivor. There must be plenty of places to hide for a short while if needs must. She just didn't see Tammy embracing the great outdoors in November. She decided to rule it out for the moment.

Keira finished her sandwich and gulped down the last of her coffee. "She was good friends with one of the guys who worked in The Ball and Chain pub in Havebury as well. It's a real dive. I didn't like it much. I only went once."

Clarke remembered the Ball and Chain as a bit of a dump, and the clientele wasn't much better either. "Can you remember his name?" she asked.

"Kroft, with a K. It's a nickname. I can't tell you his real name. Everyone calls him Kroft."

"Kroft? Does he still work in The Ball and Chain?"

Keira shrugged her shoulders. "I've never been there since."

"Do you remember anybody else?" Clarke asked.

"She's got some close friends in Dorset, but I never met them, so I don't really know much about them, except they lived on a farm." Keira picked up her handbag. "I need to get back to work. I only get a short lunch break."

"You've been really helpful. I appreciate it," Clarke said.

"I hope you find her. I'm worried she might come after me too. Is she dangerous? Didn't she murder someone?"

Clarke nodded. "I'm afraid she murdered somebody else too when she escaped from prison. So yes, if she comes anywhere near you, call the police. Just be careful, ok, but I'm sure it's me she's after, not you."

"Good luck. I really hope you find her before she hurts anyone else."

On her way back to the office, Clarke wondered what she should do next. After her last experience in The Ball and Chain pub, she really didn't want to revisit the place. She didn't remember Tammy ever mentioning anyone called Kroft, so she doubted they were particularly close. On the other hand, Katie and Ned Young were probably Tammy's only remaining friends. It was too late to go today. She would drive down to Dorset tomorrow. She just hoped they would agree to talk to her.

Chapter 9

Linda was sitting in an interview room with a prison officer when Paul and Barry arrived.

"Will this take long?" Linda asked. "I've been here for hours."

"You've been here ten minutes," the officer said.

"That's ten minutes too long."

"Have you got somewhere you need to be?" The officer didn't hide her sarcasm.

Paul smiled at Linda, trying to get her on side. He didn't need a snarky prison officer winding her up. "My name's DS Waterford, and this is DC Medway." However much he wanted to put her at ease and get her cooperating, he didn't intend to get on first-name terms with some chavvy criminal.

"And my name's Lady Godiva."

"Linda, give the detective some respect." The prison officer glared at her.

"Any chance of some coffee?" Paul asked. The interview would go much better if the officer left them alone.

"Milk, two sugars," Linda said.

The officer ignored her. "I won't be long," she said to Paul, getting up.

Paul waited until she shut the door behind her. "How long have you shared a cell with Tammy Doncaster?" he asked Linda.

"Dunno. Ever since she got here, I guess."

Two years. Tammy was on remand for a year before she got convicted. "Did she mention anything about an escape plan?"

Linda shook her head. "No. If she did, I would have bloody wanted to go too, wouldn't I?"

"So, what did you talk about? Did she mention any of her friends?" Barry asked.

"No. She didn't talk to me much about anything. She spent most of the time in the cell doing hours and hours of exercising. She became completely obsessed with it, always doing push-ups and star jumps like she wanted to win the Olympics. I dunno why she bothered."

It occurred to Paul that the fitness freak thing might have formed part of Tammy's escape strategy. Fitness and strength equal survival. She may have been planning this for a long time. It would make it much more difficult to find her if she had a well-thought-out strategy.

"What about her friends in prison? Who were her friends in here?"

"She didn't really have no friends. Nobody liked her. They're all a bit scared of her, to be honest. The only person she got friendly with was Officer Hunter."

"You mean Sadie Hunter, the prison officer?" Paul asked.

"Yeah, the screw, the one that got murdered."

"Tammy was friends with her?" This didn't tally with Archie Hunter's version of things.

"Not friends, not exactly, but they spent a lot of time talking."

Paul made a note. He would have to interview the other prison officers again. Get their take on the situation. Why did Tammy get friendly with Sadie? And did Sadie help her to escape, then got murdered for her trouble?

They were done here. He asked the prison officer to take them to the governor's office.

"Did you get anything useful out of Linda?" Janice asked when they were seated around her desk.

"Not much. She seemed to think Tammy and Sadie were friendly."

"Really? I can't imagine where she got that idea from. Sadie asked for a transfer to another wing a couple of weeks ago." She shook her head sadly. "I wish I'd let her move, but I simply didn't have enough suitable staff to risk swapping them round. If she'd told me the problem was so serious..."

Paul appreciated Janice's pain. Hindsight did that. Gave people regrets over things they could never put right. It would be a long time before Janice forgave herself for the mistake. "Can you provide a list of Tammy's visitors, please, everyone since she's been in here?" he asked, changing the subject.

"That should be easy. Only two people ever visited her," Janice said. "She only got a visit once a month, and the two people seemed to alternate, so each visited every two months. They didn't seem to be at all suspicious."

Paul smiled. In his experience, everyone was suspicious.

"I'll get you the details." Janice tapped at her computer keyboard. A few moments later, the printer spewed out a single sheet of paper. "Here's the address," she said. "They live together, according to this. We check all potential visitors before they are allowed to come. We verified the address."

Paul took the sheet of paper. Ned Young and Katie Young. "Dorset? That's dedicated, coming all this way to visit her."

"We do get people travelling long distances, usually family. It's not unusual."

"And she hasn't received any other visitors at all?" Paul asked.

"No, not until yesterday. Funny that, getting somebody different after all this time, right before she escaped. Do you think that's significant?"

"No," Paul said. It wasn't funny at all. Not to him anyway.

Chapter 10

"Make yourself at home," Rob said. "I've got plenty of room. Stay as long as you like."

Clarke decided to move in with her younger brother for a few days. It would be much more convenient for work, and she didn't want to worry their parents.

She sat down. "It will only be until the wedding, at worst, and that's less than a week away." If they found Tammy, she could go home much sooner than that.

"So, what's up? Why the big fuss? Don't tell me you and Paul have argued."

"No, of course not." Clarke hesitated, unsure how much to tell Rob, then quickly decided it would be best if he knew all the facts. "It's Tammy."

"Tammy? She's in prison," Rob said, puzzled.

"Have you not seen the news?"

"I've been busy all day. Haven't got time for stuff like that."

"Tammy escaped," Clarke said.

"What?" Rob stood up. "Are you sure? How the hell did that happen?"

"Of course I'm sure. I visited her yesterday afternoon."

"You did what?"

"I said I visited—"

"Yes, but why? I thought you'd decided not to."

"I wish I hadn't gone. Anyway, by the time I got home, she'd murdered a prison officer and escaped."

Rob appeared totally shocked. "How did that happen? That's crazy. How did she manage it? Security's tight, isn't it?"

"Apparently, she stole the prison officer's uniform and walked out bold as brass using her security pass."

"That sounds like Tammy," Rob said. "She hasn't changed."

"Well, that's the thing," Clarke said. "I thought she'd changed a lot. She was a mess, emotionally and physically. That's not like Tammy at all. She can't cope with being locked up."

"I can't say I blame her. I'd be the same," Rob said.

"Whose side are you on? You've always had a soft spot for Tammy, haven't you?"

"The only soft spot I've got for Tammy after what she did to you is right in the middle of Ranleigh Marshes," Rob said.

Clarke remembered her shock at seeing the state of Tammy. "She came across as being completely downtrodden and depressed. I assumed the pressure got to her so she couldn't cope. To be honest, I felt really sorry for her."

"Don't," Rob said. "Tammy's an actress, a good one. She should have stuck with it. She fooled you before, remember, told you all those lies, made you believe that she'd been kidnapped and locked up in that horrible flat."

"Are you calling me gullible?" Clarke asked. She'd forgotten that Tammy spent a year pursuing an acting career prior to joining Briar Holman.

"No, Sis, but Tammy's good. She'd have fooled anyone. Well, she did, didn't she?"

"I suppose so," Clarke said. Tammy deceived the rest of her colleagues, her husband, and the police, as well as her.

"The police will find her, won't they? I don't like not knowing where she is. But at least you'll be safe here. She doesn't know my address."

"No," Clarke said. "She won't be able to find out your address." Rob only moved here recently. Rob was right. She would be much safer staying here.

"Where might she have gone?"

"I'm not sure." Clarke had thought of nothing else since learning of Tammy's escape. "She knows Tredington really well. She may have gone back there or to her friends in Dorset. They're the only people who visited her in prison. Everyone else dumped her."

"That's rough," Rob said. "But I can't say I blame them. Why did you visit? You shouldn't have gone."

For once, Clarke agreed with him. She'd even started to wonder whether Tammy escaping might have something to do with her visit. But she couldn't for the life of her imagine how. "Evan wanted me to go."

"Evan? What business is it of his?"

"Briar Holman have engaged the firm to retrieve the money that Tammy stole. The police never found it. We may not find it either." The best people in the fraud squad had already failed to trace the money. Clarke lacked the arrogance to assume she might do any better. She would need a huge amount of luck and, with Tammy gone, her luck had run out. "But the thing is, they know I used to work with Tammy. So, I guess I'm the big attraction. They want me on the case. The only way we stand any chance of getting this money back is if I can get close to Tammy, so either I get into her head, which is unlikely, or she lets something slip, which is even more unlikely. So, without me, there's little chance of succeeding."

"Well, there's not much chance even with you now, not if Tammy's done a runner."

Clarke nodded. Should she be relieved or upset? Probably relieved, except that now Tammy was out there somewhere, and she didn't know where.

"Anyway, more importantly," Clarke said, "have you written your speech yet?" Rob was Paul's best man. She loved the idea of walking up the aisle towards her two best men. She'd been delighted when Paul had asked Rob.

"I've started." Rob flashed her a cheeky grin. "You might not like it much."

"I'm sure I'll love it."

"It's risqué, it's insulting, and it's rude," Rob warned her. "But it's also incredibly funny. Of course you'll love it."

Clarke made a face. "Don't overdo it."

"It's the best man's job to overdo the speech," Rob said. "That and getting the groom blind drunk on the stag night and handcuffing him to a lamppost." He laughed. "I got a couple of stories from one of his colleagues, Barry. I met up with him in a pub, and he told me loads of great stuff about Paul."

Clarke sighed. She would have to trust Rob. "If you're going to be embarrassing, it better be the funniest thing I've ever heard in my life. Otherwise, Paul will kill you, if I don't get there first."

"Paul's got a sense of humour," Rob said. "He'll be fine with it."

"Let's hear the speech then."

"No chance. It's going to be a surprise. You'll have to wait until the big day."

"I'll be waiting with great trepidation. I'm terrified already." Clarke hoped Paul wouldn't regret asking Rob to be his best man. Rob's warped sense of humour got a bit carried away sometimes. Clarke tried to smile, but it came out as more of a grimace. "Well, I'm glad you're doing it, anyway."

"You leave the speech to me and concentrate on the important stuff, like the food."

"Oh, the caterer is already organised. Don't worry, the food will be great."

"That's the only reason I go to weddings," Rob said.

"Even mine?"

Rob laughed. "I wouldn't even show up for my own wedding if the food wasn't good."

Clarke laughed, glad that Auntie Fenella had insisted on paying for some decent caterers, but there were other things on her mind. More important things, like her visit to Dorset tomorrow to see Ned and Katie Young.

Chapter 11

It took Clarke longer than expected to battle through the M25 traffic. She decided to stop for a coffee and pulled into a service station on the M3.

Visiting Tammy's friends might be a crazy idea, but she didn't have much of a choice. With Tammy at large, it would be equally mad to do nothing. Tammy had threatened her, and Clarke couldn't spend all her time looking over her shoulder, waiting to be found. She didn't trust Tammy to leave her alone. She would inevitably catch up with her, sooner rather than later.

If she was going to stand any chance of finding Tammy, the Dorset friends, Ned and Katie Young, were her only lead. She didn't even have that until yesterday, when she found the text with their address on Paul's phone.

Paul hadn't visited the Youngs yet. It would be much better if Clarke spoke to them first. They might be more likely to talk to a woman, a former friend of Tammy, rather than the police. Anything was worth a try.

As Clarke took her coffee back to the car, she realised she'd told no one where she was going. She'd made that mistake before with Tammy and didn't want to repeat the error. Grabbing her phone, she quickly planned what she would say.

"Hi, Evan."

"Clarke. I hope you've got good news because I'm not getting anywhere with locating this money. It seems to have been wired round the world a few times. We tracked the first nine bank transfers. After that, the trail went cold."

"I'm not surprised," Clarke said. Tammy was clever. She wouldn't have made it easy for them.

"Have you found Tammy?"

"No." Clarke didn't want to admit to Evan that Tammy seemed to be one step ahead of her. "But I'm on my way to see her friends in Dorset. They visited her in prison. They might know where she is." The difficult part would be getting them to tell her.

"That sounds like a good idea."

"I'll phone you when I'm on my way home."

"That's great," Evan said.

"If you don't hear from me by early evening, can you phone Paul, please?"

"Why would I need to do that?" Evan paused, then said, "You haven't told him you're going, have you?"

"He wouldn't approve."

"You should still tell him," Evan said.

"I can't." Clarke wasn't going to tell Evan that she'd taken the Youngs' address from Paul's phone.

"Are you sure you want to do this, Clarke? I'm worried now that it might be risky. What if Tammy's hiding out there?"

"I'll be careful." She didn't suppose Tammy would show up in Dorset. She'd been near Brackford yesterday. Did she even have any transport, and would too much travelling make it easier for the police to find her, with so many cameras on the roads? She wished she could work out how Tammy's brain functioned.

"Nothing's going to happen," Clarke said. "But you will tell Paul if I don't phone you later, won't you?"

"Of course I will, although he'll probably kill me for not telling him earlier. You'd better be really careful."

"I will be."

"I mean it, Clarke. If you've got the slightest worry, get out. I'd rather return Briar Holman's fee than have anything happen to you."

Clarke was touched that Evan worried about her. Luckily, she never told him the full details of what Tammy did to her when they'd both worked at Briar Holman, otherwise he'd pull her off this job instantly. "I'm sure you won't have to do that." Clarke wasn't sure at all. And, whatever Evan said, he'd be disappointed if they failed.

She hung up and drained her coffee cup. There was just time to get to Dorset before lunch. That might be her best chance of catching the Youngs at home.

Tammy's friends, Katie and Ned Young, lived a few miles outside of Blandford. Clarke pulled up outside and checked the address, wondering if this was the right house. She wasn't mistaken.

A five-bar gate of varnished wood fronted the short driveway. It would be best to leave the car out on the road, in case she needed to get away in a hurry. The property wasn't what she'd expected. Tammy always claimed that Katie and Ned owned a farm, not a smart, expensive house, with a couple of fields and some sheds next to it. This was as far removed from a proper farm as Clarke's flat was from a mansion.

Clarke clicked open the catch on the gate, admiring the front garden, with its perfectly manicured lawn and weedless flower beds. She heard dogs barking and immediately snapped the gate shut again. A moment later, two dogs raced around the corner of the house. Clarke breathed a sigh of relief as a Yorkshire terrier and an old Labrador appeared, the latter struggling to keep up with the excitable terrier.

"Don't worry, they won't hurt you." A pretty redhead came to the gate behind the dogs. "They're all bark and no bite."

"I love dogs," Clarke said.

"That's lucky. What can I do for you, anyway?"

"I'm looking for Katie." Clarke smiled, hoping that would prove reassuring.

"Who wants her?"

Clarke smiled again. "My name's Clarke. I used to work with Tammy." Clarke imagined a flash of fear in Katie's eyes.

"You'd better come in." Katie opened the gate. The dogs lost interest and hurtled off to sniff at something in the hedge. "I need to feed the geese," she said, then I'll make you a coffee.

Clarke followed her to a shed. A jumble of garden tools lay in a haphazard heap on one side, and various animal feeds were stored in dustbins opposite. Katie squeezed into the narrow gap between them, reaching for an empty bucket and filling it with corn from one of the bins. The shed certainly didn't have any space to hide Tammy. Originally, Clarke hoped to find plenty of places where Tammy might be concealed. She wondered why Tammy always called it a farm. Had Tammy, a city girl, never seen a real farm, or was this another of her many exaggerated lies?

"It's a lovely garden," Clarke said. "How big is it?"

"Around five acres. We've got the garden round the house and two fields for the horses." Katie pointed to a couple of horses grazing quietly in an adjoining field. A pair of stables flanked the edge of the field. Clarke wondered if she would get a chance to check inside them. There wouldn't be any point. It was far too obvious for Tammy to be hidden here.

Vast fields surrounded the perimeter fence. Presumably, they belonged to a neighbouring farmer.

Katie shook the bucket of feed. A moment later, a flock of geese appeared from behind the stables and ran towards them, making the most awful honking noise. Clarke stepped back.

"They're better guard dogs than these two." Katie pointed at the dogs, laughing. "They scare most people. Just stand out of the way. I've got a bucket of feed, so they won't pay any attention to you." Katie tipped the feed into a long trough. The geese quickly surrounded it and started gobbling it up. Katie disappeared into another shed. Clarke followed her, not wanting to be left with the geese, and peered in through the open door. This must be where the geese lived. Straw and goose droppings covered the floor, with some large nesting boxes taking up the whole of the far end.

"I need to collect the eggs, then we can go indoors and get some coffee."

Clarke watched as Katie picked eggs from the nesting boxes, placing them carefully in the empty bucket. The nesting boxes were numbered at the top. Her eyes wandered along the line before doing a double take. The numbers were out of order. Like everything in the shed, they were higgledy-piggledy.

Katie plucked an egg from the final nesting box, number three. "There, all done. Let's go in."

Clarke was keen to get away from the geese, although they looked a lot less vicious now that they were busy eating.

Katie led her into a big farmhouse-style kitchen. She sat down, folded her arms, and stared at Clarke.

"You're not like I imagined," she said.

"No?" Clarke was relieved that Katie seemed to know about her, but perhaps she shouldn't be. It occurred to her that Katie might easily be setting a trap for her, that Tammy might appear at any moment.

"Tammy told me lots about you. She admired you, you know."

That was news to Clarke. "No. I didn't know."

"You used to be a firefighter, didn't you?"

Clarke nodded. "A few years ago." There were some days when she still missed it. Nothing beat the adrenaline rush and the camaraderie.

"Tammy was in awe of you for that. Even after you got her arrested. She said she underestimated you. You turned out to be much braver than she expected you to be."

Clarke shrugged. She really wasn't that brave and certainly didn't feel at all brave right now.

"You visited Tammy in prison." Clarke changed the subject, uncomfortable talking about herself.

"Yes, a few times," Katie admitted. "I hated it."

"I completely understand that. I'm ashamed to say I only visited once, earlier this week." Clarke only realised now how guilty she felt about that, especially as Tammy wrote to her a few times last year, begging her to come.

Clarke looked longingly at the kettle on the worktop in front of her. She was dying for the cup of coffee Katie had promised her earlier. Katie didn't take the hint.

"The only thing that made it bearable for me was the opportunity to go back to Ranleigh Marshes. Our school organised a trip there once," Katie said. "Tammy didn't like it, but I loved every minute of it. I took up bird watching after that and spent a couple of afternoons there every month. Even dragged Ned and Tammy along a few times."

"Very different from Hackney." Clarke smiled. She easily imagined Tammy disliking the wild nature reserve, and she could pretty much guess what she would have said about the experience.

Katie grew more relaxed. Talking about old times seemed to soften her. "There was always a country girl inside me waiting to get out," she said. "That's why we moved down here. Ned worked for an investment bank, trading bonds. The job burnt him out by the time he turned thirty, but he earned massive bonuses most years. He invested it in property. So now we travel up to London once a month to keep an eye on the rental business."

"And visit Tammy," Clarke said, wanting to get the subject back on track.

"Exactly."

Clarke was warming up nicely now that she'd been indoors for a while. She pulled off her scarf and folded it up on the kitchen table.

"We took it in turns, Ned and I. That made the whole visiting thing slightly easier for both of us."

"You've known Tammy a long time?"

"The three of us lived in Hackney as teenagers."

"What was she like then?"

"Clever, ambitious, feisty, and tremendous fun. We were always getting into scrapes. I never imagined she'd end up like this, though. I blame Doug," Katie said.

"Really. Why?" Clarke would have expected Doug to be a calming influence on Tammy, not someone who would drive her to murder.

"He didn't treat her very well. Doug's controlling, and I suppose he never liked being unable to control Tammy."

"What do you mean about him not treating her well? Did he hit her?"

Katie shook her head. "It wasn't physical. It was mental torture. Tammy only ever wanted everyone to love her. He ground her down emotionally, made her stop believing in herself. What he did to Tammy was like watching someone pull the wings off a butterfly. It's a pity she didn't kill *him*. *He* deserved it."

For a brief moment, Clarke empathised with Tammy. She pulled herself together. Tammy didn't deserve sympathy, not now.

"How did she end up with Doug, if he was like that?" She always saw Tammy and Doug as a mismatched couple, her a party girl, and him, a boring old git.

"Back then, our one big aim was to get out of Hackney. Preferably as quickly as possible."

"And Doug gave Tammy a way out?"

"No. Tammy got out long before she met Doug. But she always worried she'd end up going back. She was afraid of being poor again."

Clarke remembered something Tammy said to her, when she'd locked her in that derelict block of flats, one of the things for which she'd been convicted. Tammy asked her if she'd ever lived in a tower block in Hackney. She was making a point. She'd come from poverty and feared ending up in the same state.

"You obviously understand Tammy well."

"She was one of my best friends."

Clarke noted that Katie used the past tense. Perhaps her fear that Tammy might walk into Katie's kitchen at any moment was unfounded.

"What would she be thinking now?" Clarke asked.

Katie laughed. "She'll be planning how she can spend her money."

Clarke bit her tongue, stifling the temptation to point out that the money didn't belong to Tammy. It belonged to Briar Holman's shareholders. "Do you know where the money is?"

Katie laughed even louder this time. "Don't be daft. Do you seriously believe Tammy would tell anyone that? And if she did, I would never break her trust."

Clarke caught Katie's eyes. She seemed to be telling the truth, that she wasn't aware of where Tammy had hidden the money. Clarke wondered if Tammy would come here and how much Katie would help her. She looked out the large kitchen window.

"The view from here is amazing."

Katie smiled. "Yes, that's mostly what sold the house to us. On a clear day, we can see for miles. The farms are back-to-back in that direction. Nothing to spoil our perfect view."

Clarke scanned the scenery. Katie and Ned's house, which turned out to be a tiny smallholding rather than the farm Tammy always referred to, wasn't large enough to hide Tammy. But beyond the fields lay hundreds of acres of forest, with plenty of room to hide out. Clarke would have to come up with a way to persuade Paul to search it without admitting she had visited Katie.

"I can't quite imagine Tammy in the country," Clarke said. "She's more the sophisticated townie. Doesn't like getting muddy feet. Did she visit you often?"

Katie tossed her head back and laughed. "Hardly ever," she said. "We've only been here about four years, since Ned got out of banking. She never came while she and Doug were married. He wouldn't let her. The only time she came here was when she stayed for a week after they split."

"Did she like it here?"

Katie stared at her. "Why don't you come out and ask it?"

"Sorry?"

"You know you want to. Go on. Ask me if she'll come here now."

Clarke was taken aback by Katie's directness. She'd tried not to be that obvious, but of course Katie would assume that. "Will she?" Clarke asked.

"I honestly don't know," Katie said. "In any case, that's the wrong question."

"What's the right question?"

"Will I help her if she asks me to?"

"What's the answer?"

"I love Tammy, but I'd phone the police. I can't risk her dragging down myself and Ned with her, however much I want to help her for old times' sake."

Katie certainly gave a good impression of telling the truth. She probably wouldn't help Tammy. Clarke wondered if Ned felt the same.

"Where's Ned today?" Clarke asked. "It would be good to meet him, too."

"He's sorting out one of his properties," Katie said. "Got a problem with a broken fence. He couldn't find anyone to fix it at short notice, so he decided to drive up and mend it himself."

"What a shame." Clarke wondered if it would be worth coming back another time. She hadn't expected Katie to be so open with her and she'd learned a tremendous amount about Tammy from her. Katie had told her everything, but nothing. How far did her loyalty to Tammy extend? She'd visited her regularly in prison, which was more than any of Tammy's other friends did. That must mean something.

"I should be going." Clarke glanced at her watch. If she didn't phone Evan soon, he'd phone Paul, as they agreed earlier, then she'd wish she'd told Paul this morning about the visit.

Chapter 12

Clarke parked in the village a couple of miles from Katie's house. She pulled out her phone and dialled Evan.

"I'm so glad you phoned," he said. "You got me worried this morning. I've been wondering all day if I should phone Paul."

"You didn't, did you?"

"No."

Clarke breathed a sigh of relief. Paul wouldn't approve of her visiting Katie, and she didn't want to get into an argument with him about it.

"Have you got anywhere with tracing the money?"

"No," Evan said, "but we should focus on St Kitts. You said Tammy used to dream of living there. She may have been planning that."

"You want a good holiday on expenses, don't you?" Clarke said.

"It did occur to me that one of us should go, and you're busy organising a wedding."

"I need to get home." Clarke still had a long drive home. She didn't have time to discuss Evan's dream holiday. "I'll see you tomorrow."

As Clarke hung up, she remembered her scarf. She'd taken it off in Katie's kitchen and didn't recall picking it up again when she left. A quick search of her handbag confirmed it. The scarf wasn't expensive. If she'd been further along on her journey home, she'd have left it, but the drive back to Katie's house would only take five minutes. It would be silly not to.

She turned the car around and pointed it back in the direction she came from a few minutes earlier. As she drove back, she thought about Tammy and the money, the three million pounds Tammy stole from Briar Holman when they both worked for the company. Evan might well be right. Tammy came from St Kitts. She loved it there. And when anything went wrong, it was her happy place that she visited in her head. Of course she would want to return there. It was worth a try. It might also be where she was heading now. She must have a plan to get out of the UK. Perhaps St Kitts would be her final destination.

Clarke found a parking space on the road near Katie's house. She nearly reached her front gate, relieved not to have barking dogs race up to greet her this time, when she caught sight of movement at the back of the property. Katie's mop of red hair stood out like a beacon.

Clarke was about to call out, when she saw Katie scramble over the fence behind her garden. The garden backed onto open farmland. What reason would she have to climb into the neighbouring field? She moved closer to the gate, taking care to stay near the cover of the hedge, in case Katie turned around. Katie marched across the field, striding out purposefully. In her hands, she held two brightly coloured carrier bags. Clarke longed to follow her, but the wide-open field made tracking Katie impossible without being spotted.

A frisson of excitement flared inside her. Was it possible that Katie was on her way to meet Tammy, taking her some supplies? Could Tammy be hiding out in the woods beyond the field? It seemed unlikely, given Tammy's hatred of the great outdoors. And yet... She must be somewhere. And way out here in the countryside, with no CCTV and no neighbours to wonder about her, this would be an easy place to stay hidden.

Clarke took out her phone. She brought up Google Earth and keyed in Katie's postcode. Katie was walking away from the sun, so that must be east. Clarke soon got her bearings and found the wood where Katie seemed to be heading.

The wood was huge and thick with trees of different varieties. Anyone would be able to stay hidden for months if they knew their way around and if someone took them food supplies, because she couldn't, even in her wildest dreams, imagine Tammy trapping and skinning rabbits to eat or living on wild berries. The forest provided a bounty of free produce, but Tammy wouldn't have a clue. In November, she reminded herself, even sheltered from the chilly winds, it would be difficult, but not impossible, to keep warm enough. Even Tammy could cope for a short while, until her plan to leave the country and begin a life of luxury kicked in.

Clarke glanced at her watch. It might be ages before Katie returned. Best to give up on getting her scarf back. Part of her wanted to follow Katie into the woods, to check if Tammy really was hiding nearby. But she wasn't crazy enough to risk putting herself alone in the middle of nowhere with a double murderer. She would tell Paul everything, even though confessing to him that she'd visited Katie would probably mean a row. They were getting married on Saturday. Now wasn't the time for a lovers' tiff, let alone a major disagreement, which might drag on for a few days, but she didn't have a choice. If Paul could organise a proper search team, they would soon discover if Tammy was hiding in these woods.

She walked back to her car. At least she would get three hours on the drive home to work out how to come clean to Paul.

DC Barry Medway cruised along the motorway, headed south. Paul sat in the passenger seat, staring at his phone. The address the prison governor gave him was near Blandford, in Dorset. He wondered if they would find Tammy there. Katie and Ned seemed to be her only real friends, certainly the only ones who bothered to visit. As the car sped along, Paul mulled over the logistics Tammy would face if she wanted to get to Dorset. With no car, presumably no coat, no food, no money, she would need to either hitchhike or steal some cash or a credit card. Or even steal a car. Prisons served as universities for crime. Tammy probably learned in prison how to hot-wire a car, at least in theory. So, it would be that or hitchhiking. Tammy wasn't stupid. If she used public transport, they'd be able to track her on

CCTV. No way would she take that chance. Hopefully, she hadn't hitchhiked. He was nervous she might leave a trail of dead bodies in her wake.

"Do you think we'll get any useful information from these people?" Barry asked.

"I hope so. The DCI's been on my back to find Tammy. He's worried about public safety if she's not recaptured soon. Even worse, he's worried about the embarrassment for the police if she manages to skip the country."

"She'll never get out of the country, will she, Sarge?"

"She's got three million pounds. That can buy a lot of assistance, and after two years in prison, she may have some criminal contacts." Paul wondered about that. By all accounts, Tammy didn't exactly ingratiate herself with her fellow inmates. She didn't seem to have any friends in Ranleigh Marsh. "If we don't find her soon, she'll get magic-ed out of the country, then we'll never find her."

Paul and Barry finally reached Katie and Ned Young's house at 2:00 p.m.

"They won't be expecting us," Paul said. "You go round the back, in case Doncaster's inside, but I doubt she will be. It's too obvious. The Youngs visited Tammy in prison, so they must be expecting us to show up, eventually."

Paul knocked on the door. A bronzed man answered. That wasn't the sort of suntan you got in the UK at this time of year. "Are you Ned Young?" Paul showed his ID.

"Yes."

"Can I come in?" Paul wondered which exotic holiday location was responsible for the suntan.

Ned hesitated.

"It really would be easier."

"Ok. I suppose."

Paul figured Ned's acquiescence had more to do with it being chilly on the doorstep than a genuine desire to help the police.

Barry showed up just as Paul stepped inside. Paul introduced him. He looked at Barry, raising his eyebrows in question. Barry shook his head almost imperceptibly. Clearly, he hadn't chanced on Tammy escaping out the back door. So she wasn't in the house, or Ned would have put up more resistance to keep him out.

It would be nice, after their long drive, if Ned offered them a cup of coffee. He didn't. Paul surmised that Ned didn't want them to stay long. They would need to hurry up before he asked them to leave.

"We're here about Tammy Doncaster." Paul pulled out a chair, not waiting to be asked.

"Tammy?"

"Yes, you know about her escape, I assume?"

"Escape? No. When did that happen?"

"Tuesday." Paul noticed the sweat on Ned's forehead. And the way his voice shook when he denied knowledge of Tammy's escape. He obviously lied about it, and not very well either. Paul questioned whether he was in this much deeper than he wanted to be. Was he hiding Tammy?

"When did you last see Tammy?" Paul stared at Ned, making eye contact, deliberately trying to make him feel uncomfortable.

Ned looked at his watch, as if that would give him the answer. "I don't know. Last month, I guess. We visit once a month. Katie, my wife, and I take it in turns."

Paul nodded. He knew that already. "Is Katie at home?"

"No. I don't know where she is."

"When will she be back?" He fixed the eye contact again, refusing to let Ned off the hook.

"I told you, I don't know where she is, so I can't even guess when she'll get home."

THE PAYBACK

Ned was getting flustered. Paul smiled inside. He'd make a mistake soon if Paul kept up the pressure.

"Please, can you phone her? We'd really like to speak to her too," Paul said. "It's a long way if we need to come back." He didn't want to trek down here again if it was avoidable.

Paul held Ned's gaze and, reluctantly, Ned got up and took his phone from the island unit in the middle of the kitchen. He tapped at the phone.

After a minute, he set down the phone. "No signal," he said. "It happens here. There are some good hotspots, but further into the countryside, in some areas, you get nothing."

Paul speculated on whether Katie might be with Tammy now. He gazed out the kitchen window, surveying the vast area of countryside nearby where the Youngs might hide Tammy. The chances of finding her in a search were slim, unless he managed to trip Ned up into letting some vital piece of information slip by mistake.

"Would you mind if I checked outside?" Barry asked.

"I'll show you both around," Ned said, standing up.

"I'll be fine on my own." Barry was halfway to the door already.

Ned followed him. "I don't want you frightening the horses or letting the geese out. I really need to come with you."

"I'll wait here in the warm," Paul said. He would take the opportunity to snoop around inside. Ned seemed keen to get them both out of the house. He might be hiding something.

Ned looked momentarily horrified, then recovered. "We won't be long."

As soon as the door banged shut, Paul jumped up. He trusted Barry would keep Ned out of the house for as long as possible, but there were no guarantees for how long. Paul headed upstairs, using his phone to light the way, so he didn't have to turn on the main lights, which would be seen from the garden. He glanced quickly into all four bedrooms. Why ever did they need four bedrooms for just the two of them? Probably a status thing.

Two of the rooms were virtually bare, aside from a bed, some drawers, and a few pictures on the walls. They were pretty basic guest rooms. A third, smaller room, seemed to be used for storage and was jammed full of furniture, boxes, and general paraphernalia. How would he ever find anything among all this clutter? He drew his finger along the top of a nearby box. Dust. Clearly, nothing in this room had been moved recently.

The final room was obviously the main bedroom. Paul started looking through the drawers as rapidly as possible. They were mostly full of clothes and Katie's makeup. Nothing of any use to him.

He raced downstairs, aware he would run out of time soon. Ned's garden was about five acres, with some stables and a couple of other outbuildings. That seriously limited how long Barry could make the search outside last. Paul didn't want Ned to catch him rummaging around his house without a warrant.

At the back of the hallway, Paul found a small office. He started pulling open the desk drawers. If only there was time to boot up the computer and read some of the files, but it would take too long, and, in any case, would probably be password protected.

The second drawer contained a passport, tucked under a pile of papers. Paul opened it up, expecting it to belong to Ned or Katie. The name inside was Maria Vasquez. He didn't recognise the woman in the photo. She was black, but with long blond hair. Could the passport be intended for Tammy? If she wore a blond wig, she would definitely resemble the photo.

He clicked the camera icon on his phone, watching as it loaded painfully slowly. A noise startled him, and he realised the front door was opening. Hurriedly, he shoved the passport back where he'd found it and rushed out of the office, ducking into the kitchen as Ned and Barry walked in.

He waited a few seconds, then shouted, "I'm in here."

The two men came in as Paul reached for some mugs on the shelf. "I'm making coffee," he said. He just found time to fill the kettle and switch it on before they came in. "Sorry, bit cheeky, but we've got a long drive back."

"The coffee's in the cupboard on the left," Ned said. "Let me do it."

"Milk, no sugar for me." Paul kicked himself for not being able to get a photo of that passport. He should have searched for an office before he wasted time going upstairs. Still, probably best if they got a warrant and searched the house, then they'd be able to use the passport as evidence. If the passport was intended for Tammy, they needed to take it, to stop her from leaving the UK. They needed that warrant.

"On second thought," he said, "we really should get going now. We'll skip the coffee, but thanks for the offer."

Chapter 13

"Did you find anything outside?" Paul asked Barry as soon as they were in the car.

"Not really. There's nowhere to hide Tammy there. The stables have got horses in them, and there's a shed with some pretty vicious geese in it. The only other shed is small and full of animal feed and garden tools. I didn't do a thorough search, not without a warrant, just took a peek around the place. I figured if I kept him outside for a bit, you would take the chance to search the house."

"That's exactly what I did." Again, Paul beat himself up about his missed opportunity. Barry would ask him any moment now if he'd found anything, then he would be forced to admit he'd screwed up. He didn't want to lose Barry's respect. At least he'd found something.

"Find anything?"

"Yes. And we need to get a warrant and come straight back."

They turned onto the motorway. In the dim overhead lighting, Barry looked excited. Paul wished he could get that excited too. It would make a long night much shorter. But his failure to take a photo of some vital evidence weighed on him, taking away the joy of discovering a potential lead.

Clarke got nearly two-thirds of the way home when her engine started to splutter. The car lost all power, not responding at all when she pressed her foot on the accelerator. She managed to navigate across the traffic to the inside lane of the motorway, swerving onto the hard shoulder seconds before the car chugged to a total standstill. She turned the key in the ignition and tried to fire up the engine. It made a brief coughing noise, but nothing happened. With a resigned sigh, she clicked on the hazard lights and scrambled over the passenger's seat to get out of the car and take refuge on the bank beyond the safety barrier.

Annoyed, she phoned her breakdown service, thankful that she'd remembered to renew her subscription recently, but less thankful when they informed her the waiting time would be two hours. Great. She and Paul were supposed to be having dinner tonight at her parents' house. Her mum invited Auntie Fenella over especially to meet Paul and, as her aunt was making a large financial contribution towards the wedding, Clarke really didn't want to be late.

The breakdown truck showed up well over two hours later. The mechanic spent ten minutes checking the car over before coming over to Clarke.

"You've run out of petrol."

"But that's impossible." Clarke swore she had at least half a tank left.

"Sorry, love, you were probably running on fumes for the last couple of miles."

"The tank was half full. Did it spring a leak?" Clarke couldn't fathom how else it might have happened. Maybe a stone flying up from the road had made a hole in the tank.

"Faulty petrol gauge more like." The mechanic smiled condescendingly at her, clearly not believing anything she said.

He returned a couple of minutes later. "You were right," he said. "The needle on the fuel gauge seems to be stuck halfway. Better get that fixed, so this doesn't happen again."

"But what do I do now?" She couldn't stay here all night.

"I'll tow you to the nearest petrol station," the mechanic said.

Clarke sighed. At least she would get plenty of time to decide how much to tell Paul about her visit to Katie. She hoped she wouldn't be late for dinner with her parents and Auntie Fenella. Her mum would have put a lot of effort into cooking for them.

Paul and Barry eventually got back to Dorset after nine o'clock.

Paul knocked on the Youngs' front door. He heard dogs barking inside the house, then Ned opened the door quickly, almost as if he expected someone. He seemed surprised to see them.

"Ned Young, we have a warrant to search your premises," Paul said. "Is your wife at home?"

"Katie," Ned called out. "It's the police."

Katie Young appeared in the hallway. "What do you want?" She stared at them suspiciously.

"We have a search warrant, Mrs Young." Paul handed her the paperwork. "You'll have to vacate the premises."

"May I ask what you're looking for?" Ned said.

Paul ignored the question. "We need to check everything. We'll start the search outside. You'll need to come outside with us or leave the premises completely if you prefer."

"We'll stay," Ned said.

Paul smiled. It made things easier if they found anything incriminating. He preferred knowing where they both were.

"Can't we stay in here?" Katie said. "It's cold outside."

"No," Paul insisted. "You must get out of the house." It would be so easy for Katie to destroy evidence if they left her inside alone. He wished he had brought some extra officers with him. But they simply didn't have the resources for extra officers to spend several hours trekking down to Dorset and back again. He probably should have planned ahead and asked for some help from the local plods.

"There's still only one car in the driveway," Barry whispered to Paul. "Is Tammy using the other one?"

"It's possible."

They escorted Ned and Katie out of the house. Paul headed straight for the garden shed. "What's the code to open this?" He pointed to the combination lock securing the door.

"I'll do it," Ned offered. He opened the door. The small shed seemed even more packed with stuff than earlier.

"Let's take everything out," Paul said to Barry. He hoped it wouldn't take too long. Really, he wanted to go straight to the office indoors and find the passport, but the logistics of searching the house, whilst ensuring they didn't remove any evidence from the outbuildings, would be too difficult with only himself and Barry to monitor both of them and perform the search.

"We can let them put everything back after us. That'll keep them out of our way while we search the other buildings." At least the rain held off, but the darkness made everything more difficult.

They started to remove the shed's contents. Barry stood inside, passing each item out to Paul, who inspected it before piling it into a jumbled heap. He wondered what to do with the animal feed. It would be easier to tip it out on the ground, but that seemed such a waste.

"Is there a spare dustbin?" he asked Katie.

"What for?" Her attitude remained defiant, which annoyed Paul. He suddenly wanted to tip the feed out on the ground.

He counted to ten. "It's for decanting the feed into so we can search through it properly." They might easily have buried something amongst the feed. It would provide a good hiding place.

"I don't have anything," Katie said.

Paul tipped the dustbin over and rolled it around to agitate the feed inside. He couldn't see anything. He thrust both arms into the feed, sifting through it. There didn't seem to be anything hidden in this bin. He repeated the exercise with the other four bins. Luckily, they were half empty. He found nothing buried in any of them.

Barry started to pass out the large collection of garden tools. Only a few boxes remained, haphazardly stacked at the back of the shed. Paul helped lift them out, then he and Barry emptied them one at a time onto the gravel drive.

"You can start putting stuff back in the boxes," Paul said.

Katie glared at him but got to work.

"What's in the other buildings?" Paul checked the time. They still had the house to search.

"Horses in the stables, geese in the goose shed," Ned said, as if talking to a complete moron.

"I'll need some help to search them," Paul said, ignoring the insult but resolving to make things as difficult as possible for Ned for the rest of the search. "Let's start with the stables. Can you take the horses out while we search inside?"

"Katie's the best person for that. She's the horse expert."

Katie looked up from her tidying at the mention of her name.

"Mrs Young, please remove the horses from the stables so we can search them."

Katie scowled at him. "You won't find her here. Do you really think we would hide her in the stables?"

As soon as she brought the first horse out, Paul asked Barry to search the empty stable. He wanted to keep an eye on Ned in case he tried to slip back into the house.

"When did you last see Tammy?" Paul asked Katie. The almost pure white horse she held seemed nervous in the dark, making him dance around in the dim excuse for moonlight like a huge ghost in the night. Paul kept his distance, standing close to Ned.

"I haven't seen her since my last prison visit." Katie jerked on the rope. "Steady, boy," she cooed, patting the horse on the neck.

"When was that?" Paul knew full well that Katie saw Tammy five weeks ago. Ned visited last time, not long before Tammy escaped. It would be useful to establish if she told him the truth.

"Can't remember."

"Where were you this afternoon, Mrs Young?"

"Out. I went for a walk. No law against that."

"Where did you go?" Paul didn't like her attitude. And too much protesting always made him suspicious.

"I just wandered through the woods. I needed a bit of space, ok?" Katie said. "Ned and I spend a lot of time together. Sometimes I want to be by myself."

The explanation didn't convince Paul. He wondered what she was lying about. "Do you own a car, Mrs Young?"

"No."

Her answer came too quickly and abruptly.

"I would have assumed being stuck out in the country, you would need one. How far away are the nearest shops?" Paul didn't recall seeing even a small village shop nearby when they drove here earlier.

"I used to own a car, ok? I sold it, and I haven't replaced it yet."

Paul made a mental note to check later if any cars were registered to her.

His phone rang. Clarke's name came up on the caller ID. Reluctantly, he rejected the call. He would talk to her when they finished here.

Barry came out of the stable. He shook his head. Katie took the other horse out to allow him to search the second stable but again, he found nothing.

"We need to search the goose shed," Paul said. "Can you take the geese out?"

"No, we can't," Ned said firmly. "If we let them out in the dark, we'll never get them back in again."

"So, they can stay out all night. If they get cold, they'll go in on their own, won't they?"

Ned stared at him. "It doesn't work like that. If we leave them out all night, the foxes will get them. A fox won't take just one for its dinner. It'll kill the lot of them for fun."

"There must be somewhere you can put them." It occurred to Paul that he was being far too accommodating. So much for him making Ned's life difficult! They should open the door and let the geese out, give Ned and Katie the problem of catching them again in the dark. But those geese were vicious. He didn't fancy having them come at him in the dark if they got loose. He had enough trouble with the small dog currently sniffing round his ankles.

"We might be able to fence them in," Ned conceded. He rummaged behind the stables, pulling out a couple of woven pieces of fencing. "Sheep hurdles," he said.

Katie returned from putting the horse back in its stable. "It will take them ages to settle now that you've wound them up."

"Katie, help me pen the geese in, please," Ned said. "If we take one hurdle each, we can trap them in the back corner." He opened the door of the goose shed.

Paul stood cautiously behind him. The geese woke as soon as Ned turned on the light and ran towards them, honking. Paul wanted all the geese securely penned in before he and Barry started their search. He toyed with the idea of sending Barry in alone.

Ned held out a bowl of feed and shook it at the geese. They immediately followed him into the corner, where he sprinkled some feed onto the floor. Katie and Ned quickly penned them in using the hurdles. Paul guessed they must have done this before.

Ned shouted at them to come in. Katie gave Paul the evil eye, no doubt fantasizing about letting the geese loose again. If she did, he would run like hell for the door, and then he would arrest her.

They found no hiding places in here either. Barry carried a pitchfork, and he raked through the straw on the floor. If anything or anyone was in here, the geese would guard it or them perfectly, but Paul's hopes of finding a hidden trapdoor evaporated rapidly. He examined the nesting boxes, which spanned across one end. After donning protective gloves, he started searching through the straw. Again, the search drew a blank.

The nesting boxes were numbered. But the numbers weren't consecutive. "What are these numbers?" he asked.

"The nesting boxes were second-hand," Ned explained. "The numbers were on them when we bought them, but we didn't realise until after we fixed them together, so they're in the wrong order."

"Can you move the geese into another corner, please?" Paul wanted to be thorough and check the corner where they stood, even though he didn't hold out any hope of finding anything. He itched to get back into the house and find that passport.

Ned and Katie shuffled the hurdles around, but some of the geese escaped their makeshift pen and went for Barry. Quickly, Ned rattled the feed bucket, so they ran towards him.

"Why don't we pin you in instead and keep the geese out," Ned suggested. "It'll be much quicker."

Paul disliked that idea, but Ned was right. His way would be quicker. Katie and Ned placed the sheep hurdles around Barry and Paul, leaving the geese running free around the shed. Paul wondered how they were going to get out safely now with the geese congregating around them.

Quickly, they examined the floor under the straw. As Paul expected, they found nothing.

"We need to search the house," Paul said. "Can you get us out of here?" He didn't trust them. Katie especially, would probably be delighted if the geese attacked them. She picked up the bucket of feed, waving it defiantly. For a moment, Paul imagined she intended to throw it at them, then she turned and walked to the far corner with it and threw a handful of feed on the floor.

"Out you get," she said.

Paul ran for the door, but Barry beat him to it. He wished he hadn't shown any fear. He would need to assert his authority again, to ensure Ned and Katie respected him.

"Stay out here while we search the house," Paul said as soon as Ned and Katie were both back outside.

Ned pushed the bolt shut on the goose shed, firmly locking the geese in, to Paul's relief. He wouldn't be going near them again in a hurry.

"What are you looking for exactly?" Katie asked.

"I can't tell you that."

"But it's something connected to Tammy, isn't it?" Katie glared at him. "You won't find anything."

"Then you have nothing to worry about, do you? Just stay out here."

"It's cold," Katie protested.

Ned put his hand on her shoulder. "It's all right, darling. We can sit in the car. I'm sure they won't be too long."

"We'll come and get you when we finish," Paul said, relieved that Ned had intervened. He needed to get his hands on that passport now.

Chapter 14

Clarke arrived late at her parents' house, thankful she'd phoned her mum earlier to warn her about the car breaking down. No way would she admit to running out of petrol. That would be too embarrassing, even if the broken fuel gauge meant it wasn't her fault. Paul still hadn't phoned her back. She'd left him at least three messages, asking him to call her and to come straight here when he finished work. Glancing at her phone yet again, it showed no sign of a reply. Hopefully, he might show up before they got too far through the meal.

Clarke's dad opened the front door before she reached it. He must have been watching for her.

"No Paul?"

"No, sorry. You know how it is with his job. I'm sure it will be something really important." Clarke sighed. After she married Paul, she would need to get used to apologising on his behalf. That was the nature of the job. None of the Murder Investigation Team worked predictable hours, not in the middle of a case.

"Come and say hello to Auntie Fenella." Her father ushered her into the dining room.

Her auntie immediately jumped up, rushing over to hug her. "Clarke, you look fabulous. How long is it since I last saw you?"

"It must be five years." Perhaps she and Paul would visit Auntie Fenella in Australia one day. It would make an amazing holiday.

"Well, it's great to see you. Where's your lovely fiancé? I can't wait to meet him."

"I'm afraid Paul's still working. He may not make it." Clarke wished Paul had returned her calls. If he showed up now, she would look like an idiot.

"Diana says he's a detective. How exciting," Auntie Fenella said.

"Yes, sometimes." Clarke didn't add that sometimes Paul's job got a little too exciting, although Paul would probably tell her it was boring. He spent much of his time either sitting in a car on surveillance or doing paperwork. But probably best, given that Paul hadn't shown up, that Auntie Fenella imagined his job was like on TV, with Paul racing after criminals all the time. She'd be more likely to forgive his non-appearance if she realised the importance of his job.

"I hope he'll come later, but it depends on how the job's going. If they arrest someone, they've got limited time to question them, so he may not be able to leave yet." She hoped he might have arrested Tammy, then she wouldn't mind how late he finished work.

"It's ok. I understand," Auntie Fenella said, probably not understanding at all.

"Dinner's nearly ready," Mum called from the kitchen. She appeared in the doorway a moment later. "Is Paul likely to show up? Shall I leave his dinner in the oven?" Diana Pettis already had some experience of Paul's unsociable work hours and wasn't naïve enough to assume he would walk in any minute now, if they waited for him.

"Yes, that would be best. There's no point in delaying. He might be really quick, or he might be hours yet." Clarke would bet on the latter scenario.

Her father handed her a glass of wine. "Let's sit down and get started, shall we? I'm starving."

Diana had been busy in the kitchen, laying on quite a spread, with a massive joint of roast beef and crispy roast potatoes. Clarke realised how hungry she was. With all that time spent on the motorway waiting for the breakdown service, she'd forgotten when she last ate.

Barry followed Paul into the Youngs' house. "What are we looking for, gov? Apart from that passport."

"Anything that might connect the Youngs to Tammy. If in doubt, bag it and we'll take it. Better to have too much evidence than not enough and if you're unsure, shout and I'll take a look. You start upstairs," Paul said. "I'm going straight to their office to get that passport."

Paul made a beeline for the desk where he saw the passport earlier, a frisson of excitement coursing through him as he pulled the drawer open. He removed the contents and placed them on the desk, quickly sifting through them. The passport had done a vanishing act. Surely, it must be here. Had Paul and Barry's earlier visit spooked them so much that they'd moved it? But Ned wouldn't have known they were coming back so soon. Paul flipped through every document one by one. There was no passport.

The bank statements might be useful, but it would make more sense to get all of their statements direct from the bank, to ensure no account got missed. He bagged up one statement to give him a record of the bank's address. A few bills and letters revealed nothing of interest and certainly nothing related to Tammy.

It would be great if he discovered an invoice for a new car purchase leading him to Tammy. Again, he wondered what happened to the passport. Had they given it to Tammy in the last few hours?

He should put out an all-ports warning for Maria Vasquez, to prevent Tammy from leaving the country.

Paul pulled his phone from his pocket and phoned the station. He would get someone onto the task immediately. He should have done it much earlier. It was nearly seven hours since he discovered that passport. Even with a seven-hour head start, they would be unlucky if Tammy had chosen today to slip past them and skip the country. It would still be worth trying to stop her.

He searched through the other drawers in turn. Apart from the drawers, the sparsely furnished office consisted of a bookcase, jam-packed with books, a computer and monitor that sat on the desk, and a small printer underneath it. Paul wondered whether it be worth asking the Youngs for the computer password. He fired up the computer. A request for a password appeared in the middle of the screen. Quickly, he walked back out into the garden. The Youngs sat in their car with the interior light on. The car radio blared out into the darkness. Was that for entertainment or simply so that he wouldn't overhear anything they were saying. Even in the dark, he saw their lips moving. The dogs started barking as he approached the car.

Ned wound the window down. "Have you finished already?"

"Not yet. What's the password for your computer?"

"Do I have to give it to you?"

"If you want to be cooperative, yes," Paul said.

"But I don't have to? Legally I mean."

"No, but it won't look good if you're hiding something, and if you don't give us the password, we'll need to take the hard drive away with us."

"But I need that for my business." Ned looked properly upset for the first time since they had arrived.

Paul wondered if he was onto something. He resolved to get that computer checked thoroughly. "Then give me the password," he said.

"It's *fixthefence99*," he replied reluctantly.

Paul looked at him, puzzled.

"It's Katie's idea. She sets the password to remind me of jobs around the house that I need to do," Ned explained. "When I've done it, she'll change the password to the next job."

"Good idea." Paul would be sure not to tell Clarke about that suggestion. He would need to take the hard drive, anyway. They had nothing with them to download files, and it would take too long to check everything on site. He would enjoy breaking that news to Ned when they finished the search. Anyway, the tech guys would thank him for obtaining the password. Surveying the rest of the office, Paul wondered if the Youngs owned a laptop as well. He'd ask Barry if he had found one upstairs.

Paul turned his attention to the bookcase. The Youngs owned an eclectic collection of books. Business books and autobiographies sat side by side with sci-fi novels and the complete works of Jane Austen, as well as plenty of books on horse care. He half expected to find a book on geese somewhere.

He began the tedious job of removing each book individually, flipping through the pages to check for anything concealed within them, and ensuring nothing lay hidden behind the books. Was he wasting his time? But so many times he did these searches, and at the last moment, found the tiniest piece of evidence in an unexpected place. He renewed his determination to be extra thorough. If there was any evidence connected to Tammy in this house, he would find it.

He reached the end of the top shelf of books. Three more shelves to check. He needed a break from that, so he tested the computer password. It worked. But it would have been stupid of Ned to give him a false one while they were actually on the premises.

The file explorer showed numerous folders and sub-folders, all with meaningless names. At least, the names were meaningless to Paul. He would get the tech guys to scrutinise everything. What a shame Clarke wasn't here. She would be more clued up than him about this stuff.

It might be revealing to examine all the files relating to Ned's business. Something must connect him to Tammy, something that would incriminate one or both of the Youngs and possibly even reveal Tammy's whereabouts, but he didn't have time to search through it all now.

Paul closed the computer down. He would definitely take the hard drive away with him. He smiled. The prospect of annoying Ned provided some consolation for the late evening.

The second shelf of books proved more interesting. They were mainly horse books and mostly hardbacks, which took longer to flip through. He found a couple of pieces of paper inside one of them and bagged them up, even though they may only turn out to be bookmarks.

One of the books caught his attention as it stuck out a little. Pulling it out, he noticed something behind it preventing the book from being pushed all the way in. Excitedly, he tugged out a few more books, revealing a plastic tub wedged behind them.

The tub was stuffed with twenty-pound notes. At a rough guess, there must be a couple thousand pounds in here. Why would they hide it in the bookshelf? Didn't they own a safe? He left the tub on the desk, ready to discuss with Ned and Katie. Where did the cash come from? If it came from the bank, he'd find the withdrawal on their bank statements. But, more likely, it would be payment in cash for services provided. They were probably keeping the cash instead of paying it into the bank, to avoid paying tax on it. That would be difficult to prove.

At least they hadn't given the money to Tammy, unless this formed part of a bigger stash. If Tammy got hold of large amounts of cash, it would be much easier for her to leave the country.

Where was Tammy now? He didn't believe she could be sleeping rough in the middle of the Dorset countryside, but if she was, someone would have noticed her.

It would be useful to hang around and talk to some local people. Barry wouldn't take much persuading to go for a quick half in the local pub before they headed home. Hopefully, the pub served food too. He was ravenous.

Suddenly, at the thought of food, Paul remembered he should be having dinner with Clarke's family tonight. He'd completely forgotten Clarke wanted him to meet her auntie. That must be why she tried to call him earlier. He should have phoned her back. The auntie had travelled from Australia, and she was paying for the catering for their wedding. It would seem really ungrateful of him if he didn't show up, and he was immensely grateful. He never realised when he proposed how incredibly expensive a wedding would be. But somehow, they managed to find the money for everything essential to do it properly. After all, they only planned to get married once. He didn't want to go through the hell of organising a wedding ever again.

Anyway, he needed to phone Clarke to apologise. She'd kill him, unless he grovelled like mad and begged for forgiveness. He tapped on her name in his phone.

"Paul, where are you? You were supposed to be here two hours ago. You promised."

Paul held the phone further from his ear. "I'm really sorry, darling. I'm in Dorset."

"Did you see Ned and Katie?"

"We're still here. We have a warrant to search the place."

"You're never going to get back in time to come to Mum and Dad's, are you?"

"I'm sorry. It's going to be another couple of hours at least before we can even leave here. I won't make it in time for dinner. I'm really sorry," Paul said. It would be way past midnight by the time he got home. He wouldn't admit they were eating at the local pub. Honestly, he'd rather be sampling Diana Pettis's cooking. But the pub visit was work, so Clarke wouldn't complain.

"It's ok. You're missing out on your favourite roast beef, with pavlova for dessert."

"For the Aussie auntie, I assume," Paul said.

"Yes, Mum made it specially."

"Well, enjoy. Are you staying at Rob's place?"

"Yes, at least you won't have to worry about waking me up when you get in." Clarke slept very lightly. She would normally wake the minute Paul put his key in the door. At least he could crash about when he got home and not need to consider anyone else.

"I'm sorry," Paul said again.

"I understand. We'll try to arrange another time for you to meet Auntie Fenella. It's more important to catch Tammy."

"I'm trying," Paul said.

"I know you are, darling. Love you."

"Love you too."

A movement behind Paul made him turn round. Barry stood in the doorway. "How long have you been there?"

"Just got here," Barry said.

Paul hoped that was the truth. He didn't like his colleagues around when he got all lovey with Clarke. It embarrassed him, and it was none of their business.

"Did you find anything upstairs?"

"Not really. I guess if they'd got clothes or something, they would have already given them to Tammy."

"You looked everywhere?" Paul would go upstairs and do a five-minute check himself when he finished down here, in case Barry missed anything. "What about under the carpets?" Amateurs always hid stuff under a loose floorboard.

"Yes. I've checked if any of the carpets were loose and none of them are."

"How about behind the bath panel?"

"Good idea. I'm on it, Sarge."

Paul returned to the bookshelf. Barry's big feet clumped up the stairs. He'd nearly finished here.

"We're pretty much done," Paul said when Barry came back downstairs. "Are you hungry?"

"Yeah. I haven't eaten since lunchtime."

"Me too. I'm starving. Let's go to the local pub. We can ask around if anyone's seen Tammy."

"Yeah, great idea." Barry smiled.

"I'll get the Youngs," Paul said.

Ned and Katie seemed pleased to be allowed back into their warm house.

"I hope you haven't made too much mess," Katie snapped.

Paul no longer cared. His stomach rumbled loudly. "We need to discuss a couple of things in the office." He led them into the room, walking straight to the desk to pick up the plastic tub. "Where did this cash come from?" He noticed Ned's worried expression as he held up the tub.

"We keep some cash for emergencies," Ned said, quickly regaining his composure.

"Perhaps you should buy a safe. It's not very secure hidden in the bookshelf."

Katie seemed surprised but said nothing. Paul guessed she wasn't aware of Ned's emergency stash of money.

"We're taking your hard drive," Paul said.

"You promised you wouldn't."

"That's not exactly what I said." Paul guessed Ned now regretted providing him with the password.

"I need it for my business," Ned protested.

"Then I'll inform you as soon as you can collect it." If Ned didn't keep his cash in a safe, he probably didn't back up his hard drive either. It would teach him some valuable security lessons, so Paul wouldn't sweat about it. Suddenly, he was excited to find out what might be on that computer.

Chapter 15

After dinner, Clarke excused herself for five minutes to phone Paul again. She'd forgotten to tell him about the bird hide in Ranleigh Marshes. Being so close to the prison, it would be an obvious place for Tammy to hide out. The call diverted straight to voicemail, so Paul might be on his way home now. She left a message. "Paul, it's me. Tammy may be in Ranleigh Marshes. There's a bird hide there where Katie Young used to take her bird-watching. It's very well camouflaged apparently, so it might make a good hiding place. It's worth checking. Love you. Bye."

She hung up, without adding how she came by the information. At least with a voicemail, Paul wouldn't be able to ask awkward questions yet. He wouldn't approve of her visiting Katie. But Clarke had her own investigation to follow. Somehow, she must find Tammy's money, and Katie and Ned Young were her only leads. Ned may well have invested the money for Tammy. She needed to pursue that theory further, and she wouldn't let Paul stop her.

The nearest pub was only five minutes away from the Youngs' house, in the heart of the village. Paul drove into the adjoining car park, hoping they would still be serving food this late.

"Let's get the locals talking," he said to Barry.

"Do we ask if they've seen Tammy?"

"Yes, definitely. Tammy would get noticed around here. If she's been here, someone will have seen her." Paul counted on it.

"Ok, Sarge."

"Less of the *sarge*, not in the pub." He didn't want the locals getting scared off, knowing they were police, not immediately, anyway.

Thankfully, the pub served food late into the evening. Paul's stomach rumbled as he ordered a shepherd's pie with extra chips. Barry opted for the lasagne.

"You can drive home," Paul said, getting himself a beer and ordering a Coke for Barry.

"Thanks."

Paul decided to sit at the bar until the food arrived to help them get chatting with the locals.

"Never seen you in these parts before." The girl serving behind the bar smiled as Paul handed her his credit card.

"We're here on business," Paul said. "On our way home, actually. Down here looking for someone. Have you seen an attractive black woman in her thirties?" His photo of Tammy wouldn't be of any use, not since she shaved off her hair.

The woman shook her head. "You're the only strangers I've seen around here this week," she said. "Food's nearly ready. Where do you want to sit? There's an empty table in the corner."

"That would be great," Paul said.

By the time they made themselves comfortable at the table, two steaming hot plates of food arrived.

"I'm starving," Barry said.

Paul echoed that sentiment. He counted up the hours since he last ate.

They sat with their backs to the wall to watch the pub's other customers.

"What do you think, Barry? Is it worth talking to anyone here? Can we find someone who's a bit nosy, who's into everybody else's business?"

"It's a village." Barry laughed. "Everybody's into everybody else's business."

"So, we'll talk to everybody when we finish eating." They weren't going to get home anytime soon. He tucked into his shepherd's pie, craving Diana Pettis's roast beef, even though the shepherd's pie tasted good.

"What's your opinion of the Youngs?" Barry asked.

"They're hiding something," Paul said. Katie Young definitely still had a soft spot for Tammy. Ned had been quite evasive, and neither of them was happy about their visit. If only he had managed to find that passport.

As soon as they finished eating, they sat at the bar next to a couple of farmer types. Paul nodded at them, hoping they might know some good places to hide around here. They broke off their conversation for a few seconds to stare at Paul and Barry. Paul supposed they would have to go official. He got out his ID, showing it to them discreetly. "We're looking for someone. A black woman in her thirties."

"Not seen anyone like that in these parts lately," one of the farmers said.

"Where would you hide her? There must be tonnes of places to disappear in the country. I bet you know them all."

"Aye." The older man put his pint down on the bar.

"So where would you hide her?"

"Sleepbrook Woods might be good if she liked camping. But she'd need to be a bit of a Bear Grylls type to survive in this weather. It's cold at night."

"You could live in those woods for years," his friend said, "as long as you have a hunting knife and a tent. You wouldn't starve."

Paul's heart sank, Tammy being the last person he'd pick to survive the great outdoors. "She's not the type." Paul tried to imagine Tammy lighting a campfire. "Are there any old farms around here with empty houses and lots of sheds?" He remembered that awful dilapidated flat Tammy had stayed in, so she could certainly cope with a deserted farmhouse, maybe even a shed, if somebody brought her food regularly.

"I can't think of any in this area. Plenty of places with lots of outbuildings, but it will take you a month of Sundays to search them all. They're mostly busy working farms around here, apart from a couple, where the owners gave up and sold them as lifestyle properties. All of them buildings have been turned into stables or music studios."

Paul gave him his card. "If you do see anyone who matches the description, will you phone me, please? She's dangerous, so please don't approach her."

The man laughed. "I ain't afraid of no woman," he said.

"This one's a killer." Paul didn't want him to get complacent, and he certainly didn't want any more blood on his hands. Somehow, he must find Tammy and get her locked up before she killed again, before she killed Clarke. He took a sip of his beer and wondered what Clarke's voicemail message meant. Something about a bird hide in Ranleigh Marshes. He supposed that might be worth pursuing, with it being so close to the prison, but he didn't hold out much hope of finding Tammy there, not now. That scenario was no more likely than her living rough in the woods in the Dorset countryside. Nevertheless, he decided to check out Ranleigh Marshes tomorrow morning if nothing more important came up.

Paul glanced around the emptying pub. They should go home instead of wasting their time here.

That passport, or the lack of it, niggled him like crazy. Would one or both of the Youngs deliver it to Tammy, or would Tammy come here? If only enough resources were available to keep the Youngs' house under surveillance. Or if he at least had a tracker to stick on the bottom of Ned's car. Not that a tracker would tell him anything conclusive. It didn't matter where Ned went, unless they could prove that Tammy was with him.

Barry pulled the car out of the pub car park. "I feel better now, Sarge, with some good food inside me."

"Yes, it wasn't bad," Paul said, dreaming of Diana's roast beef and pavlova. On Saturday, he and Clarke would be getting married. Would they find Tammy before then? He certainly hoped so. Otherwise, he'd never be able to relax and enjoy his wedding day. If *relax* was the right word. Perhaps he was fortunate that this case took his mind off his impending nuptials. It left him no time to get nervous. Not that he would be, not really. He was a lucky man to be marrying Clarke.

Chapter 16

Paul decided to search Ranleigh Marshes first thing in the morning. He took Barry, and uniform lent him two officers.

One of the local park rangers met them in the car park on the edge of the marshes.

"I'm Bill," he said. "I'll need to accompany you in your search. If you go off the tracks, you might get caught up in the reeds and drown."

Paul nodded. It would be useful to have a local expert with them. "Have you got anyone who can act as a guide for the others in my search team, so we can split up?"

"Yes, another ranger will arrive soon."

Paul looked at his watch. Uniform would get here shortly. "Is there a bird hide on the marshes?" If Clarke was right about the place, Tammy might be there now. He still didn't know where she got the information from, but he trusted her opinion.

"There are several. The marshes are a prime spot for birdwatching. We get enthusiasts visiting all the year round, especially to watch the widgeon and the peregrine falcons."

"What's a widgeon?" Barry asked.

"They're ducks," Bill said. "Very colourful ducks."

"Are the hides all out in the open? We're looking for something that might be concealed." As he surveyed the marshes in front of him, it struck him how flat and open they were. Were they wasting their time looking for Tammy here, when there weren't any suitable hiding places?

"There's a couple that might fit." Bill pulled a well-worn map out of his pocket and opened it up, pointing at the page. "Here," he said, "and here. One's on the edge of the forest, so it's well-hidden in the trees. The other is in a wilder part of the marsh. The scrub has grown up out of control around it, so it's completely concealed. You wouldn't even realise it's there."

Paul examined the map. There appeared to be quite a distance between the two sites. "How big are the marshes?"

"Two and a half square miles."

Paul breathed a sigh of relief. That was doable. He handed the map back to Bill and noticed the other ranger standing nearby, chatting with his uniformed officers.

"Can you take me and DC Medway to the hide in the scrubland?" That sounded like the best bet. "And your colleague can take my two officers to the hide in the woods."

"Sounds like a plan," Bill said. He walked over to pass on the information to his colleague.

Bill returned quickly. "It will be quicker if we take the boat. The others can walk. They don't have as far to go."

"Won't she hear us coming?" Paul didn't want Tammy to take off before they got the chance to apprehend her.

"Nah. It's not a powerful engine. We need it to be quiet, so as not to scare off the birds. We'll moor it downwind of the hide and walk the last few minutes, just to be sure."

Bill didn't exaggerate when he said the boat lacked power. Paul's fantasy of sweeping in James Bond style in a top-of-the-range motorboat was well and truly quashed as soon as they set off. They chugged along the waterway at a steady speed, giving plenty of time to admire the scenery and the birds, if they were so inclined.

"Keep your eyes open," Paul reminded Barry. "She may be anywhere." The only signs of life he'd spotted so far were the feathered variety. If Tammy was here, they would find her.

"Who are you looking for? Is it that escaped prisoner?" Bill asked.

"Yes. We have reason to believe she might be hiding out here."

"Who is she?" Bill asked. "Is she dangerous?"

Paul considered for a moment how much to admit. "If you don't confront her, you'll be ok, but I wouldn't recommend tackling her. She's already killed two people."

"Don't worry." Bill steered the boat into the middle of the water. "I don't want to be a hero. I've got a family to worry about. If she comes here, I'll leave it to the boys in blue."

"Very sensible," Barry said. "It's what we're paid for. Don't take any risks yourself. She's a nasty piece of work."

"Are we nearly there yet?" Paul asked. The vegetation growing on the banks of the waterway became taller and thicker, providing plenty of places to hide.

"Another couple of minutes," Bill said.

"Is it possible to stop the boat somewhere around here and walk the rest of the way? If she's here, we can surprise her." Paul still worried that Tammy would be alerted by the boat's engine and flee before they arrived.

"Good point," Barry said.

"There's a jetty a little further along. We can tie up the boat and finish on foot," Bill expertly steered the boat closer to the bank.

Paul spotted the jetty as soon as they rounded the corner.

"It's a really easy route," Bill said as he tied up the boat. "I can wait here."

"It will be quicker if you show us the way." Paul didn't want to leave the ranger alone. He would be much safer with him and Barry. Bill didn't have to tell Paul he wasn't keen. His reticence was written all over his face. But Paul didn't trust Tammy one bit, and they wouldn't be able to protect Bill if they left him here, so he would have to insist. He'd given the same instructions to the uniformed officers who had gone the opposite way around the marshes with the other ranger.

The path narrowed, so Bill led the way, with Barry bringing up the rear.

"You should go in front," Bill said.

Paul shushed him. He didn't want Tammy to hear them coming. He tried not to pin all his hopes on finding her here. She might be anywhere, probably miles away by now. But he wouldn't put it past her to be hiding out right under their noses, only a few miles from the prison.

Bill stopped abruptly. "You can see the hide from here," he whispered. "The entrance is slightly to the right. Follow the track but keep away from the left-hand side. She'll spot you through the viewing window if you approach it from that direction."

Paul nodded. "Stay here, both of you. Barry, be ready to back me up if necessary."

"Yes, Sarge."

Paul crept along the path, taking care not to make any sudden movements that might disturb the wildlife and warn Tammy of his presence. Could Tammy really be hiding out here? He hoped so, for Clarke's sake. The sooner they found her, the better.

He stopped for a moment to listen, but the cacophonous squawking of some kind of seagulls drowned out any other sounds. If Tammy was nearby, he would never hear her. On the other hand, it meant that she wouldn't detect him creeping up on her either. Suddenly, he started to like the birds.

He took advantage of the noise the gulls were making, moving more quickly towards the hide. Within seconds, he reached the door. For a split second, he hesitated, wondering if Tammy would be armed. Too late to worry about that now. He pushed the door open swiftly.

Paul immediately saw the hide was empty. He stepped inside, trying to overcome his disappointment, even though he didn't really expect to find Tammy here.

Three chairs were arranged along the viewing area, which gave a fabulous view of the water beyond. Paul realised now how many birds made their home in this area of Essex. Up to now, he'd been largely ignoring them, but now he noticed hundreds of birds. This must be a birdwatcher's paradise.

Behind the door, he found some scraps of litter. Some aluminium foil scrunched into a ball, a piece of duct tape, and a couple of empty chocolate wrappers. Paul picked them up carefully, placing them in a plastic evidence bag. The duct tape stuck to his gloves, annoying him. He peeled it off and bagged it. Forensics would test everything. If Tammy had been here, forensics would soon find out. Other than the chairs and the litter, the hide contained nothing else. Tammy surely wouldn't have survived the night out here with only a couple of chocolate bars. With one side of the hide partially open, it would have been freezing. She'd need more supplies than that. A decent sleeping bag, for a start. If she had anything else, she must have taken it with her, if indeed she had ever been here.

He walked back to where Barry and Bill waited.

"Not there," he said, turning to Bill. "When did the hide last get used?"

"A few days ago. In the spring and summer, we're inundated with twitchers, but only the serious ones are interested in freezing out there once the weather starts to turn, and those who come don't stay long."

"Do you remember who used it last?"

Bill shook his head.

"I need a name. Can you find out?" It might be important, although, if anyone connected to Tammy came here recently, Paul doubted they would have given their real name.

"Of course," Bill said. "As soon as we get back to the office. We log everyone who uses it. We don't allow anyone on the marsh unless we know where they are. They have to sign in and out, for safety's sake."

"Thanks. What about the other search party? Will they have reached their destination by now?" Paul wondered if it would be safe to phone them for a progress report. He didn't want to risk someone's ringtone giving away their approach, although he had all but given up hope of finding Tammy anywhere in Ranleigh Marshes. Now that he had come here and seen it for himself, he appreciated that it may have been a useful place to hide out for a few hours, until the initial furore died down, but it didn't provide a longer-term option.

"Give it another ten minutes to be sure, but they're more than likely on their way back by now," Bill said.

They walked back to the boat. Bill turned it around skilfully and they began the slow chug back to the rangers' office.

"Sarge, do you think she ever came here?" Barry asked.

"I'm keeping open-minded on that one until I get this stuff tested." Paul showed Barry the evidence bag. "I found it in the hide." Despite promising not to speculate, he guessed that Tammy may have been here briefly but was now long gone.

"Do people using the hide leave much litter?" Barry asked.

"They're not supposed to," Bill said. "We do ask everyone using it to keep the place clean, but sometimes they forget."

Paul nodded. He would get Erica, their scene of crime officer, to run some tests on the litter. She would soon come up with an answer.

The other ranger and the uniformed officers were already waiting for them outside the office.

"No sign of her, Sarge," the older constable said. "Should we head back to the station?"

"Yes," Paul agreed. "No point in you staying here."

Bill came out of the office holding a sheet of paper. "This is a copy of the last page of the log for the bird hides. You may as well have both of them. The one I've marked at the top is the one we visited. The other one is the one on the edge of the woods, where your colleagues searched."

Paul thanked him. He glanced at the list. Only two people used the hides recently, one in each. He didn't recognise either name, but he would send someone to check their addresses.

The marshes would give them no other useful information. Paul and Barry headed over to the prison to interview Tammy's cellmate, Linda.

Chapter 17

Clarke's phone rang. She rushed to get it out of her handbag before it automatically diverted to voicemail. The phone was definitely buried in here somewhere.

Found it. The screen said *number withheld*. She accepted the call in the nick of time.

"Hello," she said, already regretting the effort expended in answering. It would probably turn out to be someone trying to sell her something she didn't want.

"Hello, Clarke?"

"Who is this?" The voice sounded familiar. "Tammy, is that you?"

"Yes."

Clarke shivered. She would try to keep her talking. If only she could record it, or better still, trace the call. But perhaps the police would be able to trace the phone somehow via the phone company if she talked for long enough. She wished she understood how these things worked.

"Tammy, what do you want? Are you ok?"

"Am I ok?" she screamed, the piercing noise blasting into Clarke's ear.

Clarke held the phone away from her ear as if it was toxic.

"Oh yeah, I'm absolutely fine. Living in the lap of luxury now. Huh. You saw how I was, and it's all your fault."

"I'm sorry," Clarke said, wishing Tammy didn't have the power to make her feel so guilty. "But I can't do anything about that now."

Tammy snorted disdainfully down the line, making Clarke wonder whether Tammy was putting on a performance for her.

"Why are you phoning me?" Tammy must want something, which scared Clarke more than she wanted to admit.

"I need your help." Tammy sounded pitiful now.

Clarke convinced herself that Tammy was putting on an act. "I can't help you." She didn't intend to get sucked into doing anything stupid.

"Please. There's no one else I can ask."

Why would Tammy ask *her*? If she needed help, why didn't she ask Katie, who probably would help her, and maybe had already, even though she said she wouldn't? Clarke didn't trust Tammy one bit, and she didn't imagine that Tammy trusted her either.

"Why don't we meet?" Clarke suggested, losing all her resolve not to get involved. She wouldn't help Tammy. But perhaps she could help the police to catch her.

Tammy exploded on the other end of the line. "Really! You want to see me twice in the same week, after ignoring me for over a year?"

"I'm sorry." Clarke berated herself for apologising. It wasn't her fault, even if she did still shoulder most of the blame. "I couldn't face visiting before."

"*You* couldn't face it! I lived in that hellhole day after day. And *you* couldn't face it. Yeah, sure, let's meet. Let's have a good old discussion about the old days."

"Don't be like that, Tammy." She needed to convince Tammy that she was on her side, but she lacked the conviction to be able to fake that level of sincerity. If she could persuade Tammy to meet, the police would arrest her when she showed up. Someone needed to flush her out of hiding, because no one seemed to know where she was now.

"Ok," Tammy said, "perhaps we will meet. I'll call you back when I've decided."

"Why don't we arrange it now?" Clarke spoke into empty space. Tammy had already hung up.

Clarke leaned back in her chair. Perhaps Tammy would agree to meet her, but right now Tammy controlled everything. That wasn't how Clarke planned it.

If Tammy chose the time and venue, she would probably make it impossible to involve the police. On the other hand, Clarke might have misread things completely and Tammy wouldn't even call back. She was clueless about Tammy's current whereabouts, apart from the tiniest suspicion that she might be in Dorset somewhere near Katie.

But what if she did phone back to arrange a meet? Clarke hoped now that she wouldn't. What was she thinking, encouraging her like that?

Definitely, if she did agree to meet Tammy, it would need to be in a public place. She'd been caught out by her before.

Clarke desperately wanted to find the missing money. Evan promised they would find it. He really shouldn't have agreed to that, but he did, so how could she refuse to help? And if that help involved meeting with Tammy, she would have to do it.

Tammy evidently didn't intend to phone straight back. Clarke got on with trying to work out the seating plan for the wedding, yet another impossible task. She'd earmarked it to do during her lunch break. Paul should be helping her. She hadn't even met most of his relatives or his colleagues, yet he expected her to decide who to sit together. What if they didn't get on? She didn't want a punch up on their wedding day.

She'd already arranged where to sit her own family and friends. There were a couple of people she needed to keep apart, but mostly she simply needed to avoid upsetting those relatives who considered they should be put close to the top table. It needed the skills of a diplomat even to attempt this task.

She folded up the seating plan, having got as far as possible without Paul's help. Tammy still hadn't phoned back, and Clarke had no idea if she would. It pained her to realise that Tammy remained very much in control.

Clarke didn't enjoy sitting around waiting. Luckily, moments later, the phone rang. She pounced on it. No caller ID showed. She accepted the call, her whole body shaking. "Tammy," she said quietly, trying not to show the fear in her voice.

"Right, listen to me," Tammy said. "Meet me in Brackford, right at the end of Tern Road, one thirty p.m. Don't be late and come alone." She hung up.

Clarke checked her watch. One already. It would take her half an hour.

Hurriedly, she looked at Google Earth, checking the layout of Tern Road. She wasn't too familiar with that part of Brackford, and she needed to avoid getting trapped in a dead end in some remote location.

The end of Tern Road backed onto the Hale Hill estate, a maze of houses surrounded by scrub land on one side and woods on the other. Rows of identical terraced houses flanked either side of the road. Clarke was thankful Tammy's choice of venue appeared to be safe. The houses would be full of people, even during the day. But she saw nowhere for the police to hide and wait for her, unless they used somebody's house, and there wouldn't be time to set that up. There might not even be time for the police to show up at all. Tammy astutely gave her very little warning of their meeting place.

Clarke needed to get going. Even if the police didn't catch her this time, even if Tammy disappeared again afterwards, at least it proved her current whereabouts. If they stepped up the search again, they may be able to find her. Tammy wouldn't get far if they acted quickly enough. And this time she would ask her about the money. She doubted Tammy would tell her anything, but she might give some sort of clue.

The whole thing would be a real long shot, but she had to try.

She got in the car and drove towards Brackford, reaching Tern Road five minutes early.

Hopefully, she'd arrived before Tammy, so, for once, she might get the upper hand. She parked the car at the end of the road, turning it round first in case she needed to get away quickly.

Tern Road ended abruptly, morphing into Petersfield Road on the corner. The big housing estate that showed up on Google Earth stretched from the corner of the road, right across to Brackford Woods. But Clarke's search on Google Earth failed to spot the two-metre-high chain-link fence that barricaded off the whole of the housing estate from the bottom of Tern Road.

If Tammy came from Clarke's right, she would be trapped. She stood close to the car door, ready to jump in and drive off at a moment's notice, and kept looking around warily for Tammy. She didn't intend to get caught out this time. No way.

She looked at her watch again. One twenty-nine.

"Clarke?"

The voice came from behind her. Clarke turned around. Tammy stood directly in front of her, on the other side of the chain-link fence. Without hearing her voice first, Clarke would never have recognised Tammy with her head shaved. A tiny bit of stubble gave some shadow to her head. It suited her, showing off her great cheekbones and big brown eyes.

Clarke's emotions were torn. At least this way she felt safe. But equally she wouldn't be able to follow Tammy when she left. Tammy had planned her escape route carefully. No way was anyone going to catch her today.

"Tammy, give yourself up," Clarke said. "It'll be better in the long run." She was wasting her breath, but she needed to try.

"Hell it will," Tammy said. "No way. I'm not going back to prison. You have to help me. You owe me that."

Clarke disagreed that she owed her anything at all after Tammy had nearly killed her. She needed to stop these feelings of guilt about

Tammy and try to string her along for a while, but that proved impossible to do when they stood face to face.

"What do you want from me?"

"I need you to take me somewhere, help me leave the country."

"I can't do that," Clarke said.

"You owe me." Tammy kicked at the fence.

"Do you want me to end up in prison too for helping you?"

"I don't really care," Tammy said.

Clarke caught her eye. Tammy was telling the truth. She didn't care about anyone except herself. She never used to be like that, did she? Clarke doubted everything now. Perhaps this was the real Tammy. Perhaps she had never seen her true self.

"What's in it for me?" Clarke asked. Tammy had nothing she wanted, but Clarke needed somehow to connect with her on her own level.

"Well, I guess I might not kill you if you help me." Tammy laughed.

Clarke wondered if she was being serious. "You've killed too many people already," she said. "This isn't you. You used to be fun. You're not a killer? What happened?"

"Life happened," Tammy said. "Doug happened."

Even though Doug had divorced Tammy straight after the trial, she still seemed to be blaming him for some of her problems and blaming Clarke for the rest of them. The only person Tammy didn't seem to hold responsible was herself.

"I might help you if you tell me where the money is," Clarke said, seeing her chance to bring up the subject. Maybe she could get some leverage if Tammy needed her help.

Tammy shook her head. "Are you crazy? I need that money."

Clarke reflected that she wouldn't need the money at all because Tammy had probably doubled the length of her sentence when she murdered that prison officer. She would get fed and housed at His

Majesty's pleasure for many more years to come. "Well, you can at least give me some of the money. If you want me to help, you have to give me something." She hoped that Tammy would take her seriously. She might, if she assumed money motivated Clarke as much as it did her.

"How much do you want?" Tammy asked.

Clarke didn't know what she wanted. She certainly wouldn't be able to accept a single penny. If she ever got any money from Tammy, she would be obliged to return it to Briar Holman. Any amount of money would do. She figured if Tammy had to get hold of some cash to give to her, it might reveal where the money came from, assuming the police managed to keep tabs on her.

"Ten grand," Clarke said.

Tammy laughed.

Clarke immediately realised she'd pitched it much too low. She should have asked for more. "Can you get that?" Clarke asked. "How long will it take?"

"Depends what you're willing to do for it," Tammy said. "That money's my nest egg. I'm not about to share it with anybody."

Moments later, the screeching sirens of several police cars made them both jump. Clarke had phoned the police before she arrived here, but she didn't reckon on Tammy being on the other side of the fence. The police cars approached from Tern Road in a convoy of flashing blue lights, with no attempt at subtlety. There was no way they would catch Tammy today.

"You called the police." Tammy glared at her accusatorially.

"I'm sorry, Tammy. I had to."

Tammy didn't wait to listen. She ran, disappearing within seconds into the housing estate, a veritable maze, with plenty of exits. Multiple footpaths at the back led over the common and through the woods. Several roads led out of the estate, with plenty of places to hide if she opted to stay put. Tammy was getting increasingly clever.

The police would never catch her by the time they'd driven round to the other end of the estate. She would be long gone by then.

Clarke realised she'd blown her chance by calling the police. Tammy wouldn't give her another opportunity. Would today's fiasco help the police to find her hideout? At least it narrowed down the search area if they were quick enough to set up roadblocks locally. But she suspected that Tammy would have set up a foolproof escape plan to evade anything like that.

Tammy obviously didn't trust Clarke completely. She had plenty of time to plan the meeting meticulously before she phoned Clarke back to arrange things. Whereas Clarke had little time to come up with a workable strategy. Tammy still had the upper hand. If she had any sense, she'd take her money and run, use it to get herself out of the country. Fast. They may never catch up with her.

As far as Clarke was concerned, the further away Tammy stayed, the better. She really hoped never to see her again. Being so close to her once more turned out to be much scarier than she imagined, even with a high fence between them. Tammy would never change now. She'd gone too far down that route to turn back.

Whatever happened, Clarke was sure that Tammy would do anything to avoid going back to prison, and that made her extremely dangerous.

Clarke returned to the office. She needed to check in with Evan, having hardly seen him lately.

Evan seemed pleased to see her. "How's it going? Have you found anything out? Have you found Tammy yet?"

"I'm fine." If Evan stopped bombarding her with questions, she might get a chance to tell him everything. "I've just seen Tammy."

"You've *seen* her? Have the police caught her?"

"No. She gave us all the slip again," Clarke admitted. She recounted how she arranged to meet Tammy, but Tammy cleverly ensured there was a high fence between them. And when the police showed up, she managed to disappear before they even got out of their cars. She omitted to mention that the police had scuppered any chance of catching Tammy by announcing their approach with sirens blaring.

"She's clever. I'll give her that," Evan said.

"Yes, she is clever." Clarke long ago realised that Tammy was much cleverer than her. "We might never recover the stolen money."

"It's not like you to be so defeatist. Let's keep trying for now. She's not infallible." Evan tapped his fingers annoyingly on the desk. "Can you remember exactly what she said to you? Did she drop any clues at all?"

"No," Clarke said.

"She may not even realise she has."

"And I may not realise it either," said Clarke, "especially if it's something cryptic." She wouldn't put it past Tammy to be especially obscure to give Clarke a challenge she would be sure to fail at.

"Well, if we put our heads together, we might come up with the answer between us," Evan said. "Why don't you try to remember everything she said and write it down. Even the tiniest little thing might help."

Clarke nodded. "Yes, I'll do that."

"At least we're sure now that she's still in the area. It might mean that the money's here too?"

"Didn't you already track the money being transferred halfway round the world ages ago?" Clarke said.

"And I lost the trail."

"Yes, but my point is, she's not going to take all that trouble, then transfer it back into the country."

"I agree," said Evan. "The money won't be in the UK. Too easy for us to find and to retrieve it when we do. But she must have the bank codes hidden somewhere. She wouldn't have relied on memorising the numbers. There's far too much risk that she'd forget them by the time she got released from prison in another decade or more. Perhaps she's got the codes hidden in some locker at a station. And she's simply got to collect the locker key from its hiding place."

"You're clutching at straws," Clarke said.

"Ok, but we need to come up with something."

The phone on Clarke's desk rang. She picked it up. "Hello, Tebbit & Cranshaw, Clarke Pettis speaking." She used what Rob would have called her posh telephone voice.

"Clarke. It's me."

Clarke recognised Tammy's voice instantly. She waved frantically at Evan to get him to be quiet.

"Tammy, where are you?" she asked.

Evan perked up and started paying attention. He came closer and leaned over the receiver to hear the conversation.

"What do you want?" Clarke hadn't expected Tammy to call so soon. Did that mean she was becoming desperate?

"You know exactly what I want you to do. Have you thought about it yet?"

"I don't need to think. I can't do it," Clarke said.

The phone clicked.

"Tammy? Tammy? Are you there?" She had gone.

"Damn," Evan said.

"She knows where I work." Clarke had been so careful. "How did she find out?"

"Is it possible she followed you from home?" Evan asked. "Did you mention it on Facebook when you first joined us? Or are you on the internet anywhere? Have you ever Googled yourself?"

Clarke opened up Google on her computer and typed in her name. Sure enough, her name appeared as one of the employees featured on the Tebbit & Cranshaw website.

She showed Evan. "I didn't even realise they put me on the company website. I don't remember giving them permission." Tammy must have found her easily. She'd been so stupid.

Clarke wasn't sure what to do now. If Tammy found her at the office, it would be easy to follow her home to Rob's house. She resolved to be really careful. Should she go home to Paul? At least he would try to protect her, except he was hardly ever at the flat at the moment, working all hours trying to locate Tammy. Since Tammy's escape, Paul considered himself lucky if he got home for a few hours' sleep every night. Clarke had barely spoken to him lately.

Perhaps Paul would be able to finish earlier today and come over to Rob's place. She longed to discuss everything with him.

The wedding date loomed rapidly, with the days flying by. At least after that, they would be out of the country on their honeymoon. Paul refused to tell her the honeymoon destination, wanting to surprise her. He announced ages ago that she would need her passport but would say nothing more. Perhaps the honeymoon being a big secret was a good thing. If Clarke didn't know where they were going, then Tammy would never find out either, so at least Clarke would feel safe while they were away. But going on honeymoon would simply be postponing the Tammy problem. The same issues would still be here as soon as they returned home.

Paul kept saying how much he wanted to find Tammy before the wedding. Clarke didn't want them to both be constantly on edge during their honeymoon, worrying because Tammy was still out there somewhere.

Did Tammy deliberately want to spoil everything for them? *Don't be so paranoid*, she told herself. But she couldn't help it. She had waited a long time for this wedding, and now she wanted it to be perfect.

Evan interrupted her thoughts. "What did Tammy ask you to do for her?"

"Help her escape the country, I think. Drive the getaway car."

Evan laughed.

It was no laughing matter, but Clarke needed to make light of it somehow.

"Where?" Evan asked.

"Good question. She didn't say. But I'm not doing it." Surely, Tammy wouldn't want her to find out her escape route. If Clarke called the police, they would apprehend Tammy before she arrived at her destination. Did Tammy's plan involve getting rid of loose ends like her? Suddenly, she didn't feel very safe. She didn't want to become a loose end.

"I agree," Evan said. "She's dangerous. You don't want to be in a car alone with her. And besides, you'd get arrested for aiding and abetting a criminal."

"Exactly." Clarke fidgeted in her chair. Evan wasn't assuaging her worries.

"But next time she phones, you might string her along a bit. She doesn't need to know you won't help her escape. Tell her you're considering helping her for old times' sake, that sort of stuff."

"I'm not a very good liar," Clarke said. "She'll see through me."

"It's a lot easier on the phone, when they can't read your body language or the expression on your face."

"You sound like you speak from experience." She resolved not to believe everything Evan told her from now on.

"Don't tell my girlfriend that." Evan laughed. "Anyway, it's not that difficult. You should try it. You just need a bit of practice. Give Paul a call and tell him a few white lies."

"That's no way to start married life," Clarke said, feeling guilty that, although she'd never exactly lied to him, she sometimes omitted the truth, when she did something that he wouldn't approve of, and right now those things Paul wouldn't approve of all concerned Tammy.

Paul would be horrified, but only because he worried about her. But the last couple of years had taught her a lot. She no longer trusted Tammy. Her previous dealings with Tammy would make her extra careful.

"I want you to stay away from the office," Evan said. "You can work from Rob's house until Tammy's caught."

"But that might take forever." Clarke didn't have much confidence that Tammy would be recaptured soon.

"Well, not that long. Surely they'll catch her before you come back from the honeymoon?"

"I'm counting on them catching her before we go." Clarke hoped they would. She wished she believed that. "Are you sure? It doesn't seem fair that I never have to come into the office."

"You can work equally well from home. We've got all the technology. And you'll probably get more work done without me interrupting you all the time. Anyway, it's Tebbit & Cranshaw's fault that Tammy tracked you down. We need to keep you safe."

"Thank you. I appreciate that." Was Evan's decision driven by worry for her or concern for the company in case she sued them? "Can I go early today, please? It's not a great idea to leave at normal going home time, in case Tammy's waiting for me and follows me to Rob's house."

"Of course. And you don't have to work at Rob's house if you'd rather not stay there on your own." Evan's phone pinged with a text message. He glanced at it, then ignored it. "But don't come here. Can you go into Rob's office?"

"I'm sure he wouldn't mind." Rob owned the company. He could easily let her work there, but Tammy might track down Rob's office. "It's probably much safer working at his house. He's got good security, and Tammy won't have Rob's address. He only moved in recently."

Clarke turned her attention to the piece of paper on the desk. She'd written a few things down. Things that Tammy said. Clarke didn't remember much, not about the money anyway. She only said her stash was safe but gave no clue where it might be. Possibly anywhere in the world. Clarke wondered what had happened to the money over the last couple of years. Three million pounds sitting in a bank account earning a pathetically tiny rate of interest would be quickly eroded by inflation. That would make it worth a lot less by Tammy's official release date.

Ned used to work in the City, earning millions trading bonds. Would Tammy have given some of the money to him to invest for her? If he traded bonds or foreign currency with it, he may have turned that money into a much larger amount already.

Equally, he might have lost the lot, but Clarke didn't think Ned was incompetent. Not that she'd ever met him, but from what Katie told her, he was very good at his job. He'd certainly earned enough big bonuses for them to retire early and move to Dorset, and he'd bought a lot of properties in London to rent out.

What if the properties weren't really his? What if he'd bought them with Tammy's money? But that would be complicated if she planned to leave the country. On the other hand, she couldn't possibly have been planning to escape right from the start of her sentence. She'd have been crazy to bank on that happening, so she probably had a longer-term plan for the money. Maybe Ned invested it in property, ready for when she got released. Perhaps that explained why Tammy still hung around. If all the money was tied up, she may not be able to start a new life until Ned sold some assets for her. Clarke needed to go back to Dorset.

She decided to ask Paul to start investigating Ned's finances. He could access a lot of information that she couldn't. How would they track down the properties Ned owned? They probably wouldn't be registered in Ned's name and definitely not Tammy's. Ned would have set up a company to invest Tammy's money, wouldn't he? Clarke looked up the Companies House website and searched for companies with Ned Young as a director.

The search came up blank. Of course, *Ned* must be short for *Edward*. Quickly, she searched again. Three companies listed Edward Young as a director and the only shareholder.

She scrutinised the dates. One of the companies was incorporated eight years ago. Clarke guessed that must be his own property company. He probably would have started buying properties while he still worked in banking, as somewhere to invest his huge annual bonuses.

The other two were investment companies, both set up in the last eighteen months. Was one of them Tammy's? They wouldn't risk putting Tammy's name on anything, or it would immediately pinpoint it as being stolen money. Or both companies might be hers, if Ned considered it safer to split the money. The Companies House website didn't give any further information, and the first set of accounts for each company wasn't due to be filed yet, making it impossible to tell the value of each company's assets.

Did Paul find anything on Ned Young's computer? She needed to ask him if it contained records of the companies' assets. That was definitely worth investigating further.

Clarke texted Paul quickly, asking him to leave work a little earlier tonight and come over to Rob's house. The three of them could brainstorm everything. Surely, between them, they would get some bright ideas. Rob had a good brain, Paul had access to a lot of resources, and Clarke, what did she bring to the equation?

The only thing in her favour was potentially her access to Tammy. Would Paul let her act as bait to lure Tammy in for the police to arrest? She doubted Paul would ever allow that in case she got hurt. There was no disputing that Tammy was dangerous. It would be madness, even if Clarke found the nerve to do it. Could she? Not simply to recover the money. No amount of money would be worth putting her life in Tammy's hands. She'd been in that position once before and never intended that to happen again. They needed to catch her soon before the constant stress broke her.

Tammy must be hiding somewhere. If not at Katie and Ned's house, then where? Was she local to Brackford? Where would she hide in this area?

Clarke racked her brain. Something would come to her, eventually. If she slept on it, she would wake up with a brilliant idea.

Chapter 18

Clarke left the Tebbit & Cranshaw offices at 2:45 p.m. If Tammy intended to wait and follow her home, that would be an unlikely time for her to choose.

This entire situation made her paranoid and illogical. Tammy wanted to be driven somewhere, so surely that meant she didn't have a car, in which case, how could Tammy follow her to Rob's house? Was she worrying about nothing? Rob would tell her to chill. But her paranoia might keep her safe.

She pulled out of the office car park, indicating left. To be really cautious, she should take a different route home. So, at the T junction at the end of the road, instead of turning left again, she turned right.

Her petrol gauge still hadn't been repaired. Clarke tried to remember how much mileage she had done since last filling up. There must be at least half a tank left, plenty enough for her to take a longer route. She turned right again. This road provided a shortcut to the dual carriageway. At this time of day, few people used it, so she should easily spot anyone following her. She kept checking her rearview mirror. There were no other cars in sight.

Reassured, Clarke relaxed and headed to Rob's house. Twenty minutes later, she arrived safely, locking the door behind her as soon as she got inside. Tammy wouldn't find her here.

Clarke and Rob finished eating long before Paul phoned to say he was leaving work. Clarke took a pizza out of the fridge, pepperoni, his latest favourite, and got it ready to put in the oven as soon as Paul showed up.

"You don't treat me that well," Rob said.

Clarke laughed. "I'm not just about to marry you."

"Fair point."

Paul arrived right on time, giving Clarke a big hug as soon as he walked through the door. "I missed you this week," he said.

Clarke cooked the pizza in ten minutes. It smelt delicious as she handed the plate to Paul.

"Tammy found out where Clarke works," Rob said.

Clarke glared at him. She wasn't going to tell Paul that yet in case it worried him.

Paul frowned. "How do you know?"

Clarke realised she would have to tell him everything now. "She phoned me on my work number."

"How did she get that?" Paul asked.

"Apparently, I'm on the Tebbit & Cranshaw website. It's easy to find me if you Google my name."

"That's awful," Rob said.

"Evan offered to get it taken off, but the damage is done now. He says I don't have to go into the office until Tammy is caught."

"That's good. You'll be ok here." Rob put a glass of wine on the table in front of her.

"Are you sure Tammy won't find you here? What if she followed you from the office?" Paul asked.

"No," Clarke said firmly. "I did worry about that, so I took a roundabout route home and checked that nobody tailed me."

"That's smart." Paul smiled at her proudly. "Could she get Rob's address from anywhere?"

"No," Rob answered immediately.

"Rob, you need to be careful too, in case she tries to follow you from your office."

Rob nodded, handing Paul a cold beer.

"What else have you been doing? Are you anywhere near tracking down Tammy yet?" Clarke asked Paul. She seemed to be making more progress than the police. At least she'd seen Tammy once and spoken to her twice, even if it had proved fruitless.

Paul shook his head. "I can't tell you everything, except that we haven't had a lot of developments."

Rob glared at Paul. "Look, you guys, you're getting married on Saturday. You need to get Tammy locked up again before the wedding. So why don't you stop being so damn stupid, tell each other everything you know, and pool resources. It's the end result that counts. Sod the rules. No one's going to find out."

"He's right, Paul," Clarke said. "Tammy needs to be locked up. It doesn't matter how it happens."

"I worry about you getting involved. That's half the reason I don't want to tell you anything," Paul said.

"I won't get any less involved just because you tell me something. It will probably work the other way. If you've already done something, I won't need to do it, will I? I just want that woman off my back. I want to stop worrying. And I don't want her ruining our wedding."

"Ok," Paul said, "but it's all off the record."

"Of course." Rob and Clarke both spoke together.

"We visited Katie and Ned Young."

"I know. You must have arrived soon after I left," Clarke said. "I only met Katie. Ned was apparently up in London, checking one of his properties. He owns a lot of properties that he rents out."

"What time did you leave?" Paul asked. He finished his last mouthful of pizza and pushed his plate to one side.

"One thirty."

"We got there at two," Paul said. "There was no sign of Katie. Ned didn't seem to know her whereabouts."

"Ned was home? He must have got back from London quickly."

"Yes, that's odd," Paul said.

"What did Ned tell you?"

"Not that much, really," Paul said. "But he showed Barry outside, so I poked around the house quickly. I found a passport that might be a fake passport for Tammy."

"I knew they were helping her," said Clarke. "I knew it."

"The passport name was Maria Something-or-other. Does that name mean anything to you?"

Clarke shook her head.

"If you've got the passport, Tammy can't leave the country," Rob said.

"We don't have the passport. It's not acceptable as evidence if we poke around without permission, then steal it. We drove all the way to Brackford to get a warrant. Went straight back and searched the house. By that time, the passport was gone. We didn't find anything."

"Did you search the sheds outside?" Clarke asked.

Paul took a gulp of his beer. "We searched a shed that was crammed full of tools and animal feed. Took everything out. I couldn't find anything to prove a connection to Tammy."

"What about the stables and the goose shed?" Something about her visit to Dorset niggled at the back of her mind, but she couldn't quite recall what.

"We searched them too. It was pitch-black outside by then, so it's possible we missed something. But there really is nowhere to hide anything with any of the animals."

"You're probably right," Clarke said. She probably would have been more thorough than him, but she would still have bet on finding nothing. Katie and Ned would be crazy to hide anything there. The police would obviously search the premises, eventually. She wondered how they managed to slip up with the passport.

"When I left, I forgot my scarf," Clarke said. "I drove straight back and Katie had just gone out. I saw her walking across the fields at the back of the house with a couple of carrier bags. She may have been taking food to Tammy."

"It's possible," Paul said. "Where would she have been headed?"

"The land at the back doesn't belong to them. The fields lead to a massive wood. There might be any number of places Tammy could hide."

"Can you use dogs to search the woods?" Rob asked.

"Maybe," Paul said. "The problem is, Katie might have simply been taking a shortcut to get somewhere else without being seen. Without evidence that Tammy might be there, I'm not sure the DCI would sign off the extra expense."

"We're all forgetting something," said Rob, thumping his fists down on the table. "Tammy's been seen in this area recently. Is she really driving up and down the motorway every day? It's a three-hour journey each way. Has she even got a car?"

"She may have," Paul said. "We can't rule out anything."

"Somebody must be helping her," Clarke said.

"If anyone else is involved, it's probably Katie and Ned. They're the only ones who bothered to visit her in prison."

"Have they both got cars?" Clarke hadn't seen a car in Katie's driveway when she'd visited.

"We saw Ned's car," Paul said, "but no sign of Katie's car."

As far as Clarke recalled, Katie's car wasn't parked in the driveway when she visited either. She would have paid more attention if Paul had mentioned the possibility of Tammy having a car before.

Paul interrupted her thoughts. "Katie claims she sold her car. We're following up on that, but it might not mean anything. Tammy may just as easily have stolen a car. That would make more sense, then it wouldn't get traced back to her friends. She could steal a different car every day if she wanted to keep us off her trail."

"Is it really that easy? How would she start it without a key?" Clarke asked.

"You hot-wire it," Rob said. "Simple enough when you know how, if you pick the right sort of car."

Clarke wondered how Rob learnt to hot-wire a car. "I can't imagine Tammy doing that."

"Tammy may have learned in prison," Paul said. "The inmates pick up so many things as soon as they mix with other criminals. If I had my way, they would spend their entire sentences in solitary confinement."

"Bit harsh," said Rob.

"I'm only half serious," Paul said. "But you get my point. They all learn stuff inside, whether they want to or not. I bet Tammy would be perfectly capable of stealing a car, and if she kept stealing a new one every day, no one would know what to search for."

"Could Katie or Ned have bought a car recently, especially for Tammy?" Clarke asked.

"It's possible," Paul said, "and, with a private cash sale, the registration wouldn't have gone through yet and there would be no trace on Katie's bank statement, but would she take the risk of being found out, eventually?"

Clarke shook her head slowly. Katie had said she wouldn't help Tammy, at least not if it meant risking herself or Ned.

Rob stood up and walked around the room. "You said Katie and Ned always visited Tammy separately, and when each of you went to Dorset, you only saw one of them, not both at once."

"What are you getting at?" Clarke almost heard Rob's brain ticking over.

"Has it occurred to either of you that only one of them may be helping Tammy? The other may not be aware of it."

"But which one?" Paul asked.

"Katie would be the obvious choice," Clarke said. "She's Tammy's oldest friend."

"I thought all three of them were friends at school," Paul said.

"Yes, but Tammy and Katie were particularly close."

"I still wouldn't rule out Ned," Paul said.

"There is someone else."

The two men stared at Clarke expectantly.

"One of Tammy's friends, ex-friends, told me she used to be very close to a man called Kroft, another old friend from school."

"Kroft?"

"It's a nickname. He works in The Ball and Chain pub in Havebury." Clarke had intended to go there and try to talk to him, but she hadn't been able to face it yet. Remembering her last visit to that pub made her shudder. It must have been two years ago, when she went to meet Bradley Acres. That didn't end well. She didn't want to go back.

"Barry drinks there sometimes. I'll ask him. We can pay Kroft a visit tomorrow," Paul said.

Clarke was relieved to let Paul take charge of that task. DC Barry Medway wouldn't have the same hang-ups as her about visiting that place.

"What, I don't get it." Rob handed Paul a can of Coke. "Tammy's really intelligent, and Katie or Ned obviously got the passport for her. So, why didn't she leave the country immediately? That would be far safer for her."

"Beats me." Paul opened the can and took a gulp of the cold drink. "I'm worried that she wants revenge on Clarke. She's already instigated a meeting. And she tracked her down at work. She didn't need to do that if all she wants is to flee the country."

"You think all this hate's been festering inside of her while she's been in prison? That might be the most important thing to her now," Rob said.

"She's arrogant. She probably believes she can do both, get revenge and then leave the country. But the longer she stays in the UK, the more chance of us catching her." Paul looked across the table at Clarke.

Clarke hoped Paul was right. "Tammy said she wanted my help. She wanted me to drive her somewhere. That might mean she doesn't have a car."

"Or more likely, she wants to get you on your own. Please don't be tempted to do it, Clarke." Paul stared at her pleadingly. "Tammy's dangerous. She's already killed two people. It would be easy for her to kill you if she trapped you in a car with her."

"I'm aware of that," Clarke said. "I'm not stupid."

"Sorry. I didn't mean you were." Paul took another mouthful of his pizza. He'd been talking so much, he was still only halfway through it. "This is delicious."

"What do we do next?" Rob asked.

"Can you use me as bait?" Clarke suggested. "I won't get in a car with her, but perhaps I can ask her to meet me again. If you surrounded the area with police, you would capture her this time."

Paul looked shocked. "Remember what happened when you met her before. She only gave you the location at the last minute so the police wouldn't have time to get there. And even if we got officers in place earlier last time, we wouldn't necessarily have positioned them on both sides of that fence. That was clever of her. She planned her getaway carefully, with multiple escape routes. We would have needed a lot of officers to cover all of them and we simply don't have that resource. No one would sign off deploying dozens of police officers, with no guarantee she will even show up."

"It won't need dozens," Clarke said.

"Whatever. It would be impossible to guarantee apprehending her. Anyway, it would be far too risky. Tammy could get you up close and stick a knife in your back in seconds. Remember what she did to that poor prison officer. Don't underestimate her."

"I did have some more thoughts about the money." Clarke conceded on the bait idea. "Ned Young used to be an investment banker, a very good one, apparently. What if he invested the money for Tammy? If she left it in a bank account, earning a tiny amount of interest and then didn't get out of prison for fifteen years, inflation would eat away at the value and it wouldn't be worth even half as much in real terms by that time. I checked Companies House. Ned set up two new companies about eighteen months ago. He may be using them to invest Tammy's money. Can you check them out?" she asked Paul.

"Yes, that's worth investigating," Paul agreed.

"If you find any company bank accounts with evidence of Tammy's money going through them, we can work backwards from there, follow the trail from the end point instead of the start point. If we can get the two halves of the money trail to meet in the middle, we can tie it back to the Briar Holman money."

"If Ned made some good investments," Rob said, "it would already be worth a lot more. What happens then? If Tammy stole three million, but now it's worth four million, will she only have to give the three million back or will they take all of it? Who gets the extra hypothetical million?"

"That's a good question," Clarke said. "The answer is, she would have to give all the money back, four million instead of three."

"In the meantime," Paul said, "if Tammy contacts you at all, you must phone me immediately. I wonder if we could get your mobile number rerouted through Rob's home phone and put a trace on it. That might work. I'll talk to the Techies at work. Then you simply have to keep talking until the call gets traced."

"Good idea," said Clarke. "I'll be here for most of the day."

"Are you safe here on your own?" Paul asked.

"I've got a really good security system," Rob assured him. "It's linked into my phone, so if anyone tries to break in, I'll get the footage on my phone immediately and I can call the police."

"That's good," Paul said. "Make sure you keep the phone with you, even if you're in an important meeting."

Rob nodded.

"What can I do?" Clarke asked.

"Nothing. Stay out of trouble," Paul said. "I'll start investigating stolen cars. If nothing else, we might recover a few stolen vehicles, so something good will come out of this." He laughed.

"I need to visit Ned," Clarke said. "I can ask him about those companies."

"You've got no jurisdiction to do that. He doesn't have to tell you anything," Paul said. "Let me do it."

"But you don't know anything about finance," Clarke pointed out. "How will you ask the right questions?"

"So, make me a list of questions," Paul said. "I'll make sure I ask them."

Clarke promised to email the questions first thing in the morning. She still intended to go back to Dorset. Maybe she wouldn't send Paul the email until later.

"More importantly," Paul said, turning to Rob. "How's the best man's speech coming along?"

Rob smiled. "It's top secret. It'll be a surprise on the day."

"He won't tell me anything either." Clarke started to clear the table.

"You'd better not embarrass me too much." Paul looked worried.

"Embarrassing the groom is in the best man's job description." Rob drained his glass. "There's no escape."

"Don't say that, Rob. He might not show up on the day."

Paul took Clarke's hand and squeezed it. "Perhaps we should elope."

"Don't you dare," Rob said. "Mum would never forgive you."

Clarke knew he wasn't joking. Their mother was even more excited about the wedding than Clarke. "Don't worry," she said. "After all the work I've put in to organise it, nothing's going to ruin our wedding."

Chapter 19

Paul let himself into the flat. He grabbed a beer from the fridge and sat in the living room. He needed to relax. Talking about Tammy had wound him up.

He took a swig of his beer. Why couldn't he find her? Him, the supposedly brilliant detective. And Tammy? Just another no-good criminal. How difficult could it be to catch her? He had underestimated her, but she underestimated him too. Sooner or later, she would slip up.

Clarke worried him. She was getting far too involved, visiting Katie in Dorset. What if Tammy had been there? Clarke never liked being told what to do. She was too headstrong for her own good. Sometimes he loved that side of her, but other times that same quality made her a liability to herself. He didn't want Clarke putting herself in danger, and somehow, he needed to keep her safe.

The only way to do that was to find Tammy. When Tammy escaped from prison, she had nothing. No food, no transport, no clothes. Her only two friends lived miles away. And surely, if it was easy for Tammy to access the money she stole, she'd have skipped the country by now.

So why couldn't he find her? He must be missing something.

Suddenly, a loud crash of breaking glass made him jump to his feet. Someone had lobbed a brick through the front window. An icy wind blasted him to full alertness in an instant. He grabbed his keys and ran to the front door.

Scanning the road outside, a flash of movement on the pavement caught his eye. Quickly, he slammed the door behind him and ran towards the road.

The person he'd spotted began to run. That alone marked them as guilty, especially with nobody else in sight. Paul raced after them, thankful he still wore his trainers.

"Stop," he shouted. "Stop, police."

The figure ahead ran faster. Paul needed to reach them before they turned the corner and disappeared out of sight. They wore dark clothes and a hoodie, nothing to identify them if he let them get away. His first thought was Tammy, but Tammy wasn't a runner. She would never run this fast. This person was flying, and they were smaller than Tammy too. Paul put on an extra spurt of speed, lengthening his stride and pumping his arms like crazy, determined to catch the culprit.

He started to gain on them, making up ground rapidly until he was only a couple of metres away.

"Stop," he gasped, his breathing so heavy the words barely came out. He lurched forward, managing to grab the runner's arm. In one swift move, he pulled the runner towards him and quickly turned them around to face him, keeping hold of their arm. To his surprise, a young girl stared up at him.

"What's your name?" His breathing was laboured from his exertion, so he paused for a moment to get some air into his lungs.

The girl remained silent.

"I'm a police officer," Paul said. "If you don't tell me who you are, I'll have to arrest you."

Still no reply. The girl looked scared.

"You threw that brick, didn't you?" Paul noticed her gloveless hands. "It will have your fingerprints on it, so you may as well tell me what's going on. What's your name?"

"Lizzie."

Paul smiled, trying to put her at ease so she would continue to cooperate. "Ok, Lizzie, tell me, why did you throw that brick?"

Silence again. This wasn't getting him anywhere. He guessed Lizzie must be about fifteen years old. Where were her parents? Did they realise what their daughter got up to? Did they care?

"If you won't talk to me, I'll have to take you down to the station."

"Someone made me do it," Lizzie said suddenly.

"Who made you?" Paul's immediate thought was Tammy.

"I don't know. I didn't recognise her."

It must be Tammy. "Was she black, with a shaved head?"

Lizzie shook her head. "Blond hair, but yeah, she was black."

"That's good." Paul smiled at the girl. "Can you tell me anything else about her?"

Lizzie considered for a moment. "She was quite pretty and nice at first, but then she got scary."

"How did she get scary?"

"She threatened to break my arm if I didn't do it. She said it would be all right. If I threw the brick and ran, it would be all right. No one would come after me. I'm sorry."

Paul took his phone out of his pocket, not lifting his gaze from the girl for a moment. He still didn't trust her not to run if she saw a chance.

He quickly pulled up an old photo of Tammy, from when she'd had glorious hair. It sounded like Tammy might be wearing a wig now. He showed Lizzie the photo.

"Try to imagine this woman with blond hair," he said. "Do you think it might be her?"

"Yes, maybe," Lizzie said.

"I need to take you to the police station to make a statement. If you cooperate, I promise not to arrest you. It's this woman I want, not you." It wasn't really necessary to frighten the girl any more, but the end justified the means.

Paul walked her to the flat's front door and double locked it. He'd have to take a chance on the broken window. No one would see it from the road and, in any case, he'd left the light on, so it appeared he was still home.

Barry Medway was getting ready to leave the station when they arrived.

"You in a hurry to get home, Barry? I need a bit of help with this one." He wasn't supposed to interview her without having a parent present. They wouldn't do a formal interview. If she made a statement and signed it, he would take her straight home. The DCI would have left by now. Paul didn't mind bending the rules a little when the end justified the means, but he never would risk being alone in a room with an underage girl.

They entered the interview room. Barry looked concerned. He knew as well as Paul did they should have an appropriate adult present.

Lizzie sat down.

"How old are you?" Paul asked.

"Thirteen."

Thirteen? Paul would have sworn earlier that she looked older. And, if she said thirteen, that probably meant eleven. Under the harsh strip lighting in here, she did appear younger than she had in the darkness outside.

"And what's your full name?"

"Lizzie Thompson." She gave her address on the Hale Hill estate.

"Tell me what happened, in your own words." Paul decided not to record the interview. That would make it too official. Barry wrote everything down. He would get Lizzie to sign it at the end as her statement.

"This woman came up to me."

"When?" Paul asked.

"This afternoon."

Damn. Hours ago. Tammy might be anywhere by now.

"And what did she say to you?"

"She said she'd give me fifty quid if I threw a brick through someone's window."

Paul raised his eyebrows. That conflicted with what she said before. Did Lizzie do it for the money?

"I said no. But she said if I didn't do it, she'd break my arm."

"So, you agreed?" Paul said. "Did you take the cash?"

Lizzie looked frightened, and suddenly she did appear much younger. "We really need the money," she said. "Dad's got no job, and Mum left us. If we don't pay the rent, we'll be chucked out on the streets."

Poor kid. Paul noticed now her clothes were old, and her face sported a gaunt appearance, as if she didn't get enough to eat. He believed her. "It's ok," Paul said sympathetically. "I understand." He saw too many kids like this, and most of them turned to crime because either their parents or the system let them down.

Barry scribbled Lizzie's words into his notepad.

"I wanted to refuse." Lizzie still looked afraid. "But she frightened me. She would have hurt me. And we really need the money. Will I have to give it back?"

She looked more worried about the prospect of losing the money than anything else. It wouldn't help anyone to take it off her. Paul decided to ignore it.

"So, what happened next?" Paul asked.

Lizzie shuffled in her chair. "She said I must wait outside the flat all evening until someone came home. Then she told me to throw the brick through the window as soon as the lights went on, then run."

It took several minutes between Paul arriving home and the brick flying through the window. He imagined Lizzie agonising with herself outside, trying to make the right decision.

"Where did you meet Ta—her?" He'd nearly said Tammy's name. Lizzie didn't need to be told that.

"The park near your place. I was going home from school."

Paul checked the address she gave him. "The park's a long way from where you live."

"I can walk it in half an hour. It saves the bus fare."

"Where do you go to school?"

"Taylor Park."

Paul was familiar with Taylor Park, the local comprehensive. He made a separate note to check the route between Taylor Park school and Lizzie's home, certain it would be more than a half-hour walk.

"Do you remember where the woman went after she spoke to you?"

"I don't know. She walked the opposite way to me. I just wanted to get away from her."

Barry finished writing. Paul quickly read through the statement before passing it to Lizzie. "Can you read through this and, if you're happy with it, sign it at the bottom, please?"

She read it slowly, then reached for the pen and signed.

"Thank you." Paul took the piece of paper, unsure whether to file this officially yet. "I'll take you home now."

"I can walk."

"I'm not letting you walk home in the dark at this time of night. I insist. Don't worry, it's not a police car. We won't set the neighbours gossiping." He wanted to take her home, to check that she'd given him her correct address. Plenty didn't and he might want to get in touch with her again.

Half an hour later, he got back to the flat. He still needed to deal with the broken window. If he called a glazier early in the morning, he might not be too late getting into work.

While deciding what to do, he fetched a dustpan and brush from the kitchen to sweep up the worst of the glass. Then he got the vacuum cleaner out, worrying briefly that the noise might wake up the neighbours. Tough. He didn't want to leave broken glass on the carpet. He didn't have anything to board up the window, but it wasn't easily visible from the road. He would go to bed and risk that it would be all right.

The temperature in the living room had dropped dramatically due to the cold air blasting through the broken window. The sooner he fixed this, the better. Once the glazier mended the window, he wouldn't mention it to Clarke. He was grateful she was staying with Rob. Tammy threw a brick through that same window once before, so it would freak Clarke out if she found out Tammy had organised a repeat performance. There was no harm done, not really, so best to put it behind him and never admit it happened to Clarke, for her own good.

The girl's statement might prove useful, but it didn't get him anywhere near tracking down Tammy. He needed to find her, fast.

Chapter 20

It was mid-morning by the time Paul got the window fixed and arrived at the police station. After his late night, he appreciated the couple of extra hours' rest. A Post-it note from Erica, the scene of crime officer, was stuck to his computer screen, asking him to come to her office.

He found Erica's door already open.

"You wanted to see me?" Paul hoped she'd made a breakthrough. Having such a huge role in this case gave him an opportunity to prove himself. He didn't want to blow it by failing.

"Yes, sit down." Erica gestured to an empty chair by her desk.

Paul plonked himself down on it, pulling it closer to the desk. Erica's coffee mug sat steaming on her desk. He wished he'd brought his own drink with him. It would be cold by the time he got back to the MIT office.

"I've analysed the rubbish you gave me."

"The Ranleigh Marshes stuff?" Paul almost salivated with anticipation. Erica wouldn't have made him come down here to tell him she'd found nothing.

"Yes. The food wrappers. They've got Tammy Doncaster's DNA on them."

"Are you sure?" Paul couldn't stop his face from morphing into a huge, cheesy grin, even though it only told him that she'd been there. It gave no indication of where she might be now.

"Certain," Erica said.

The expression on her face dared him to doubt her. Paul wouldn't dare to try. "That's great," he said.

"There's more."

"More? What?" Even connecting Tammy to the bird hide in Ranleigh Marshes was more than he'd hoped for.

"It looks like someone used that little piece of duct tape to tape a car key to something, maybe to the underneath of a table or chair."

So, Tammy did have access to a car. Had Ned or Katie Young left the key for Tammy?

"I can't be completely sure, but the car may be an Audi," Erica said.

Paul smiled. "That might help narrow it down." Did either of the Youngs own an Audi? He would get Barry back on the CCTV later, to check if any Audis were in the area near Ranleigh Marshes on the day Tammy escaped.

"How sure are you about the make of car?"

Erica pursed her lips, hesitating for a few seconds. "Ninety-five percent, at a guess, but I hate guessing. That's the best I can do. The tape was too screwed up to be more certain than that. A lot of car keys are similar, but there's a faint impression of part of Audi's four circles logo on the tape." Erica pulled up a photo on her computer, enlarging it on the screen.

"Yes, I see what you mean," Paul said, examining it closely. This was great news. Find the Audi, and perhaps they would find Tammy.

"Did you find any other DNA on the rubbish?" If Erica found proof linking one of the Youngs to Tammy, he could put pressure on them to tell him where she was hiding.

"A minuscule amount, but so little, it may have been the shop assistant who sold the food. The tape only had Tammy's DNA on it, so it's highly likely that whoever else touched it wore gloves," Erica said.

"Thanks for this, Erica. It may have given us a break," Paul said. They certainly needed one.

Paul's coffee was completely cold by the time he returned to his desk. He didn't have time to tip it away. It would be easier to catch Kroft before the pub opened at lunchtime. He'd nearly reached his car when he ran into Barry, on his way back to the station.

"If you're not busy, we've got a new suspect to go and interview." He would put Barry on searching for the missing Audi as soon as they got back. Interviewing Kroft was his top priority now.

"Sure. Where are we going, Sarge?" Barry got in the car with Paul and pulled on his seat belt.

"We're going to the pub," Paul said. "The Ball and Chain in Havebury. You drink there a lot, don't you?"

"I do occasionally. My mate, Shaun, is more of a regular. Why are we going to that dump?"

Paul ignored the question. "Do you know anyone who works in The Ball and Chain? How about a guy called Kroft, with a K?"

"I don't know any names, but I might recognise him if I saw him. What does he look like?"

"No idea," Paul said.

"Shaun would know. Do you want me to call him?"

"That would be great." Paul pulled out onto the dual carriageway. It wouldn't take long to get to Havebury.

"Shaun, mate." Barry put the phone on speakerphone and held it in front of him.

"Hi, Baz."

"Shaun, you know everybody in The Ball and Chain, don't you?"

"You make me sound like I spend all my time there." Shaun laughed. "But yeah, I know most people."

"Do you know a guy called Kroft?"

"Yeah, Kroft is the manager. He lives above the pub."

"Do you know much about him?"

"Not really," Shaun said. "He's a nice guy. Except he supports Man United."

"I'm surprised you even talk to him in that case," Barry said. "Seeing as you're a Liverpool supporter."

"Well, I need to get served drinks occasionally, so I can't completely blank him, can I?"

"Shaun, I'm Paul, Barry's sergeant." Paul butted into the conversation. "How long has Kroft worked at The Ball and Chain?"

"It's been a few years. I must have been drinking there for five years. He worked behind the bar then. He's only been made manager in the last year."

"Thanks. That's really useful."

"What's he done?" Shaun asked.

"Oh, he hasn't done anything," Barry said. "We need him to help with our inquiries."

"Yeah, right," Shaun said. "Has he murdered someone?"

"Why did you say that? Do you think he might?"

"No, course not. He's a nice guy. But you are in the murder squad, aren't you?"

"MIT, yes. But no, he hasn't murdered anyone. Anyway, thanks, Shaun. I'll catch you at the weekend." Barry hung up the call.

"Why are we going to see this Kroft guy?" Barry asked.

"Apparently, he's an old friend of Tammy Doncaster."

"Aha."

"And he may have seen her since she escaped," Paul said. "We need to talk to him."

A few minutes later, Paul pulled into The Ball and Chain car park.

"Ironic if we found Tammy here, since they built the pub on the site of an old prison." He laughed. He didn't seriously expect to find Tammy. That wasn't why they were here.

At nearly midday, the manager should be in the pub. Paul hoped it wouldn't get too busy for lunch yet, so they could talk to Kroft out the back in private. He marched up to the bar, with Barry following close behind, and pulled out his warrant card.

THE PAYBACK

"We're looking for Kroft."

The barman hesitated for a moment, then said, "I'll get him." He disappeared out the back.

Paul wondered if he should follow him in case Kroft ran. He whispered in Barry's ear for him to run round to the rear of the pub, in case Kroft tried to get away.

The barman quickly returned with a tall black guy.

"You looking for me?" he asked. "What's it about?"

"Kroft?"

The man nodded. "Yep, that's me."

"Can we talk in private?" Paul said.

"Sure."

Paul glanced at the door, seeing Barry on his way back. "My colleague's here as well. Hold on a second." He waited for Barry to join him.

They followed him into a small office.

"Sorry, I've only got two chairs in here." Kroft jumped up and sat on the desk facing them.

"You're an old friend of Tammy Doncaster," Paul said. He may as well get straight to the point.

"Yeah, I used to know Tammy. Sure. We were at school together."

"Have you seen her much since?"

Kroft swung his legs back and forth under the desk. Paul wondered if it was a sign of nerves.

"She used to come in here occasionally." Kroft's legs swung faster. "Not really her kind of place, though. She's more the upmarket type. Likes a nice wine bar or restaurant. It's a bit rough here."

That tallied with what Tammy's friend told Clarke. "So, when did you last see her?"

"She's in prison, isn't she? I haven't seen her for ages. Must be a couple of years."

"Are you sure about that?"

"Of course I'm sure."

"If you were such good friends, why did you never go and visit her in prison?"

"She's a murderer," Kroft said. "She's not really someone I want to associate with anymore. Bad for the image."

Privately, Paul thought having a murderer for a friend would improve his image by several notches in this dive of a pub, but he kept that to himself. "What car do you drive?" he asked.

"It's an Audi," Kroft said. "The Sportbac."

Paul raised an eyebrow. Could this be the Audi they were looking for? "When did you last go to Ranleigh Marshes?"

Kroft hesitated. "Haven't been there for years."

"Where is your car? I'd like to see it." Suddenly, Kroft had become a person of far greater interest. Paul would get the forensic team to collect the car. They would soon confirm if Tammy had ever been in it.

"It's gone in for repairs." Kroft's legs started to swing again.

"What's the name of the garage?" Paul snapped back. The excuse seemed a bit too convenient to explain the missing car, making Paul instantly suspicious. If he piled on enough pressure, Kroft might crack.

"It's a mate doing it."

"What's his name?" Paul didn't even give Kroft time to take a breath.

"I don't know. He's one of my regular customers."

"So, you gave an expensive car to someone you hardly know, who doesn't have a proper garage. Really?" Audis weren't cheap. He would expect him to be more careful who he entrusted the car to. Being a pub manager must pay better than he thought, if Kroft wasn't worried about such an expensive vehicle. Or perhaps he dealt drugs on the side. That wouldn't surprise him in this dump. He resolved to ask around at the station if there were drug issues in this pub. He may be able to use that as leverage to make Kroft give up Tammy.

Paul stared at Kroft, who avoided eye contact.

"Loads of people in here use him. He comes highly recommended," Kroft said.

"When did you give him the car?"

"A couple of days ago. I expected it to be finished by now. It's a bit inconvenient without it."

"When you get it back, give me a call," Paul said. "In the meantime, what's the registration number?"

"I don't understand what my car has to do with anything," Kroft said.

"The registration number, please." They would check CCTV for it. Perhaps that would help them prove that Tammy had used it to make her escape. Unfortunately, the car might be anywhere by now. Paul very much doubted that Kroft's mechanic acquaintance possessed it.

Kroft gave him the registration number. He would verify later that the registration was in Kroft's name. The fact that Kroft owned an Audi may just be a massive coincidence. Paul found it odd that Kroft didn't even visit Tammy in prison. So, did he really care enough to lend her an expensive car? And, if he did, did Tammy still have the car? She may have dumped it somewhere. Did Kroft plan on claiming it on his insurance? Well, with such a useless cover story, he probably wouldn't get away with that.

"Do you live upstairs?" Paul asked.

"Yes."

"Can we see?"

"Have you got a warrant?"

Kroft appeared more confident now. Either he would get cocky and make a mistake, or Paul would get nothing more from him. It was too early to judge which way things would go. "No, but we can get one very quickly. How about you save us the trouble if you've got nothing to hide?" Paul said.

Kroft shrugged. "I guess so." He slid off the desk and opened the office door. Paul and Barry followed him up the stairs.

Kroft opened the door of the flat. A pretty black woman came out of the kitchen towards them.

Paul stopped dead, staring at her dyed blond hair. Maria Vasquez. He glanced at Kroft, who seemed equally surprised to see her.

"I thought you'd already gone," Kroft said. He turned to Paul. "This is my girlfriend. She's just leaving."

"What's your full name?" Paul asked her.

"What's it to you?" Maria scowled at him.

"Babe, they're police."

"I haven't done anything wrong."

She seemed suspicious. Paul wondered why.

"She's right," Kroft said. "Maria is practically a saint. She hasn't done anything wrong. She's never even got a parking ticket."

"I'd still like you to tell me your full name, Maria," Paul said.

"It's Maria Vasquez. Ok?" She folded her arms defiantly.

"Do you know Tammy Doncaster?" Paul asked.

"Never heard of her."

"Where's your passport?" Was the passport in Ned's house a copy, or had Maria provided her own passport for Tammy?

"I'm here legally," Maria protested. "Just because I'm black, it doesn't mean I'm an illegal immigrant."

"I'm not suggesting that you are," Paul said, wishing she were less defensive. "I still want to see your passport."

"I don't have it. I've sent it off to be renewed."

THE PAYBACK

"She hasn't done anything," Kroft said. "This doesn't concern her. If you must know, she's a one-night stand, and I would really like her to leave." He turned to Maria. "You should go home now, babe."

Maria's face screwed up, and she started to cry. She turned to Kroft. "You used me." She avoided eye contact with him. "How could you do that?"

"Just get out." Kroft made no attempt to apologise.

Maria barged past Barry towards the door.

"Sarge?" Barry looked at Paul.

"Let her go." He didn't need a hysterical woman to deal with.

Maria slammed the door behind her.

"Women!" Kroft said, sounding exasperated.

Paul ignored him. He wondered how Maria's passport had come to be in the Youngs' house. If Maria was really a one-night stand, when would he have got the chance to take her passport? It didn't make sense. He had to be lying about something. "I want you to come down to the station with us," he told Kroft.

"Why? I haven't done anything," Kroft said.

"We think you've been helping Tammy Doncaster." Paul would arrest Kroft if he refused to come with them to the police station.

"Seriously? No way," Kroft said.

"Are you going to come to the station with us and make a statement voluntarily, or do I have to arrest you?"

"Ok. I'll come, but it's voluntary."

Paul and Barry led Kroft out to the car. They would need to question him immediately once they got to the station, although Paul would love to let him stew for a bit while they ate a sandwich. Except that he wasn't under arrest yet, meaning he might walk out anytime he liked. They needed to get on with things. Paul's stomach rumbled. Lunch would have to wait.

They drove back to the police station in silence. Paul went through in his head what he planned to ask Kroft about the passport at Ned and Katie's house. It surely was no coincidence that they used Maria's name and the photo in it looked like her. He must have taken Maria's passport for Tammy. It surely wouldn't be a forgery. It would be madness to choose a friend's name deliberately. So, the passport must be the real thing. Tammy could easily achieve a sufficiently similar appearance with a blond wig. He suddenly remembered the woman Lizzie had described. Blond hair. Tammy must already have changed her appearance to resemble the passport photo. That meant she might be ready to leave the country very soon.

Paul wondered if Tammy knew Maria. "How long have you been with Maria?" he asked Kroft suddenly, breaking the silence. Perhaps he could trip him up.

"I already told you, she's a one-night stand," Kroft said.

Paul didn't believe him. He should have brought Maria Vasquez in too. Maybe she wasn't as innocent as she'd seemed.

Chapter 21

"I didn't expect to see you again." Katie answered the door promptly.

"I forgot my scarf," Clarke said, cringing inside at the lame excuse. She really wanted to see Ned, but his car wasn't outside. Perhaps she should wait until he showed up.

Katie looked puzzled, perhaps realising the scarf wasn't worth the long drive to retrieve it. "You'd better come in."

Clarke shivered as she entered Katie's house, despite the warmth, apprehensive that perhaps Tammy would be here. But surely Katie wouldn't have invited her in so readily if that were the case.

Katie gestured for her to sit at the kitchen table while she searched through a drawer. "Here it is. I wondered if you might come back for it. Ned wanted to throw it out, but it's a nice scarf."

"Thank you for rescuing it," Clarke said.

Katie took some cups from a cupboard. "You better have a coffee while you're here. It's a long way to drive."

Clarke wondered if she should make some excuse for being in the area, but she'd missed the moment for that, and Katie would never believe her, anyway.

"Have you found Tammy yet?"

Clarke shook her head. Either Katie was a pretty good actress or she didn't have a clue where Tammy was hiding. If she did, she surely wouldn't risk asking Clarke if she'd found her. "I did see her," Clarke admitted.

"Where? How is she?" Katie sounded concerned.

Clarke figured she must still genuinely care for her friend. That would give her all the more reason to help her.

"When I first realised I lost my scarf, I came straight back," Clarke said, changing the subject. "About ten minutes after I left you. You were walking across the fields with some carrier bags." Clarke figured she might as well confront Katie now, otherwise her journey would be for nothing, unless Ned materialised soon.

Katie appeared surprised at the accusation.

"Where were you going?" Clarke asked.

Katie smiled. "Birdwatching. Why? Did you really imagine I might be hiding Tammy in the woods?"

"Would you blame me for assuming that?" It had looked odd. Naturally, Clarke assumed that it might involve Tammy. She still didn't believe Katie.

"Let's settle it. I'll take you there as soon as we've finished our coffee. I can prove I'm telling the truth. I've got nothing to hide."

For a moment, Clarke wondered if she should go with her. What if Tammy really was in the woods? She wouldn't be very safe, stuck in the middle of nowhere with the two women.

"Yes," she said. "I would like to see it." At least it gave them the chance to talk on the way. She had plenty more questions. And if she saw any sign of Tammy, she would run and phone for help. Clarke gulped down her coffee, keen to get going before she changed her mind.

"Do you know a friend of Tammy's called Kroft?" Clarke asked.

"Yes, of course I do. We were all friends back in Hackney when we were at school. Karl Croft. Karl with a K. Croft with a C."

"Do you still see him?" Clarke asked.

"Haven't seen him in years. But I'm sure Tammy did. He works at some god-awful pub, near Brackford. Never been there and don't want to."

"Why didn't you keep in touch?"

"He was a bit of a latecomer to the group, I guess. Perhaps we never really bonded enough."

"Or did you fall out?"

"Me, Ned, and Tammy were like The Three Musketeers. Kroft coming along kind of upset the balance. He was nuts about Tammy. She kept leading him on and he and Ned ended up fighting over her."

Clarke wanted to ask who won but didn't quite dare. Clearly, Katie won in the end. "So, they were both keen on her then?"

"All the boys were keen on Tammy, but I got Ned." Katie smiled smugly.

Clarke wondered if Ned still had feelings for Tammy.

"Anyway," Katie said, "Tammy's mum had fallen out badly with Kroft's mum, so we always met either at my house or Ned's house."

"Why did they fall out?"

Katie laughed. "Allegedly, Kroft's mum had a fling with Tammy's dad, but nobody really knew for sure. Tammy liked to pretend she and Kroft were together. She said it made her feel like Maria in West Side Story, the forbidden relationship, and the family feud. She always fancied herself an actress. She would have loved to play that part, but I'm not sure if anything actually went on. She just liked teasing Kroft. And it wound up her mum."

"I thought then that she had her eye on Ned."

Clarke drained her coffee cup.

"Let's go bird watching, then," Katie said. She opened a cupboard and grabbed a couple of bags out of it. "This is what you saw me taking before." She opened the bags, revealing a cushion in one bag, some bird seed and binoculars in the other. She took a couple of bottles of water and some biscuits from another cupboard and added them to the bags.

"I'll lend you some wellies," Katie said. "It can be a bit muddy at this time of year."

"Thanks," Clarke said, wondering if this would turn out to be a massive waste of time. But the more she talked to Katie, the more she hoped that something useful might slip out. Something that might give her some clue to Tammy's whereabouts. Someone must be helping Tammy. It would be impossible for her to have escaped and remained hidden on her own.

"We'll have to climb the fence," Katie said. "There's no gate. The farmer doesn't mind me going across his fields as long as we walk along the edge, but he won't let me put a gate in the fence."

"That's ok." Clarke scrambled over the fence, being careful to lower herself down gently so she wouldn't have to jump onto her dodgy ankle and aggravate her old injury.

They set off across the field. The stunning view from Katie's garden made Clarke long to move to the country, but Paul would hate it. She pushed the idea from her mind before it took root.

"Where's Ned today?" Clarke asked.

"He's gone up to London. Checking on the property business," Katie answered quickly.

Clarke's hopes were dashed instantly. She really wanted to talk to Ned. This must be at least the second time in a week that Ned had gone to London. She distinctly remembered Katie saying last time they only went once a month. Was Ned helping Tammy? Was he still keen on her? If only Clarke could meet Ned. Paul had met him, but Paul wasn't the most empathetic of people. He wouldn't necessarily pick up on things like that.

Clarke got her phone out, trying to be careful. She quickly typed in a short text to Evan, explaining her plan. The phone pinged a few seconds later, telling her the message had failed to send.

"The signal is non-existent once you get away from the house," Katie said.

Clarke tried to relax. Everything would be fine, apart from it being a total waste of time. She wondered how fast she could run, if necessary, in wellies that were a size too big.

"Tell me more about what happened when you were at school," Clarke said, trying to take her mind off of anything bad that might happen in the present. "What was Tammy like back then?"

"Pretty much the same as when you worked with her," Katie said. "Lively, larger than life, always getting into trouble. She set her heart on becoming an actress, so she was always doing impressions, funny voices, and singing. Have you ever heard her sing?"

"No, I haven't," Clarke admitted.

"Tammy's got a great voice. She acted in a couple of school plays too. Although she did have a strop, the first time when they wouldn't give her the starring role, but the second time around, she was definitely the leading lady. Three standing ovations she got."

"It's a shame she didn't make it professionally," Clarke said. "She would have been good." She'd certainly proved that many times over with all the lies she told. Her acting ability had come into its own. What a pity she didn't make a career of it. Perhaps things would have turned out very differently for Tammy if she'd followed that path for longer.

They reached the edge of the woods. "It's through here," Katie said, pointing to an opening in the hedge. "A couple of local people use the bird hide. The farmer is very good about it, as long as we keep things tidy and don't trample his crops."

A big group of trees and bushes concealed the hide, so Clarke never would have found it on her own. It would make a fabulous place for Tammy to hole up, although it would be bitterly cold at night. She opened the door cautiously.

Katie followed her in. It was quite small inside, with the only furniture being two chairs and a small table. If Tammy had been staying here, she clearly left ages ago.

"I'll go and throw some food down," Katie said. "That should attract a few birds." She shut the door behind her.

Clarke took the opportunity to search the tiny hut for any signs that Tammy might have been there. Forensics might get something, some fingerprints or DNA, from the bare hut. But it appeared to her that no one had been in there for a long time. Perhaps Katie really did come here to watch birds.

Katie came back, opening the door noisily. She pulled the cushion from her bag. "Sorry, I should have brought a cushion for you as well."

"I'm fine," Clarke said. The chairs did look hard, but she wouldn't stay much longer. "I probably should be getting back soon."

"You do believe me now, don't you? Tammy would hate it here." Katie laughed.

"She must be somewhere," Clarke said. "Where do you think she might have gone?"

"If she's got any sense, she'll have left the country by now. That's what I would do."

Clarke agreed, but something was making Tammy stay. "Would Kroft help her?"

"I doubt it. Kroft never visited her in prison. Not once. So no, I can't imagine why he would. Tammy used to be pretty good at getting people to do what she wants, but I imagine being in prison changes things."

Maybe chasing after Kroft would be a waste of time. Keira was probably wrong about him. Clarke checked her watch. Paul must have visited Kroft by now. Hopefully, something useful had come out of it, but she doubted it.

"What happened when you saw Tammy?" Katie asked.

"I only got to talk to her for a couple of minutes. I stupidly called the police, but all they achieved was to scare her away." Clarke stared out the window. She had yet to see any birds. "She blames me for everything."

"Why didn't you just leave things alone in the first place?"

"How could I? Tammy stole millions of pounds. Did you really expect me to ignore that? Besides, I didn't even realise it was her at first. By the time I learned she was responsible, I'd left it way too late to back off." It wouldn't have made any difference. Tammy committed a crime. "She shouldn't have done it. It's her own fault." The words sounded hollow. Clarke still blamed herself, even though there was no logic to that. Katie's guilt-inducing stare didn't help. She would beat herself up about it all the way home.

Chapter 22

Paul arrived early, after promising to bring Ned's bank statements to Rob's house. Clarke had only just arrived back from Dorset.

"What have you got for me?" she asked Paul, keen to examine everything. Hopefully, she would spot something to connect Ned with Tammy's money. He must be involved. It occurred to her now that Ned might have been collaborating with Tammy all this time, possibly even putting her up to defrauding Briar Holman. Perhaps he gave her the idea in the first place.

"I contacted Ned's bank. I've got just about every bank statement for every account he's ever had there. And we found another bank statement in his house, so I contacted that bank too, and he's got another three accounts with them. You've got plenty of work to do looking at these. Maybe that'll keep you out of trouble."

Clarke laughed nervously. She hadn't even told him yet that she'd ignored his request for her not to go back to Dorset. "How is everything else going? Any sign of Tammy yet?"

"You were right, she did go to Ranleigh Marshes," Paul said. "The rubbish we found in the bird hide had her DNA on it, and we also think someone left her a car key."

"Somebody's helping her, then," Clarke said, pleased that, at last, Paul was readily sharing information. They needed to work as a team to stand any chance of ever finding Tammy. Whether Paul liked it or not, Clarke was totally involved in this.

"Yes, she never could have done this on her own."

"Do you know who gave her the car?"

"We're assuming Kroft. He's got the same make of car. And he made up some cock and bull story about sending it to the mechanic."

"You saw Kroft then?" Clarke sighed with relief that she didn't need to go back to The Ball and Chain pub. She still suffered from the bad memories of her last visit. Even thinking about it set off a sharp twinge as the built-up tension in her shoulders made her muscles spasm.

"Yes, we met his girlfriend too, Maria. He swears she was only a one-night stand, but her name was on the passport I saw in Ned and Katie's house."

"Did the picture on the passport resemble Tammy?"

"Hard to tell. I haven't seen Tammy since she shaved her head, but if she wore a blond wig, there would be a reasonable likeness, enough that passport control wouldn't question it."

"And the woman you met? Maria? Did she look anything like Tammy?"

"I suppose there were similarities. I guess Kroft must have given Ned her passport for Tammy to get out of the country. We didn't find it when we went back to the Youngs' house with the search warrant."

"What was Maria's surname?" It would be useful to know what name Tammy might be using now.

"Maria Vasquez," Paul said.

Clarke leapt up from her chair as if she'd suffered an electric shock. "Are you sure? It was definitely Vasquez?" She spelt out the name, wanting to be certain.

"Yes, of course I'm sure."

"You saw Maria Vasquez? You met her for real?"

"Yes, I already said that."

"How long were you with her?"

"What's with the twenty questions? Not long at all, actually. We took Kroft into the station for questioning. We didn't have any reason to take his girlfriend, if that's what she was. She left pretty quickly."

"We need to find her," Clarke said. "This may sound nuts, but Maria might have been Tammy."

"Really? Yes, that is nuts. I would have recognised her."

"What makes you say that?" Rob asked, staring at Clarke as if she was mad.

"Something Katie said. Tammy used to be obsessed with Maria Vasquez."

Rob and Paul both looked puzzled.

"Maria Vasquez is a character in West Side Story, the musical." Clarke despaired of the two men. Didn't they know anything? She shouldn't have to work this hard to explain her thoughts. It was so obvious to her now.

Both men still looked blank, so Clarke carried on. "Katie said Tammy and Kroft had a thing going at school. Tammy's mum and Kroft's mum fell out, so it was that forbidden love, feuding family scenario."

"Like in Westside Story." Rob finally got it.

"Exactly. And sometimes, when Tammy got into trouble, she gave a false name and Katie said she always used the name Maria Vasquez. Tammy really identified with her. She actually might be that woman you met."

"No." Paul looked incredulous. "I would have recognised her."

"She's a good actress. With a bit of makeup and a wig, she would fool you easily. You're not used to seeing her like that, and no doubt she would have been putting on a different voice too."

"Even so."

"You didn't see her after she shaved her hair." Clarke recalled their brief meeting at the Hale Hill estate. Tammy had been almost unrecognisable. "I used to see her every day. And she did her hair in so many different ways. It altered her appearance completely even doing that. If she changed her hair colour and put on some clever makeup, I doubt even I would recognise her, so she would certainly fool you."

Paul took out his phone and dialled a number. "Guv, is anyone free to go to Havebury?"

Clarke leaned over to listen to the conversation. Paul made a shushing sign with his fingers. She guessed it must be his DCI on the phone.

"Can you send them to The Ball and Chain pub? We need to pick up Karl Croft again and Maria Vasquez."

Paul listened while the other person spoke. "I can be there in twenty minutes. Tell him to wait outside for me." He hung up the call. "Barry's still at the station," he said to Clarke. "He'll meet me at the pub. If she's still there, we'll get her."

"I should come with you," Clarke said.

"No," Paul and Rob shouted in unison.

"If you find her, I can identify her."

"I'll call you if we need you," Paul said, "but please don't go anywhere near that pub. I don't want you getting hurt."

"I'm amazed that Tammy had the audacity to pull off a stunt like that," Rob said after Paul left. "Paul's going to look stupid if you're right."

"Paul will look great when he catches Tammy." It wasn't Paul's fault. Tammy would have fooled anybody. "It may not be her, anyway. I might be wrong."

"Let's hope not. We'll all be much happier when she's locked up again," Rob said.

"I doubt she'll still be there." Clarke guessed Paul's earlier visit would have spooked her. "Even Tammy wouldn't be arrogant enough to push her luck like that twice."

"Yes, that's what worries me," Rob said. "She'll be long gone by now."

Clarke nodded, still trying to work out why the passport would be in Ned's house, if Tammy was staying with Kroft, assuming Maria Vasquez really turned out to be Tammy. Did Ned obtain the fake passport for her? That begged the question: who had the passport now?

Paul parked his car on the road outside The Ball and Chain pub. He didn't want anyone to see him coming. He phoned Barry. "Where are you?"

"I'm just coming down the road, Sarge."

"Ok, don't go into the car park. Stop on the road, behind my car." He wondered if they should have brought extra backup. Tammy had already murdered twice, and she would have Kroft to help her now.

The trouble was, Paul was far too embarrassed to admit Clarke's crazy theory to DCI Price. Clarke might be right. They had surprised Tammy, so she'd probably ad-libbed, hoping she could bluff her way out of the situation. But Paul needed to impress Jonathan Price before he took this case away from him, and it sounded so ridiculous. Not to mention how stupid he would look meeting Maria Vasquez and not recognising her as Tammy. He and Barry would just have to manage alone. Two against two gave good odds, especially as he and Barry were trained police officers.

"What's the plan, Sarge?" Barry asked.

"We need to arrest Maria Vasquez. Kroft as well if we can, but concentrate on Maria."

"Will she still be there? Kroft chucked her out. Why her, anyway?"

Paul hesitated. Barry needed the full facts. It would be negligent not to tell him everything. He took a deep breath. "This may sound really stupid, but Maria Vasquez may be Tammy."

Barry laughed. "Seriously? You're right, Sarge, it does sound stupid."

Paul glared at him, wiping the smile off his face. "Clarke said Tammy had a thing about Maria Vasquez. She's a character in West Side Story."

"Never seen it, Sarge."

"Well, anyway, it's possible that Maria might be Tammy, so don't take any chances with her. If we can arrest Karl Kroft as well, that would be great."

"Yes, Sarge."

Paul relaxed. Barry might think he was barking mad, but he would follow orders. "I'm going to go to the bar to check if Kroft's there. You go straight upstairs to the flat. Break the door down if necessary." The door to the flat seemed pretty flimsy. Barry would have no trouble kicking it in. "Don't bother knocking. Get in fast, in case she escapes down the fire escape."

They entered the pub separately. Paul immediately spotted Kroft serving behind the bar and approached him directly. He only needed to distract him for a couple of minutes. "We need to talk to you," he said. Hopefully, if he finished serving this customer, that would allow Barry the time he needed to get upstairs.

"Sure," Kroft said. "Just give me a minute." He finished pulling a pint and took payment for it.

Paul went behind the bar to block off Kroft's exit. "Where's Maria?" he asked.

"Maria?"

"Your girlfriend, Maria?"

"Oh, she's not here," Kroft said.

Paul noticed he didn't deny Maria being his girlfriend. "Well, where is she?"

"No idea. She didn't say."

"When did she leave?"

Kroft shrugged his shoulders.

"Let's go upstairs, shall we?" He would check for himself and make sure Barry didn't need any help. He followed Kroft upstairs. The door to the flat was open. Paul was pleased to see no damage. It must have been unlocked.

"Barry," Paul shouted.

"There's no one here, Sarge."

"Have you got a search warrant?" Kroft asked.

Paul ignored the question. "Where's Maria?" He stared Kroft in the eye. "Is she Tammy? Where's Tammy?"

"I really can't help you. I wish I knew."

"Have you got your car back yet?" Paul asked. Kroft was lying. He'd definitely flinched when Paul mentioned Tammy. He must be lying.

"It's in the car park," Kroft said.

"Barry, get forensics to take the car away and check it." They would soon find out if Tammy ever used it. "And get a warrant to search the flat. As soon as possible."

"I haven't done anything," Kroft protested.

"We need to take you to the station." Paul had no intention of letting Kroft go. Right now, he was their only lead.

"I'm supposed to be working. We're short-staffed tonight."

"I'm sure they'll cope without you. If you cooperate, we might not be long."

"And what if I don't cooperate?"

"I'll have to arrest you." Paul wondered whether he should arrest him, anyway. It would give him a reason to cuff him.

"What for? I haven't done anything."

"What about aiding and abetting a fugitive?"

"You got any evidence for that?"

Paul realised he lacked hard evidence yet. His gut instinct said that Kroft was guilty as hell. He might have to take a chance on this one and arrest him. At least it would give them time to get a search warrant and get forensics in the flat. No doubt, he would suffer the consequences later, unless the drug squad had any dirt on him he could use. Then he would simply need to find an excuse to prevent Kroft from seeing his solicitor for an hour or so. It shouldn't be difficult. Last time, Kroft used the duty solicitor. It would be very easy to delay her.

Earlier, he didn't quite believe Clarke's theory. But now, with Maria missing and Kroft being uncooperative, he agreed Clarke might actually be onto something. He pinned his hopes on her being right, because he was running out of options. If his instinct let him down now, he would look like a complete idiot, and the DCI would never trust him again.

Chapter 23

Rob pulled out of his driveway. He had insisted on giving Clarke a lift tonight. "You're looking good, Sis."

Clarke had made an effort for her hen night. "Did the girls tell you what they've got planned for this evening?" she asked, terrified that her friends would have organised some really embarrassing entertainment. "I'm hoping for a civilised meal and an early night. You know how much I hate typical hen nights."

"Yeah, but that's half the fun, doing all that embarrassing stuff."

"Fun for them, not fun for me," Clarke protested. "It's my hen night. I should be allowed to do what I want. I'd rather not have one at all, but Gina and Mum insisted."

"I'm sure they won't have planned anything too bad, if you're lucky. Mum's going, so that might rein them in a bit."

"I doubt that. Mum will be egging them on."

"Would it be so bad?"

Rob stopped at some red traffic lights. Clarke considered getting out of the car and running home. "Yes," she said. "It would be bad. I refuse to dress up in silly clothes, and there had better not be any embarrassing rude stuff. I've already told the girls I've banned plastic penises and L plates."

"Well, that's no fun, is it? I've got loads of great stuff planned for Paul's stag night." Rob laughed.

"That's what I'm worried about." Paul's stag night would take place tonight as well. Clarke had spotted Rob loading a big box into his car earlier. She would love to find out what was in it. "Please bring him back in one piece."

"It's my job as best man to make sure he has a good time."

"That depends on your definition of a *good time*. Please don't tie him to a lamppost naked and leave him all night. And don't put him on the train to Aberdeen, or he won't get back in time for the wedding." She silently hoped Rob was joking.

"He's got two days."

"So, you are planning something like that. Am I going to have someone to actually marry? Your job as best man is to get him to the wedding on time, in a fit state."

Rob ought to be responsible. He wouldn't do anything too outrageous, would he?

"Sis, you clearly don't understand the role of best man at all. The best man's job is to make an extremely embarrassing speech and make sure the groom-to-be has an absolutely riotous stag night, the sort of night that will go down in the stag night history books as a legend."

"You are planning something dreadful, then? You won't hurt him, will you? I don't want to be walking up the aisle next to a man with a broken arm." Clarke felt like a real killjoy now, but the situation with Tammy gave her more than enough stress. She didn't need another problem to worry about.

"Stop fretting. Anyway, technically, you won't be walking up the aisle with Paul. It's Dad who walks you up the aisle."

"Stop being pedantic."

"Ok. I promise I'll take care of him. But we do have some fun planned and huge amounts of beer."

"Well, I'm hoping my hen do won't be nearly as unruly as Paul's stag night. A quiet, civilised meal will suit me fine."

"Yes," Rob said, "but you know that's not going to happen, don't you?"

"Then you should turn around and take me home now. I'll tell them I've got a headache."

"You wouldn't dare. You know how upset they'd be. Don't be such a spoilsport."

"I'll do my best. I'll try to enjoy it, as long as no one pins an L plate on my back."

They were getting near the restaurant.

"Promise me, Clarke, that you'll get a taxi back to my place after. I really don't want you walking around on your own with Tammy still at large. Are the police getting anywhere with finding her?"

"No." Clarke was as worried as Rob. "She might be anywhere. It's impossible even to guess."

"Perhaps she's got out of the country."

"How? She left the prison with nothing but a prison officer's uniform. She doesn't have any clothes of her own. She doesn't have anywhere to go. All her friends in this area have long since dumped her. They don't want anything to do with her, so they certainly wouldn't help an escaped prisoner. What's she going to do? She's got no food, nowhere to sleep, no transport."

"She's got three million pounds," Rob said, "and we're already pretty certain that someone is helping her. We just don't know who."

"Yes," Clarke said, "she still has the money, but she's got to get access to it. She'll need her bank account numbers and passwords, stuff like that." Tammy would never have predicted her arrest two years ago. Clarke was sure she wouldn't have prepared for the possibility. She reminded herself that Tammy was intelligent enough to memorise all of her bank account details.

"So, you've not found the money yet?"

"No. Evan's been working on it in the office, but he's made no progress. The plan for me to visit Tammy in prison and persuade her to tell me where she'd hidden the money obviously isn't going to work now."

"No way she'd ever do that, anyway," Rob said.

"No, I agree. But she might have accidentally dropped some clues, which would help us find the money. It was always a long shot. But it was the only shot. And now I can't even do that."

"Secretly, you're quite pleased you don't have to visit her again, aren't you?"

"Absolutely," Clarke admitted. "I hated seeing her like that, and knowing that I put her in there made me feel so guilty."

"It's not you who's guilty," Rob said. "Tammy's the guilty one. You shouldn't keep feeling bad about something that's not your fault. Get over it. You didn't murder anyone. She did."

Clarke decided against telling Rob about her latest trip to Dorset. He wouldn't approve and he'd only worry and would undoubtedly tell Paul as well. She would probably give up on searching for Tammy anyway until after the wedding. They were getting married in two days, and she still had plenty to organise. She really didn't have time to chase after Tammy now. At least when they were on their honeymoon, she would be safe from her.

"Where is the stag do?" she asked, trying to change the subject.

Rob grinned. "Well, we're starting off almost right next to the restaurant you're going to. I thought that would be easier, so that I can chauffeur you."

"Isn't the best man supposed to pick up the bridegroom for the stag night?"

"Probably, but it made more sense for me to take you, and one of Paul's other friends is collecting him. I'll take him home after."

"Ok. And where are you going on to next?" Was Rob planning some sort of laddish pub crawl? Clarke wondered.

"I'm not telling you that, Sis."

"Oh, go on."

"No. You'll have to wait until Paul tells you tomorrow. That's if he doesn't have a two-day hangover."

"Well, it better not be three days."

"Stop worrying. Paul will be fine. But it's my responsibility to make sure he has a great time, and I take my duties very seriously."

"Ok, but please make sure he's in a fit state for the wedding."

"Of course I will, Sis." Rob turned into the car park. "I'll walk you into the restaurant," he said. "I'm not letting you go anywhere on your own."

"Don't be ridiculous." Rob made her feel like a prisoner. "I'll be fine. Brackford is full of people."

"Yes. And you know what Tammy's like. I'm walking you all the way inside. And you need to promise me you'll get a taxi back to my house later."

"I don't want to run into Tammy any more than you want me to. But I honestly don't think she'll be anywhere around here. The middle of Brackford will be far too busy for her to risk coming here. Wherever she is, she'll be hiding out or trying to travel out of the area."

"Well, let's hope you're right. But please be careful, anyway," Rob said. He locked the car and walked with Clarke towards the restaurant across the road.

Rob opened the restaurant door for Clarke to go in. "Don't wait up for me," he said. "We're sure to be back much later than you. We've got plans."

"Be careful," Clarke said.

"I'll have to be," he said. "I'm driving, so I can't drink. If I change my mind, I'll leave the car and get a taxi back. I can easily pick up the car in the morning."

"Have a good time," Clarke said, suddenly distracted by a wall of pink balloons on the other side of the restaurant. Her mum and several of Clarke's friends sat at the table in front of it. As she got closer, she noticed pink glitter sprinkled all over the table. They had really overdone it with the pink. Hopefully, that would be the worst thing they had done. She still dreaded rude toys and L plates. She scanned up and down the table, but thankfully, didn't notice any such thing. They'd promised not to embarrass her. If they produced any humiliating props now, she swore she would walk straight out of the restaurant.

"Clarke." Her best friend Gina greeted her with a hug. "We've saved you a seat right in the middle of the table, so you can talk to everyone."

They all began greeting her at once.

"Congratulations. Paul's a lucky man. I hope he appreciates that." Auntie Fenella air-kissed her. Clarke was delighted to see her.

"I'm sure he does." Clarke sat down, surveying the table again for any unwanted items. "I trust you didn't organise anything like a stripper." If anyone was going to do that, it would be Gina.

"Damn." Gina laughed. "I'll have to cancel him. His muscles are amazing. I was really looking forward to it."

Clarke hoped she was pulling her leg. Knowing Gina, she probably booked two strippers, one dressed up as a policeman because she was marrying one, and the other as a firefighter as a nod to Clarke's former career. She still dreaded the rest of the evening, but the dread was gradually fading. Perhaps she would enjoy it after all.

It took ages to greet everyone and open her presents. Eventually, somebody thrust a menu in front of her and they ordered some food.

"I suppose as it's a hen night, I'll have chicken. That would be appropriate, wouldn't it?" Clarke said.

They all laughed politely.

"As long as it's washed down with plenty of wine," Gina said.

Diana Pettis reached for the nearest wine bottle and poured a glass for Clarke, nearly knocking over one of the candles on the table. "It's your favourite, darling. Sauvignon Blanc."

Clarke smiled. If they'd booked a stripper for later, it would be much easier if she got drunk. She picked up the glass. It would help her get through the evening. She might even enjoy it if they reined in the *fun* aspects.

"The balloons are fabulous," she said, fervently hoping that would be the only bit of rubber she would see this evening.

"Thank you. Your mum organised most of it. We got here early to set up the decorations," Auntie Fenella said.

"Thanks, Mum. What a lovely thought." They did bring a party mood to the gathering, Clarke admitted to herself.

The waiter arrived with their starters. Clarke was starving and grateful to get some food inside her to start mopping up the wine. It would be good to have an enjoyable evening and forget all her problems. She would try to relax and enjoy it.

The evening passed quickly and, before long, Clarke found she did actually enjoy it, even joining in a raucous game of *Marry, Date, or Shag*.

"We need the balloons," Diana said, as they waited for the bill to arrive. "We all wrote messages on them for you." She reached up behind her and started taking them off the wall, handing them one by one to Clarke.

Congratulations on landing such a hunk. The first balloon was from Gina.

Diana quickly passed her another one. Every balloon had a message written on it, one from everyone present.

"One more," her mum said. "I've lost count of how many messages there were."

Clarke took the balloon, turning it around in her hands. This message was written with a

different colour marker pen. This one was red. She read the message.

It's payback time.

"Who wrote this message?" Clarke asked.

Diana looked at it. "I don't remember this one." She showed it to the girls. "Which one of you wrote this? What does it even mean?"

Everyone denied it. Clarke didn't doubt them. The message and the vibe it gave off were all wrong. None of her girlfriends would write that as a message. Not today. Not ever.

Clarke reached for her wine glass. She really needed a drink now. If it wasn't any of her friends or her mum or auntie, a message like that could only have come from one person. Was she being paranoid again? She had no idea how Tammy might be watching her? Did Tammy know she was here right now? She must do, surely. Who else would write something like that? It even looked a little like her writing, although possibly Clarke's memory tricked her. If she took the balloon home, she could ask Paul tomorrow to get the handwriting checked out.

She forced a smile, not wanting to worry her mum. "It's been a lovely evening," she said, so happy that her friends had given her the nice, civilised meal she wanted. "It's been a wonderful evening. And thank you for not arranging anything embarrassing. I hate all that hen night stuff."

"Your mum insisted you would kill us if we did anything like that," Gina said. "We so wanted to. It's not too late, if you've changed your mind."

Clarke shook her head. "No, I really don't need anything embarrassing. I can't wait for the wedding now. I hope you're all looking forward to it." She got up and started to gather together her gifts. She would take the balloons home too, all of them, not just the one, so her mum didn't suspect anything might be wrong. She collected them up, arranging the strings in her hand one by one.

"Here, let me help." Diana Pettis snatched the balloon strings out of Clarke's hand. They danced in the air as she pulled them across the table.

Suddenly, three loud bangs sounded in lightning quick succession. Clarke ducked down behind the table, pulling her mother with her. *Tammy.* The first thing that came into her head was Tammy. *Where is she?*

Diana Pettis laughed out loud and got up from the floor. "Calm down," she said, holding up some pieces of string with wrinkled rubber remnants attached to the ends. "I must have let the balloons get too near the candle. I may possibly have drunk too much."

Clarke relaxed. For a moment, she really imagined Tammy might be trying to shoot her. She felt so stupid. Tammy wasn't even here. The one saving grace was that her rather tipsy mother wouldn't remember exactly what happened.

"Are you ok?" Gina asked.

Clarke got up. Everyone else had left. "It's been a tiring week," she said. "I should get a taxi and go home."

"There's one waiting outside," Gina said. "It's going to drop me off, then take you on to Rob's house."

Clarke smiled. "What would I do without you?" She gathered up the remaining balloons, which had floated up to the ceiling. She looked at them one by one, rereading the messages. The one from Tammy was among the three balloons that popped. Damn.

Chapter 24

Paul's hangover was a real headbanger. He wished now that he'd booked a day off of work after his stag night. But he would be getting married tomorrow, and they hadn't found Tammy Doncaster yet. He couldn't let up.

As he walked up the stairs to the MIT office, Barry almost ploughed right into him.

"What's up?"

"There's been a sighting of Tammy, Sarge. Brackford Woods."

"I'm coming with you." If it was Tammy, they needed to hurry. At least the fresh air might help clear his head.

"You drive." Paul thought he was probably under the drink-driving limit, but, to be honest, he had little recollection of what happened last night. Best to be on the safe side.

"Some woman phoned the special phone line," Barry explained as he reversed out of the parking space. "We assumed at first it was a hoax call because it's unlikely that anyone would recognise Tammy now."

"So why the rush?" Paul's head pounded. He'd drunk a whole carton of orange juice and taken a couple of painkillers before he came out, in an attempt to combat the effects of last night's alcohol. It wasn't working yet.

"The woman described Tammy's clothes."

"So?"

Barry stopped at a red traffic light, tapping his fingers on the dashboard in frustration. "They were exactly the same clothes Maria Vasquez was wearing when we saw her."

"You need to speed up." Paul wished they'd taken a patrol car. Flashing blue lights and a siren would be a godsend to cut through this traffic. This sighting of Tammy might be their lucky break, if they could get there in time. They certainly needed a break, although

Paul didn't have a clue how they were going to find Tammy in Brackford Woods. He phoned DCI Price to request some backup. If it really was Tammy, and it sounded likely, they would need to cover all exits from the woods.

At last, Barry pulled up at the nearest entrance to where Tammy had been spotted. Uniformed officers would be getting into place by now at the other entrances to the woods, with enough officers to search the area and keep watch on the exits.

Several cars were already parked up, reminding Paul that Brackford Woods was a prime spot for dog walkers. They would need to be careful that none of the dog walkers ended up as collateral damage if Tammy put up a fight. All officers knew to warn any members of the public they encountered to leave the woods immediately and go home.

They took the main path into the woods. "We need to search the smaller side tracks," Paul pointed out, reluctant to leave the main gravel path and get his shoes muddy. "Tammy will never stay out in the open. She'll be hiding somewhere." Something in the back of his mind told him that Tammy wouldn't want to get her shoes covered in mud either. He pushed the thought to one side.

"How about this path?" Barry asked, indicating a narrow track leading off to the left.

"Good idea." This would take them deeper into the woods. Paul took the lead.

"Should we split up, Sarge?"

"We can spread out a bit, but we need to stay within sight of each other." The undergrowth in this section of the woods would make that difficult. "Don't forget Tammy's dangerous. Don't take any chances." He made the mistake of underestimating Tammy Doncaster before and didn't intend to repeat the error.

"I'll head further into the trees, and you can stay on the path," Barry volunteered.

THE PAYBACK

A few moments later, Paul heard Barry curse as he got tangled in one of the many brambles entwined across this part of the forest floor. Tammy wouldn't be hiding amongst this thick, scratchy undergrowth. They needed to think more strategically. He waved at Barry to come over.

"If I'm not mistaken," Paul said, "we're heading towards the school. If there's a way through the hedge, Tammy might leave the woods unseen."

"Yes, if we carry on down this path, we'll get close to the school."

Paul wished he knew the woods better, but at least his general sense of direction was good. "We should hurry, in case she gets there before us." How long since the woman had called the phone line? Would Tammy already be miles away? He started to run. Barry needed no urging to keep up with him. The school was just visible in the distance.

"Did the woman caller leave her name?" Paul asked, puffing lightly between the words. They may need to contact her again.

"No, Sarge. She said she didn't want to get involved."

Anonymous callers frustrated Paul immensely. He couldn't fault the woman's public spirit for wanting to help, but so often the follow-up enquiries made all the difference to an investigation.

A stream blocked the path, which by now had turned into more of a deer track than a footpath. Paul stopped. "It's not very wide. I reckon we could jump if we got a run at it."

Barry nodded, still getting his breath back.

"I'll go first." Paul ran towards it, trying to pick up some speed. One stride in, he realised he wasn't going to hit the bank in the right place to jump from, so he put in a short stride to take him to the bank's edge. Instantly, he wished he hadn't done that. The short stride made him lose momentum, and he completely failed to push off the bank with any power.

A moment later, he landed several inches short of the top of the far bank. His feet slipped on the mud and he slid inelegantly down the bank, coming to rest with both feet dangling in the water.

He heard Barry laughing as he scrambled up the bank. "It's not funny, DC Medway."

Barry put his hand over his mouth to stifle the sound.

"Let's see you do it better." Paul lifted up each leg in turn to drain the water from his shoes, finishing just in time to witness Barry Medway leaping the stream like a gazelle.

"Well done," Paul muttered grudgingly. His shoes squelched, and his feet were freezing. At least his hangover seemed to have gone.

"What now?" Barry asked.

"The school is on the other side of that hedge." Paul pointed to a thick hawthorn hedge very close by. "Let's go in opposite directions and check for a way through." His phone vibrated in his pocket and he quickly read the incoming message. "The DCI says the dog handlers are at the north entrance. They're going to search the woods now."

"That's great," Barry said. "So, all we need to do is make sure she doesn't escape through the school grounds."

"That's right." Paul hoped it wouldn't take too long. He wanted to swing by the flat on the way back to the station and change his shoes and jeans.

Paul pushed through the undergrowth, being careful not to trip over the brambles that grew thickly across the forest floor. In some parts, it was impossible to pass, forcing him to detour and return to the boundary hedge further along. The sound of the police sniffer dogs barking intermittently encouraged him onwards. Hopefully, they would hit Tammy's scent soon. His feet were cold and wet, and he wanted to get this over with as soon as possible. Paul had taken the direction that would get him closer to the car when he reached the end of the hedge. Except now he kicked himself for not taking the car keys from Barry before they split.

Hopefully, Barry was having better luck than him. The hedge appeared to be dense with thorns along its entire length. He wondered how much kids had changed since he attended that school. He and his friends often used to squeeze through holes in the hedge and bunk off into Brackford at lunchtime. At least, if the hedge remained impenetrable along its entire length, then Tammy wouldn't be a risk to any of the children at the school.

He checked his phone for missed messages. Surely the dogs would have picked up a scent by now. Perhaps the anonymous caller was mistaken. Without knowing exactly what she said, he couldn't judge how accurately her description applied to Tammy. Perhaps the woman she saw wore clothes in similar colours, but different. He cursed himself for not taking a few minutes to listen to the recording before they rushed over here.

Eventually, Paul reached the car and leant against the door, hoping Barry wouldn't take too long to get back. He sent him a text to hurry him along. The sooner he got into the car and put the heater on full blast, the happier he would be.

Paul's feet were completely numb by the time Barry showed up.

"Sorry, Sarge. I thought you'd want me to check in with the dog team. There's no sign of Tammy Doncaster anywhere in the woods. They didn't pick up a scent at all."

Paul silently cursed. "That's bad news," he said, relieved that it wasn't him who called in the dog team or DCI Price would complain about his budget.

Paul directed Barry to the flat, keen to change his soaking wet shoes. The car heater helped but would never warm and dry his feet completely.

"You'd better come in." Paul would take a while to find some clean clothes and wash the filthy river water off his feet. He didn't want Barry sitting out in the car when he might be doing something useful, like making them coffee.

Paul delved into his pocket for his keys, but just as he located them, he realised that the lock was broken, and the door already open. He snapped into full alertness. "Someone's broken in," he whispered to Barry. The lock had been fine when he'd left the flat this morning.

Cautiously, he entered the flat, listening for any sound from inside. "I'll take the bedrooms, you check the kitchen," he told Barry. "Kitchen's on your right."

They went in fast. If anyone remained in the flat, Paul would use the element of surprise to his advantage.

The flat was empty. This must have happened while they were searching Brackford woods.

"Why don't you see if any of the neighbours are home. They may have seen something. I'll check what's missing." Paul dispatched Barry to check on the neighbours. Most people on this road worked. He doubted anyone would be in at this time of day.

He put on some gloves before he began his search, although the police rarely found a burglar these days who didn't wear gloves themselves. At first glance, nothing appeared to have been disturbed. He checked all the obvious things. The small amount of cash on the bedside table that he'd emptied out of his pockets when he got home last night still sat where he'd left it. His passport remained in its usual drawer. And the few electrical goods that may have been of interest to a burglar hadn't been touched. There wasn't anything else worth taking. Clarke's jewellery consisted mostly of affordable chain-store stuff. To his embarrassment, he realised he'd never bought her anything expensive, apart from her engagement ring and, thankfully, she would be wearing that.

Paul pulled off his gloves. Perhaps he broke the lock himself last night. Was he still too drunk to notice it even this morning when he left for work? He dismissed the idea as improbable.

His feet still squelched as he walked, reminding him he needed to change. Quickly, he grabbed some clothes from the bedroom and took them into the bathroom, turning on the shower to warm up. It would take a couple of minutes. Just enough time to put the kettle on so it would be ready as soon as he got dressed. Opening the kitchen door, he made a beeline for the kettle, stopping dead in his tracks in front of it.

A plain white envelope addressed to Clarke stood propped up against the kettle. That definitely hadn't been here this morning. He reached for it, remembering just in time to fetch some gloves before he touched it.

"None of the neighbours are in." Barry came back as Paul was putting on a clean pair of gloves. "I've got some CCTV from the shop down the road, but I doubt it will show anything."

Paul quickly debated with himself whether to tell Barry about the envelope. He decided he might need Barry's help. "Nothing's been taken, but I found a letter."

Barry followed him into the kitchen. Paul suddenly realised he'd left the shower running. He sent Barry to turn it off. He opened the letter carefully, despite it being addressed to Clarke, eager to get an initial look at it before Barry returned. A sudden fear that it might contain something dangerous, anthrax, for instance, made him hesitate. No. He needed to see the contents now. He eased out the single folded sheet of paper just as Barry came back.

"What's in it, Sarge?"

"Give me a moment." He unfolded the paper slowly, dreading what it might say.

Three words, in enormous lettering, filled the piece of paper. *IT'S PAYBACK TIME.*

Paul shuddered. Surely it had to be Tammy. Who else would send a threat like that to Clarke? "Barry, can you fetch an evidence bag from the car, please?" He would get Erica to check for fingerprints and send the message to the handwriting expert. But he realised that was unlikely to yield any results.

As soon as Paul safely bagged the piece of paper, he sent Barry back to the station with it. Paul would take ages sorting things out. Barry would pick him up later. He phoned a locksmith, then got into the shower.

Was this what this morning was all about? He could just imagine Tammy putting on a fake voice to phone the special hotline and describing herself, knowing that would clear the way for her to break in here. Had she expected to find Clarke at home? Thank God she wasn't here. Tammy was playing with them and Paul didn't know what to do next. Somehow, he had to keep Clarke safe.

Chapter 25

Clarke arrived at the hotel early. She'd spent the morning with her bridesmaid Gina, going through all the last-minute wedding preparations that she'd forgotten to do, then the afternoon packing her wedding dress and everything else she'd need, followed by a tedious hour at the hairdresser's. The end result looked worth it, although it meant a swim in the hotel's pool would be out of the question. At least her day off had relaxed her, especially with Gina making her laugh at every opportunity. After the events of the last few days, she needed that. Gina had given her a long pep talk before she left, insisting that she should forget about Tammy until after the honeymoon and let other people worry about it instead. It was almost working.

Her mother would arrive later, in time for dinner. Mum had booked a room for the night. They planned a nice, relaxing evening and an early night, then Dad would join her tomorrow morning.

The tension in her shoulders hadn't completely disappeared. Was it a symptom of pre-wedding nerves? More likely worry about Tammy. She'd so hoped that the police would have caught Tammy and returned her to prison by now. With an enormous sigh, she resolved to take Gina's advice and try to forget about Tammy. She decided to lie on the bed in her room and watch a film until Mum arrived. A nice comedy would be perfect, definitely nothing scary. She needed to forget about Tammy and not allow her to ruin her wedding day.

She lifted her suitcase onto the bed, carefully taking out her wedding dress and hanging it in the wardrobe. Tomorrow would be perfect.

The film, a lovely rom-com with a happy ending, was exactly what she needed. Clarke checked the time. 7:55 p.m. Mum should be here by now. The restaurant was booked for 8:00 p.m., so Mum might be already waiting downstairs. Clarke pulled on her shoes and considered brushing her hair but worried she might mess up the carefully coiffured styling. Then she headed down the corridor to find the hotel's restaurant.

She stopped off at the hotel's reception desk on the way. "Has Diana Pettis checked in yet?"

The receptionist stared at her blankly.

"She's my mother. I'm supposed to be meeting her."

The girl seemed to wake up. "Of course. I'll check." She tapped at the computer keyboard a few times. "I'm sorry. She doesn't appear to be here yet."

Clarke didn't want to lose the table. She sent a quick text in case Mum was stuck in traffic. She would go to the restaurant, and her mother could join her as soon as she arrived.

She ordered a glass of wine, hoping she wouldn't have drunk too much of it before Mum got here.

"Would you like some garlic bread or some olives?" the waiter enquired.

"Yes, please. Both," Clarke said, then remembered she would have to fit into her wedding dress tomorrow. "No, just the olives, please."

Her phone beeped as the olives and wine arrived. *Sorry, running very late. Don't wait up for me. See you in the morning. xx*

Clarke sighed. Mum was normally so efficient and hardly ever late for anything. She hoped there wasn't a problem. It looked like she would have to spend her wedding eve eating alone. What a pity Gina wasn't here to keep her company and take her mind off of everything.

Chapter 26

Clarke rolled out of bed, feeling excited. This was it, her wedding day. There was a time when she had doubts about Paul. But not anymore. He'd matured and become the man she loved so much now. She couldn't wait to get married.

She wondered if Mum would be up yet. Someone needed to help calm the butterflies in her stomach. Currently, the butterflies were turning backward somersaults and doing the splits. She wasn't sure if it was wedding nerves or excitement. She checked her alarm clock. It was still only 6:50. Far too early to disturb Mum. The text Mum sent last night said she would be late getting to the hotel and not to wait up for her, so she would probably still be asleep this early.

The excitement, or whatever it was, continued to build until she couldn't stay in bed a moment longer. She grabbed some clothes, eager to be doing something. She would go out for a walk and get some fresh air, then meet her mother for breakfast. She pulled on some jeans and a fleecy top, then grabbed her coat.

As Clarke was about to leave the room, she noticed an envelope on the floor. Someone must have slipped it under the door. Probably a note from Mum.

She picked it up, reeling in horror as she opened it. The envelope contained a wedding card. The picture of the bride and groom on the front was mutilated, the groom untouched, but the bride's head obliterated with ink. Her blood ran cold. She opened the card with trepidation and read the message inside.

Clarke sat down, feeling breathless, and read the note again.

Your mum can't come to the wedding. She's tied up. Take a trip down Memory Lane if you want to see her again? Come alone.

The card wasn't signed. She immediately thought of Tammy, but what did the massage mean? Clarke pulled her phone from her coat pocket and called her mother's number. It diverted immediately to voicemail. Without thinking, she phoned her dad.

"Hi, darling. Your mum forgot to take her wedding outfit last night. Tell her I'll bring it to the hotel. I've tried phoning her, but it keeps going to voicemail."

Clarke hesitated. She'd had a sudden thought. "Thanks, Dad. See you later." She blurted the words out quickly so her voice wouldn't have time to shake, then she hung up. She'd figured out what the message meant. *Memory Lane.* The way it was capitalised. She Googled a map of Tredington, her hands shaking as she zoomed in on the address she had spent the last couple of years trying to forget.

She scanned the map and found what she was searching for within seconds. She put her finger on the position of the derelict block of flats, the flats where Tammy had imprisoned her. The next road along was called *Remembrance Road.* There was a war memorial at one end where people put poppy wreaths on Remembrance Sunday every year.

Was Tammy really holding Diana Pettis in one of those flats? Clarke wondered briefly if it was a hoax. But her mother should be here, at the hotel. Her failure to show up and the fact that she obviously wasn't still at home with Dad convinced Clarke. Tammy proved before that she was more than capable of doing something like this.

Come alone. An image of Sadie Hunter sprang into her mind, reminding her of exactly what Tammy was capable of now. Phoning the police would be taking an enormous risk. She would have to play along with the instruction on the card. What option did she have? This was her mother. She couldn't take that risk. It would be daylight, so there would be people near the flats. She would be careful. It would be ok.

The drive from the hotel to Tredington would take nearly an hour. Clarke thought of her mother tied up in that awful flat with

Tammy, remembering all too vividly what that felt like. The card specifically said *tied up*. Clarke had no doubts it was meant literally. There was no time to waste.

She ran downstairs. Reception was empty. Her stomach rumbled, reminding her of the breakfast she would have to skip, as she pressed the buzzer on the desk several times. A young woman appeared.

"Please, can you confirm if Diana Pettis checked in last night? She's my mother."

The receptionist typed something into her computer, not seeming to notice how much Clarke's voice shook.

"Please, hurry."

"Computer's a bit slow this morning." The girl looked as if she couldn't care less.

Clarke balled her fists and dug her nails into her palms, trying to manage her frustration.

"No. She's a no-show," the woman confirmed at last.

"Are you sure?" Clarke's hopes that the card would prove to be a sick wind-up were instantly destroyed. She rushed outside and headed for her car, which she'd left in the far corner of the car park. As she ran towards it, she tried to stay calm, but inside, she was reliving her ordeal of two years ago.

Thankfully, traffic was light at this time in the morning. Clarke checked her mileage and tried to calculate how much petrol might be left in the tank, cursing the stupid broken fuel gauge. She should have got it mended. Performing a rough calculation in her head took her mind off Tammy for a moment. The car would get to Tredington all right, but she would need to fill up the tank before driving back to the hotel.

Approaching Tredington, the traffic slowed. Clarke rapped her hand on the steering wheel in frustration, terrified of what might happen to Mum if she didn't find her on time. The delay turned out to be caused by a broken-down car. After a few minutes, the traffic started to move again.

Thank God she was soon back up to speed and approaching Tredington. She pressed her foot hard on the accelerator. Now was not the time to worry about a speeding ticket, although getting stopped would delay her, which would be a disaster. She kept glancing in her rear-view mirror for any sign of traffic police.

Clarke reached Remembrance Road at 7:50 a.m. The road turned out to be even closer to the derelict block of flats than it appeared on the road map. Dreading meeting Tammy again but fearing far more that Tammy might have hurt her mum, she drove down the entire length of the road holding her breath, whilst searching for a parking space.

At this time of day, the residents' cars filled most of the roadside spaces. If she waited an hour, they would start to go out for the day, and their coveted parking slots would be snatched up by shoppers. This wasn't an easy place to park at the best of times.

She found one space, but someone had placed traffic cones across it, probably one of the adjacent flats attempting to save a space for a visitor. Well, she needed it more than they did. Quickly, she got out of the car and moved the cones, then reversed into the space. She walked swiftly towards the flats.

When she saw them close up, she was shocked. They were in an even worse condition than they had been a couple of years ago. But more distressing than that, they brought back memories of the time she'd spent trapped inside with Tammy, memories she had tried to forget. Did Tammy choose this place deliberately to torture her?

She really didn't need a repeat of those dreadful few days. But she'd been naïve then. She wouldn't make the same mistakes this time.

Clarke checked around the outside of the building, trying to find an entry point, in case... In case of what? Her mum had to be somewhere. If Tammy was holding her inside the flats... Whatever happened, Clarke had no choice but to go inside.

Metal fencing surrounded the building. Clarke pushed at the fence panels before eventually finding a loose one. She could probably squeeze through if necessary. Did Tammy discover the same loose panel and take her mother inside?

A plastic-covered notice tied to the fence fluttered in the slight breeze. Clarke began to read it. The first couple of sentences told her the entire block was going to be demolished.

A sudden movement behind her startled Clarke, and she began to spin round, but she was too late. Something hard bashed against her head. In a few short moments, dizziness overtook her, and the world turned black.

Clarke regained consciousness, not quite sure where she was. She gazed at the hazy block of flats above her. Slowly, she got to her feet, trying to piece together what had happened. She patted at the pockets in her coat, trying to find her phone. Every pocket was empty. Her phone was gone. Her keys and purse were missing too, but she had no memory of being mugged.

Her car was parked in the next road. She remembered that. Her head throbbed as she walked lethargically down the street.

The car was gone. Did she misremember where she parked it? Impossible. She recognised the traffic cones she'd stacked to one side next to the empty space. This was definitely the spot.

Now she recalled why she came here. The thought flew into her head like a bad nightmare. Tammy. She came here to meet Tammy. And to find her mum.

Tammy must have taken everything from her pocket. She must have found the car. But if Tammy had left, where was her mother? Clarke was becoming increasingly worried. She looked over at the flats in the distance. Surely there was a reason why Tammy brought her here, to this exact place. Maybe her mother was inside. She had to check.

Her mother may have been in those flats since last night. Who knew what state she might be in by now. She had to find her.

It was too early for anybody to be about yet. No one to ask for help. In any case, Tammy had warned her not to involve anyone else. If her mother wasn't in the flats, that meant Tammy still had her. She wasn't prepared to risk breaking Tammy's rules.

Clarke pushed at the loose spot in the fencing enclosing the flats until she made the gap big enough to crawl through. Now she simply had to get inside the building.

Everything was boarded up more professionally than the last time she was here. She walked around the back of the block. A solitary board was missing from a ground-floor window. Quickly, she heaved herself up and climbed through the glassless window frame.

As she stood in the stairwell inside, she wondered if she should call out. What if Tammy hadn't left? What if Tammy was waiting for her inside? If that was her plan, a showdown between the two of them, it would be better to surprise her. She kept quiet.

She started up the staircase, tiptoeing on the concrete steps so as not to make any noise. All of her senses were heightened as she remained alert for any signs of Tammy, any signs of trouble, and, most of all, any signs of her mum.

The most obvious place to search would be in that same flat, on the fifth floor, but she wasn't sure which door to take as she never got to see it from outside. When Tammy brought her in here two years ago, she'd been dragged in unconscious. Then when she escaped, the only possible way out had been through the window, climbing down an old fire escape ladder from the fifth floor. She shuddered at the frightening memory, hoping she would never have to do that again.

Four different doors led off of the fifth-floor landing. Which one? Quickly, she tried them all.

Three of them were locked. The remaining one wasn't. The lock was broken and looked to have been forced open at one time. She remembered how she and Tammy had fought and lost the key, getting trapped inside. This must be the one. The police would have forced it to get to Tammy. She pushed the door open tentatively, listening for any signs of life.

A faint groan made her jump. *Mum?* She ventured further into the room. Fear of being locked in again made her panic, but she forced herself to think logically. It would be impossible to trap her inside with the lock broken. She took a deep breath. Somehow, she had to do this.

A big, dirty pink heap on the floor drew her attention. It moved slightly. Clarke jumped back a step, her heart racing with fear until her eyes focused more clearly.

"Mum?" Clarke ran towards the heap. A filthy duvet. Something moved beneath it. She snatched at the duvet, pulling it away, afraid of what it might reveal.

"Mum. Are you ok?" She knelt down to hug her, wanting to cry with relief.

Her mother opened her eyes and blinked. She must have been in the dark under that duvet since yesterday.

"It's ok, Mum. I'm going to get you out of here. You're ok now."

Clarke took hold of the tape across Diana Pettis's mouth. Diana winced as Clarke ripped it off.

"Sorry."

Diana took a few deep breaths. "What time is it?" she asked.

"Nearly nine a.m.," Clarke said.

"Saturday?"

"Yes, Saturday."

"The wedding?"

"Don't worry about that." Clarke was surprised that she had forgotten about her wedding. Her heart sank. They would have to cancel it. There was no way they could go ahead now, not with Mum in this state. "We need to take care of you."

"Clarke, you're getting married today. I wouldn't miss it for the world, so hurry up."

Clarke recognised her mother's *I must be obeyed voice*. It was a long time since she'd used it. She would have to humour her, but she would do the sensible thing, the right thing. And no doubt, when they got safely home, she would have a damn good cry about it.

"What happened?" Mum's hands and legs were tied with rope. How could Tammy have got her up here?

"I don't know." Diana shook her head. "I woke up here, but I don't remember anything before that."

Clarke worked at the knots, starting with the rope around Diana's legs. The red marks beneath the rope evidenced it being tied too tightly. When Tammy had brought her here, she had used chloroform to knock her unconscious. Could she have done the same thing to her mum? She tried to wriggle the rope free, worrying it may have restricted Mum's circulation and done some damage, but it was a slow process without anything to cut it.

"I'll be right back," she promised, reluctant to leave her mum, even for a minute. Clarke dashed out of the flat door towards one of the other flats on this floor, forgetting that all the other doors were locked. There must be a kitchen in this flat.

She searched around and found what was once a kitchen. The cupboards were falling apart, and the sink was missing, leaving an array of rusting pipework. Some of the cupboards still contained oddments of crockery. Clarke dived for a bank of drawers and began to pull them open, swiftly finding what she'd been searching for, a cutlery drawer. She rummaged through the contents, finding some rusty cutlery. Some old dinner knives appeared too blunt to be of any use, but plenty of other utensils might help. She pounced on a carving knife and some scissors that seemed to have escaped the rust, hoping that neither was completely blunt.

"Where have you been?" Her mother was in a panic.

"Don't worry. I've found something to help us." She brandished the carving knife, trying to stay calm to reassure her mother, and slid it underneath one of the pieces of rope around her mum's legs. She started to saw at the rope.

It was a slow job, but it was having an effect. Once she had broken through part of the rope, she picked up scissors, managing to dig them in between the remaining strands of rope, hacking through a few strands at a time.

"Hurry up," Mum urged. "We need to get out of here. We are absolutely not going to miss your wedding."

"Don't worry about that." Clarke eased the carving knife under the last few strands of rope. "It's more important to make sure you're all right." She sawed at the rope. It didn't take long to break through. She pulled the remnants of rope away.

Diana rubbed at her legs. The bright red marks around them looked sore.

"Give me your hands," Clarke said. It had taken far too long to release Mum's legs. It might be quicker to get the rope off her hands. She would use the same tactics. Carefully, she slid the carving knife underneath the rope around her mum's wrists, being ultra-careful to avoid nicking a vital artery. They had plenty of time. Tammy wouldn't be coming back, not if she'd stolen Clarke's car, and it would take a while for the circulation to return fully to Mum's legs, so she would take as long as she needed.

Suddenly, a huge crash made her mum scream. Clarke jumped at the same time.

"What was that?" Diana sounded scared.

"I don't know." Clarke ignored it and kept carefully sawing away with the carving knife.

A few moments later, another crash made them both scream.

"What's going on?" Diana tried to get up, wobbling before her legs gave way under her.

"I'll go and find out," Clarke said. "Try to wriggle your legs to get your circulation going again, so you can walk." Her mum must have been tied up all night. No wonder her legs refused to work. Clarke ran to the window on the far side of the room. She saw no sign of anything outside.

"I'll be right back," she said. She went back out onto the landing, racing to the window at the other end.

Gasping at the sight outside, she stepped back from the window. A huge crane filled the garden, and a giant wrecking ball swung straight towards the flats. Today must be demolition day. How had she not noticed that? They needed to get out fast.

Clarke remembered now that she'd been reading the notice outside when she'd been knocked unconscious. If only she'd been able to read it to the end. But then she might not have come inside. She might not have found her mum. She might have lost her. Clarke pulled herself together. She might still lose her if she didn't act quickly.

Her mum was walking around slowly when she got back.

"Come on, we need to leave," Clarke said.

"What's going on?"

"It's nothing," Clarke lied, not wanting to panic her mother. "Let's go."

"Can you untie my hands first?"

"We can do that later." There really was no time. Clarke picked up the scissors and took her mum's arm.

"We need to get outside." They headed for the stairs. Another crash echoed through the empty building. A fine mist of dust fell from the ceiling, making Clarke sneeze loudly.

Clarke pulled her mother towards the stairs. She was walking too slowly. Clarke bent down in front of her and leant her over her shoulder in a fireman's lift. It was a long time since she'd done this.

She clung onto her mother with one hand and held the banister with her other, descending two flights of stairs.

More crashing noises, closer now, encouraged her on. Clarke turned away as rubble flew towards them, showering them in dust. They fell back onto the stairs.

"Oh my God."

Diana opened her eyes and screamed as a gaping hole appeared in the wall next to the stairwell.

Clarke linked her arm through Diana's. "Come on. We need to hurry." Her mum walked faster now, and Clarke half dragged her down another flight of stairs.

A thunderous bang nearly deafened them, covering them in a cloud of brick dust. Clarke kept going. Only one more flight of stairs to go.

Again, the terrifying crunch of metal on brick signalled that time would soon run out. A gaping hole opened up in the stairwell wall. Three of the steps below them had disintegrated.

They stopped abruptly. Clarke quickly surveyed the damage. They would need to jump down.

"I can't do it," Mum protested, "not with my hands tied."

"I'll lower you down. Come on, you have to try. Hurry." Clarke grasped her by the shoulders and lifted her until her feet dangled only a few inches from the lower stairs. Thank God her mum was lightweight. Clarke was grateful for her well-muscled swimmer's arms. She would need to hold her steady and lower her gently.

"I have to let go now. Bend your knees when you land. You'll be fine." Clarke leant over as far as possible.

She let go. Diana fell back and rolled down several stairs. For a moment, she lay still. Clarke worried that she was hurt. Then she got up, struggling to regain her feet without being able to use her hands properly.

Clarke forced herself to hurry. That wrecking ball would be straight back any second soon. Clarke's terror of landing on her bad leg made her hesitate, even though she had the banister to hold on to. She psyched herself up to jump.

Another almighty crash beside her made her leap back against the banister. She closed her eyes to protect them from another shower of dust and grit. Below her, Diana screamed.

When Clarke opened her eyes a couple of seconds later, several more stairs had disappeared.

"Clarke? Are you ok?"

"I'm fine," she shouted. Seeing the carnage below her, she was anything but fine, but she didn't want to panic her mother.

"You can't get down now. You'll have to find another way."

Clarke gulped. There wasn't another way. She pulled at the banister. It still felt pretty solid. Any moment now, that wrecking ball would strike again. Taking a deep breath, she leant over the banister and let go.

She slid slowly several yards down the banister, then suddenly picked up speed. She shot off the corner of the banister as the stairs turned the corner, losing her balance and landing in an ungainly heap on the floor.

She gazed up at her mother walking towards her and jumped to her feet, rushing to help her mum. They ran to the bottom of the stairs just before the wrecking ball punched another hole in the wall. The whole of the stairwell started to crumble behind them.

Clarke searched for the window where she had entered the building. The wall above it had collapsed into a pile of rubble. There would be no chance of getting out that way. It put them right in the firing line.

"Come on, this way." She dragged her mother through the building, running to the corner opposite the demolition site.

There must be other windows. She vaguely recalled that all the others were firmly boarded up, but somehow, they must escape this death trap. She found a window on the other side of the flats. As expected, it was boarded up. She pushed against the board as hard as she could, shoving her shoulder into it. The board moved slightly.

She examined it further. It was screwed on much too firmly for them to push it off.

Chapter 27

Clarke stared at the boarded window. How were they ever going to get such a solid board off? Suddenly, in a flash of brilliance, she remembered the scissors. They were still in her back pocket. By some miracle, she'd managed not to stab herself when she fell off the banister, but they were still firmly wedged in. She pulled the scissors from her pocket. They might work as a makeshift screwdriver.

Clarke started to undo the screws. They were stiff, but opening the scissors out enabled her to use them as a lever. With a bit of work, she managed to remove one of the screws.

The carnage behind them became worse with every minute. How long before the whole building became unstable? Or the wrecking ball moved to this side of the building? They really needed to hurry.

Clarke worked three more screws out. Her fingers were starting to blister.

"We can push the board out now," Diana said. "There'll be a gap."

"Just one more." The gap didn't look big enough yet.

The dust was choking them, although Clarke worried more about the ominous creaking sounds as the building tried to decide when to give up its fight and crumble to the ground. The ceiling would collapse soon. If they were still inside when it did... She worked the scissors urgently, taking out the next screw more rapidly than the first.

A big hole gaped in the far wall, so now the noise of the machinery outside deafened them, their fear amplifying the sound still further.

"Let's both push on this part of the board as hard as we can. Put your shoulder into it," Clarke said.

They both leant against the filthy piece of wood. It started to give. Clarke thumped her shoulder hard against it.

"It's moving," Diana said. "Come on, keep trying."

"After three," Clarke said. "One, two, three." They gave it a huge push, leaning their combined weight into the board. It began to move before splintering and giving way.

Clarke helped Diana to climb out. She found it difficult with her hands still tied together and landed in an ungainly heap on the ground outside. Clarke hoisted herself up and scrambled through the hole. Quickly, she helped her mum to her feet, and they ran towards the perimeter fence.

Clarke turned and surveyed the building. The place where she'd got through the fence was behind the crane. There was no way to reach it safely. But they were too close to the building to stay here. When it fell, it would create no end of rubble and dust.

She took her mother's arm and ran towards the crane, waving her other arm in an effort to get noticed. Her shouts were drowned out by the noise and, as she got closer, she noticed the driver's earmuffs. He would never hear anything. She kept waving. They just needed him to glance this way.

The building looked unstable and started to collapse in places. They needed to get further away. They needed to be outside the perimeter fence. It wouldn't be safe to stay here much longer.

At last, the driver looked in their direction.

Clarke waved her arms at him, hoping he would notice her through the haze of dust. A moment later, the noise stopped as the driver turned the engine off. He climbed down from the cab and walked towards them.

"You shouldn't be in here," he shouted angrily. "Are you crazy? It's dangerous."

"I'm sorry," Clarke said. "Please, how do we get out?"

"Come with me."

Clarke and Diana followed him gratefully. He didn't seem to notice that Diana's hands were tied together. He was too intent on berating them and escorting them off the premises as quickly as possible.

"As soon as we get out of here, can you please untie my hands?" Diana whispered.

That was the least of their worries. Clarke began to realise how lucky they were. Buildings like this were usually demolished by setting explosives at the base of the building. If that had happened, the whole building would have imploded on top of them. Tammy must want them both dead. Clarke was frightened now that she would come after them again once she realised her failure.

The crane driver pulled back the fencing to reveal a tall gate. He undid the padlock and pulled it open. "I should report you to the police," he said.

"We're really sorry," Diana said. "My daughter's getting married today." She nodded at Clarke.

"So, what was this, some sort of hen night prank? They might have killed you both. Didn't they realise we were going to demolish these flats today? There are notices everywhere." He shook his head in disbelief.

"It won't happen again, we promise, and thank you for your help," Clarke said. "Just one more thing. Do you have a phone? We've lost ours and we really need to phone for help."

"You're not wrong. Look at the state of you." Reluctantly, he took his phone out of his jacket and thrust it at them.

Clarke took it gratefully and dialled her dad's number, one of the few numbers she knew by heart. "Can you come and collect us, please?" She gave him the address, ignoring his requests for more information.

She looked at her mum, covered in brick dust, tired, and scared, with who knew what injuries. Dad would be horrified by the state of them.

It was nearly ten o'clock. Clarke had noted the time from the crane driver's phone. They sat down on the pavement outside the building site and Clarke took out the scissors to work on the rope around Mum's wrists.

"We've still got a wedding to get to," Mum said, wincing as the scissors dug into a sore spot.

"I'm taking you to the hospital first. You need to get checked out properly." She needed to contact Paul. He would understand.

"I'm absolutely fine," Diana insisted. "I'm not going to be responsible for my daughter missing her wedding. I've waited a long time for this."

"You've been tied up all night, and you're not fine." Clarke finally cut through the last strands of rope, pulling them away. Diana's wrists were red, and the ropes had drawn blood on one wrist, which had congealed into a dark mass where the rope dug in.

"Thank you. That's much better." Diana touched her wrists cautiously, examining the damage. "I'll get checked out afterwards, but really, I'm ok, apart from my wrists and my legs being a bit sore and being covered in dust. A long, hot shower and some breakfast will soon sort me out."

"But—"

"I'm fine. Are you ok?"

"Yes," Clarke said. Her ankle hurt, but a couple of paracetamol would remedy that. She wondered what to do about Tammy. Mum was right. They should get on with the wedding. If she cancelled it now, Tammy would have won.

She tried to work out how quickly Dad would get here. He would probably be another forty minutes. At least that would give them time to calm down and make a plan.

"We need to get organised. What do we need to do?" Her mum said, as if reading her mind.

"We'll have to go back to your place first to pick up your clothes." Dad intended to bring them to the hotel. Would he worry that something was wrong and forget?

"Why don't we both have a shower at ours? We've got two bathrooms and I can lend you some clothes."

"That's a great idea." At least they would look vaguely respectable when they arrived at the hotel. Clarke's wedding dress and everything else was there already.

"Ok, that's the plan," Diana said.

"Are you sure you don't need to go to the hospital and get checked out first?" Clarke was still concerned about her mum. "Does it hurt anywhere?"

"Stop worrying. It's only a bit of soreness. I can put something on it when I get home. Everything will be ok."

Clarke hoped her mum was right. She tried to put Tammy out of her head for now and concentrate on the wedding. The ceremony was scheduled for one thirty. Now she started to worry that they wouldn't make it on time. She couldn't even phone Paul yet to tell him what had happened.

Dad would be ages yet. She needed to phone the police. Tammy must have taken her car. If they found the car, they would find Tammy. It was the best chance they'd had so far. They might be able to catch her before she did any more harm.

A young woman came out of one of the nearby houses.

Clarke walked up to her. "Excuse me. I need to phone the police. My car and phone have been stolen."

The woman looked wary and Clarke remembered the state they were both in. She smiled, dreading to think what the woman must think of her appearance, covered in building-site debris.

"What happened to you?" she asked, taking a step back.

"We had an accident." It wasn't strictly the truth, but she needed to persuade the woman to help. "Please, I need to call the police urgently. It's really important."

The woman took her phone out of her bag, unlocked it, and handed it to Clarke.

Clarke dialled 999, quickly giving her location. She told them her car registration number. "I think Tammy Doncaster has stolen it," she said. "She took my keys."

The operator didn't appear to recognise Tammy's name.

"Tammy Doncaster," Clarke repeated. "She escaped from Ranleigh Marsh prison a few days ago."

"We'll send somebody out to you," the operator said.

"No," Clarke said. "We can't stay here. We need to leave, but you must find Tammy Doncaster." She hung up the call before the operator got the chance to argue and handed the phone back to its owner, thanking the woman for her help.

Her mum seemed to be a little better already. Clarke hoped she would be all right and the pain in her legs and wrists was just temporary soreness, with no serious damage. Hopefully, there would be no lasting psychological effects from the experience, but Clarke understood how traumatic it could be, being imprisoned by Tammy. And it must have been worse for Mum, tied up and scared right from the start, knowing what Tammy had previously done.

Dad's car drew up sooner than expected. He got out and stared at them. "What have you done? Look at the state of you. What happened? Are you all right?" He spoke quickly, hardly allowing either of them to get a word in anywhere.

"Please take us home, love," Diana said. "We'll explain on the way."

Dad opened the car door for Diana. Clarke got in the back and fastened her seat belt. This was going to take one hell of an explanation.

"What about the wedding?" Dad asked.

"We need to go straight to the hotel, as soon as we're cleaned up," Diana said. "I won't let Clarke miss her wedding."

"Will we get there before the ceremony?" Clarke asked. Disoriented without her watch, she'd completely lost track of time. She tried to work out how long it would take to make herself look presentable enough to get married. She leaned over to get a look at herself in the rear-view mirror, shocked at what she saw. She'd need more than a hairdresser to sort this out. Paul would change his mind and run as soon as he saw her.

"It will be tight," Dad said.

Clarke trusted him to do his best.

They were silent as they drove out onto Tredington High Street and headed north. Clarke was relieved at first that her father didn't press them for details. She broke the silence at last. "It was Tammy."

"That woman." Her father banged his fist on the steering wheel. "Did she hurt you?"

"We're ok," Diana said. "The police may catch her. She stole Clarke's car."

"That woman's been nothing but trouble. She's dangerous, and I don't want you going anywhere near her. She needs to be locked up again."

Clarke silently agreed, but it was her that Tammy wanted. She only took her mother as a way of getting Clarke to come to the old block of flats. She must have wanted to kill her. Why else would she choose that place on demolition day? If Tammy was so hell-bent on revenge, Clarke didn't know what would stop her. How could she get married, with Tammy still free, or go off on her honeymoon, worrying that her mother might still be in danger?

She thought of Paul. For his sake, she would have to put this behind her for the rest of the day and show up to marry the man she loved. Time enough to worry about Tammy afterwards. Paul would know what to do for the best.

"How did you get covered in dirt? You're filthy," Dad said.

"It's a long story." Clarke started to relate some of the morning's events.

Diana interrupted. "Can we concentrate on the wedding today, please? It's supposed to be a happy day. And if you don't put your foot down a bit, love, we'll be too late. We've got to go back to our place, take a shower, then get to the hotel in time for Clarke to get dressed."

"We need a miracle," Dad said as he turned onto the dual carriageway.

Clarke hoped there weren't any traffic police around because she was sure her father was vastly exceeding the speed limit.

Chapter 28

After what seemed like an eternity, they pulled into her parents' driveway. They all piled out of the car at once, and her dad rushed to unlock the front door.

Her mother took charge as soon as they got upstairs. "One bathroom each. Let's get cleaned up."

The warm water running all over her was the most wonderful sensation in the world to Clarke. She turned it up to full power, trying to rinse off every last bit of dust, every last bit of Tammy. Then she washed her hair at a record speed, worrying she wouldn't have time to dry it properly before they left for the hotel.

Her dad was right. It would take a miracle to get to the hotel on time. What would happen if they were late? Would the registrar be booked for another wedding? Saturday was their busiest day. She'd booked the hairdresser to come to her hotel room to put her hair up. No way would she get there in time for that. The hairdresser was going to do Gina's hair too. Gina would be waiting for her by now, worried that she hadn't shown, not even able to get her on the phone as Tammy had taken it. Suddenly, she wondered if Tammy would use her phone, sending texts, like she'd sent Clarke that text from Mum's phone last night. Clarke never bothered locking her phone as she so rarely let it out of her sight. She got frustrated having to unlock it every time she wanted to use it, so she simply never did.

What would Tammy tell Gina? Or maybe she'd text Rob instead. Maybe she'd completely misdirect them. She told herself not to be so stupid. Tammy would have dumped the phone, afraid she would be traced if she kept it.

She speedily rinsed off her hair, grabbed some towels, then wrapped her hair in one and herself in the larger one.

"Dad," she yelled down the stairs.

Her father poked his head out of the spare bedroom. "I'm here. No need to shout so loud."

"Please, can you phone Rob? Explain things but tell him not to worry Paul. And tell him Tammy has my phone." She went to her mum's bedroom, tapping at the door before she opened it.

"I'm nearly ready, love. I'm just getting dressed. Raid my wardrobe for something to wear to the hotel."

Clarke opened the wardrobe and dragged out a top and a skirt. Not the trendiest gear ever, but she would only be wearing it briefly. She pulled the clothes on quickly.

"Have you got a hair dryer?"

Diana pointed to the dressing table.

Clarke tried to dry her hair. It was thick, so it always took ages.

Her mother was dressing. As soon as she was ready, they would have to go. She didn't want to rush her, but she willed her to hurry.

"We need to put something on your wrists," Clarke said, noticing the soreness.

"There's some ointment in the bathroom cabinet. Can you fetch it, please?" Diana said, gingerly pulling on her tights over the sore spots on her legs. At least the dark-coloured tights would hide any telltale marks.

Clarke found some antiseptic cream in a cupboard in the en suite bathroom. That would have to do.

Diana had bought a lovely pale-yellow dress for the wedding. Clarke gasped. She looked stunning in it. What a transformation from the dirty, ravaged woman of twenty minutes earlier. Perhaps there was hope for her too. For the first time this morning, Clarke looked forward to her wedding.

Diana took the antiseptic cream and smoothed some onto her wrists, popping the tube into her handbag for later.

Clarke's hair was still damp. It would probably go frizzy. Damn Tammy. This wasn't how she'd imagined getting ready on her wedding day.

Her mum came over to her. "You've got a nasty scratch on your arm," she said. "That's going to show when you're wearing your wedding dress."

"Can we cover it up somehow?"

Diana opened one of the drawers in her dressing table and pulled out some silk scarfs, picking a lovely turquoise one. She wrapped it around Clarke's arm, tying it in a pretty bow. Then she selected two cream-coloured scarves.

"Can you tie these around my wrists?" she said. "There's no way I can disguise these marks. I wanted to use bracelets, but they'll rub on the wounds and make them worse."

Clarke tied them on, not making such a neat job of the bows as her mother had done on her. Then, quickly, she pulled on some clothes and put her dirty shoes back on.

"We need to go. I hope your dad's changed and ready."

"Yes, he's dressing in the spare bedroom," Clarke said. "Don't forget your hat," she added. Clarke had been shopping with her mum when she bought her outfit and helped her buy a very expensive feathered yellow hat to match her dress. As mother of the bride, Diana wanted to really splash out and look fabulous, but if they didn't hurry, there would be no bride and no wedding.

Dad waited at the bottom of the stairs. "Ready?"

Her mum grabbed a couple of towels from the airing cupboard. She passed one to Clarke. "Spread that over the car seat. It will be filthy from all that dirt we brought in when we came back." She arranged her own towel over the front seat, tucking it in carefully to protect her dress from getting dirty.

"Let's go," she said.

The hotel where the wedding was being held was almost an hour away, with the wedding due to start in an hour, and Clarke still wasn't dressed.

Clarke held her breath the entire journey.

"I phoned Rob," her dad said. "He's going to try to make sure the registrar can stay a bit longer."

"Thanks, Dad." Clarke breathed a sigh of relief. She didn't want to ruin the wedding ceremony by worrying Paul. This gave her plenty of time to tell him everything later. It was no way to start married life, lying to your husband before you've even taken the wedding vows, but it couldn't be helped. Besides, at this rate, there still might not be a wedding.

As they pulled into the hotel car park, DC Kevin Farrier ran out to meet them.

"We found your car," he said. "It looks like it ran out of petrol only a few miles out of Tredington."

"What about Tammy?" Clarke asked.

"There's no sign of her."

Clarke's heart sank. She'd desperately hoped that the police would manage to pick Tammy up with the car. At least Clarke was thankful she didn't get that petrol gauge fixed. Otherwise, Tammy might be miles away by now. Although, in reality, that was what she wanted. Clarke realised how terrified she was of Tammy coming back for her.

She pushed the thought aside and raced into the hotel. Halfway up the stairs, she realised she didn't have her room key. Tammy must have taken that too.

For a moment, she wondered if Tammy would be sitting in her room, waiting for her. She shuddered. No, she should rein in her imagination. Tammy would want to get away. She wouldn't risk coming here.

She passed her dad on her way downstairs. "Keep going, I'll meet you outside my room," she said.

She pressed the bell on the reception desk several times. "I've lost my key," she blurted out. "I'm really sorry. I need to get in quickly. I'm getting married five minutes ago."

The receptionist gave her a spare pass key. "Don't lose this one, please," she said, but Clarke was already through the door to the stairs.

She ran up and a minute later, she burst into the hotel room. Her dad followed her in.

"Dad, can you find Gina and send her up here to help me get dressed? Then find Paul. Don't tell either of them anything to worry them. I'll meet you at reception as soon as I'm dressed. I won't be long." She would need a lightning quick change or she would be very late indeed.

Gina was brilliant. She'd known something was wrong, and Clarke didn't have time to tell her the full story. Gina worked magic with Clarke's hair and did her makeup perfectly in no time at all.

They walked towards the big reception room where the ceremony was to be held.

"Calm down," Gina said. "It's traditional for the bride to be late."

Clarke smiled and tried to breathe deeply. It was all going to be ok.

Dad was waiting for them outside the door. "What's the scarf for?" he asked, pointing to the silk scarf Mum had tied around her arm earlier to hide the scratch.

"Something borrowed, something blue." Clarke smiled at him.

He opened the door and took her arm. At the front of the room, Paul turned towards her and grinned. At the sight of him, Clarke immediately relaxed. Everything was going to be all right.

After the ceremony and the tedious photo session, Clarke and Paul still had half an hour free before the meal. The guests seemed happy chatting with each other.

"Shall we pop up to our room and freshen up?" Clarke suggested. It would be nice to have a few minutes to themselves. "It's getting a bit much being the centre of attention after the morning I've had."

"Yes, what morning have you had?" Paul asked. "You still haven't explained."

"Let's slip away now before anybody spots us, and I'll give you the quick version," Clarke said. There wouldn't be time yet for the full story.

They managed to sneak out without anyone noticing. As they reached the room, Paul stopped her outside the door and kissed her.

"I can't believe we are Mr and Mrs Waterford now."

"Me neither." Clarke was far more incredulous than Paul. Earlier today, she wasn't convinced she'd even make it to the wedding.

Paul put his key card in the door and pushed it open. The curtains were drawn inside, making the room dark. He fumbled for the light switch. It didn't work.

"Doh," he said. "I forgot you have to put the card in the slot to make the lights work."

The lights came on as Clarke entered the room behind Paul.

As the door clicked shut, a whirling shape appeared in front of them.

Clarke gasped. Tammy waved a knife threateningly towards Paul. She looked wired. Paul stopped abruptly.

"Keep away from me," Tammy screamed. "I'll kill you if you come any closer."

Clarke breathed in deeply, trying to stay calm. "Tammy, please don't do anything stupid. We can talk about this."

"What is there to talk about? You ruined my life."

"No," Clarke said. "You ruined it yourself." Tammy was ruining their wedding day too. "I didn't steal that money. And I didn't murder anybody either." Had she really wasted the last two years feeling sorry for this woman? Clarke finally began to realise that her mother was right. Tammy had brought everything upon herself. It was time she faced up to that.

"I'm not going back to prison."

"Let's talk about this sensibly. It won't help you if you kill anybody else." Clarke shuddered, terrified that Paul would rush in bullheaded and get stabbed. Now she couldn't erase the image from her head. She couldn't lose him now, not after less than an hour of being Mrs Waterford.

"Tammy, put the knife down," Paul said.

Tammy ignored him.

"Things will be much worse if you don't come quietly."

"I'm not coming at all." Tammy moved closer to Paul.

"Clarke, go outside and call the police," Paul said.

Clarke didn't want to leave him, especially knowing what Tammy was capable of. A roomful of police officers waited downstairs for the wedding reception. The irony of that wasn't lost on her. But they would never realise what was going on up here until it was too late. Unless she fetched them. She started to inch towards the door.

"Stop," Tammy shouted. "Nobody's leaving this room. If you leave, I'll kill him, I swear."

Clarke froze and turned back towards Tammy.

"Clarke, go," Paul said.

"I'll kill him if you do."

Paul was an experienced police officer who could handle himself well, but he was no match for a crazed woman with a knife. He always told Clarke he would rather face a gun than a knife.

"Tammy, what are you doing here? You could have left the country by now." Clarke still didn't understand it.

Tammy glared at her. "Unfinished business," she said. "I don't want you following me. You're so damn persistent. You never give up, do you?"

It was true. Clarke realised she was far too persistent for her own good. If only she'd let things go when she first suspected someone was embezzling money from Briar Holman. She might have died because of her dogged tenacity. Her mother had suffered tremendously in the last few hours because of her pig-headedness. And now Paul was going to suffer too. Would she have done anything differently if she'd known? She let the question hang in her mind, not daring to answer it in case she didn't like the response.

Paul tried again. "Tammy, put the knife down."

"Oh, shut up," Tammy snapped.

Clarke wasn't sure what to do. Tammy wasn't open to negotiation. In fact, she appeared to be on the edge of losing control altogether. Clarke couldn't let Tammy kill Paul, but how could she stop her? She glanced down at her dress. The beautiful slinky satin sheath that earlier made her feel like a film star, now impeded her every move, with its long, tight skirt and accompanying high-heeled shoes. Her feet were aching already, and her ankle pained her, especially after this morning's events.

Paul moved almost imperceptibly towards Tammy.

She spotted the movement. "Don't come any closer."

Clarke worried that Paul might be planning to tackle Tammy and wondered how to distract her, but the layout of the room enabled Tammy to watch both of them at the same time. She seemed more focused on Paul now, so Clarke risked a small step forwards.

Without anything to defend herself if the worst happened, she would be useless. If she moved closer to the dressing table, she might manage to pick up something to throw at Tammy. And that might give Paul a chance to disarm her.

"Tammy, let's sit down and talk about this sensibly," Paul said.

Tammy held the knife, her fingers almost pale as she gripped it tightly. "There's nothing to talk about. I win, you lose. That's the only possible outcome."

"There aren't any winners in this, Tammy. It's not a game."

Clarke was amazed at how calm Paul remained, but then he'd been trained for exactly this sort of thing. "Tammy, please, you've got all that money. You don't need to do this. Leave us alone," Clarke pleaded.

"I can't."

"You know we never found the money," Clarke said. "You were very clever at hiding it, so I'm sure you must be clever enough to have left the country by now. I can't believe you're still here. You can't have stayed just for me. What's really going on?"

Tammy shrugged.

Clarke wondered if someone had let her down. Like last time, when Tammy couldn't get away because she was waiting for her fake passport to be produced.

"I thought you were my friend," Tammy said. "You turned on me."

"I'm sorry," Clarke said. Part of her wasn't sorry at all, not anymore. "I had to do the right thing."

"Why must you have principles?"

Clarke ignored the question. Tammy appeared to have few principles, and look where it had got her. "Where did you hide the money, Tammy?"

"I'll never tell you. You're not getting your hands on my little nest egg."

Paul shifted from foot to foot. Clarke sensed he was getting restless and wondered when his patience would give out. Patience wasn't his greatest quality. She willed him not to do anything stupid.

"I wish things could go back to how they were," Clarke said. "Back at Briar Holman when we were working together. We had fun."

"Yes." Tammy looked wistful for a moment. "Yes, we did."

"I loved our time together. We were a great team." Clarke's tactic of talking about the old days seemed to be getting through to Tammy. Perhaps it would make her realise what she'd lost.

"I hated it there, especially the last few months, with Doug upstairs. Ken's lazy and Andrew's a prat. You were the only good thing about the job."

Clarke smiled at her and let her carry on talking.

"Anyway, we can't go back. Not now. It's too late."

"I didn't want to stay after you were gone," Clarke said. "It wasn't the same anymore."

"You moved out of the flat too, didn't you? Where have you been staying?"

Clarke had no intention of letting on to Tammy that she was staying with Rob. "In London," she said. Evan was right. She found it easy to tell little white lies.

Clarke's alarm clock sat on the dressing table, reminding her that in another five minutes, people would start to miss them. She supposed they would search up here, eventually. The heavy metal alarm clock sat almost within reach. She considered whether she could throw that at Tammy. If she hit her in the right place, it might disable her long enough for Paul to grab hold of her and take the knife. She slid along the wall a few more inches.

She was behind Paul, so he hadn't noticed her moving. Slowly, Clarke shuffled along the wall, hoping Tammy wouldn't spot her change in position. Tammy was too busy feeling sorry for herself, and she was focused much more on Paul, the main threat to her.

Clarke edged closer. A few more inches and she might be able to reach out and grab the alarm clock. She would aim for Tammy's head. Even if she missed her target, it would probably still be enough to distract her. If Paul took advantage of that, then they would be all right. She wondered how to communicate her intentions to Paul. Weren't couples in love supposed to sense these things? If only Paul were more perceptive.

Suddenly, Tammy lurched forward, screaming. Paul ducked, trying to avoid the knife, then, in a slick move, he knocked her to the floor and twisted her arms behind her back. "Tammy Doncaster, you're under arrest for the murder of Sadie Hunter."

Tammy struggled underneath Paul. Then, with no warning, he fell backwards. Clarke stared at him, horrified. Blood seeped from his stomach, his white shirt turning bright red. Tammy wiggled out from underneath him and quickly got to her feet.

"What have you done?" Clarke asked, moving towards her. Tammy dived for the knife. Clarke reacted instinctively, grabbing a perfume bottle, the nearest thing to hand on the dressing table. Instantly, she regretted her snap decision. It wasn't big or heavy enough to do any damage, not with Tammy still in possession of the knife.

She glanced at Paul. He lay on the floor, clutching his stomach. There was so much blood. In that moment, Tammy ran at her with the knife. Clarke screamed as she sprayed perfume in Tammy's eyes. Tammy dropped the knife, clasping her hands to her eyes.

"You've blinded me," she screamed. "Help me, I'm blind." Clarke saw her chance and pushed Tammy to the floor. Tammy curled up in a ball, still clutching her eyes and screaming. Clarke pulled at the scarf on her arm. The bow undid easily.

Clarke grasped Tammy's wrists, yanking them behind her back. She tied them tightly with the scarf. Quickly, she grabbed a towel from the bathroom, folded it, and put pressure on Paul's wound. She took his phone from his pocket and called for an ambulance. Then she called Rob, telling him to bring police and first aid urgently.

Paul's silence worried her. "Paul, Paul, can you hear me? Please say something. Please." She pressed the towel with all her strength, trying to stop the blood. She couldn't lose him. Not today.

Across the room, Tammy groaned. Clarke ignored her.

Someone knocked at the door. "Clarke?" It was Rob.

Clarke realised the door was locked. She leapt up and opened it, racing straight back to Paul to reapply pressure to his wound. It didn't seem to be bleeding anymore. She hoped he hadn't already lost too much blood.

"What happened?" Rob asked, kneeling down next to her.

Within seconds, the room filled with off-duty police officers. They piled in on Tammy. She wouldn't escape now.

"Tammy stabbed him," she said, her voice shaking. "The ambulance is on its way. Can someone go downstairs and wait for it?"

Rob dispatched someone. He put his arm around Clarke. "He'll be all right. Paul's strong."

Clarke wasn't so sure. Tears ran down her cheeks. How could she remain so calm and strong for other people's emergencies, but be such a wreck when the man she loved was lying in front of her unconscious and probably bleeding to death?

The paramedics arrived quickly. Clarke watched in a daze as they put a line into Paul's wrist and pushed a bag of fluid through.

"You should go with him," Rob said. "I'll drive to the hospital. I'll meet you there."

Chapter 29

Paul was in surgery by the time Rob found Clarke. Shortly after that, two detectives arrived. They offered to come back later, but Clarke wanted to talk to them while she waited. It helped. Much better than moping about dreading the worst. She recounted everything that happened since her trip to visit Tammy in prison.

"Can you think of anything else?" the female detective asked.

"There is one thing," Clarke said. It had been nagging at her for the last hour. She wasn't even sure she had the confidence to say it out loud. What if her hunch proved wrong? She might waste everybody's time and look really stupid. And yet, she was sure she was right about this. Tammy told her where the money was. She'd always thought she was much cleverer than Clarke, although she would never have said it outright. Was this what this entire mess was about, Tammy pitting her wits against Clarke, arrogantly expecting to win? She'd actually told her where the money was hidden. Clarke just hadn't realised it until now.

She gave the detective Katie's address in Dorset. "The money Tammy stole. The bank account code is written on the nesting boxes in their goose shed," she said. It sounded ludicrous now that she said it out loud, but she'd never been more sure of anything. It was Tammy's nest egg, she had said. Of course, three million pounds was a great nest egg, but there was something about the way she'd said it, emphasising the words, taunting her with them. The answer was in plain sight all this time.

"We'll need to get a warrant." The detective promised to let her know what happened.

It was three hours before Paul's surgery finished. The consultant came to talk to her.

"He was lucky. He should make a full recovery. Why don't you go and sit with him, so you'll be there when he wakes up."

Paul looked peaceful. He was still sleeping. The nurse in the recovery room kept a watchful eye on him. Clarke took his hand gently, and he opened his eyes.

"Are you ok?" Paul whispered.

Clarke gave him her biggest smile ever. "I should be asking you that."

"What happened? Did Tammy get away?"

"No. They got her. They've taken her to a high-security prison. She won't escape from there."

Paul reached out for Clarke's arm. "What did you do to your arm?" He pointed to the scratch on her upper arm, the one previously covered by the scarf. It was hardly significant compared to the wound Tammy had inflicted on Paul. Clarke realised she still hadn't found a spare moment to tell him about the morning's events. That would have to wait until he felt better.

There was a knock at the door. "Can I come in?" DCI Jonathan Price entered the room.

"Sorry, sir," Paul said.

"We're not at work now. Call me Jonathan." Jonathan Price sat on the spare chair at the end of the bed.

"Yes, sir, I mean Jonathan."

"Anyhow, what are you apologising for? We've got Tammy Doncaster, thanks to you and your amazing wife. And we've got the money too."

"You have?" Clarke was more surprised than anyone, having spent the last couple of hours doubting her hunch about where Tammy might have hidden it.

"Well, not the actual money, but we have the bank details. We traced some of it to a bank in St Kitts."

"That's where Tammy's from," Clarke said.

"That's brilliant news," Paul said, looking much perkier now. "What about the rest of the money?"

"Ned Young invested most of it in property," Jonathan said.

"Is that why Tammy didn't leave the country immediately, because Ned tied up most of the money in property, not expecting Tammy to need ready cash anytime soon?" Clarke didn't want to believe what Tammy said, that she'd stayed to make sure Clarke wouldn't pursue her anymore. She preferred to ignore the fact that Tammy might have wanted to kill her.

"We've arrested Young. He's confessed to everything. He and Karl Croft both helped Tammy after she escaped, and Ned was handling the stolen money."

"What about Katie?" Clarke asked.

"We don't think she was involved. She had no idea what her husband was doing," Jonathan said.

Clarke smiled. She had grown to like Katie Young. But even though Katie wouldn't face any charges, her life would still be destroyed by this.

"What about Sadie Hunter? We were sure she must have helped Tammy escape," Paul said.

"Tammy admitted to blackmailing Sadie, threatening her mother. She also said Sadie was friends with one of the security staff, and he helped her to smuggle stuff into the prison. We still don't know who it was, so they may still get off scot-free."

"And Maria Vasquez?" Paul asked quietly.

"Tammy Doncaster's new identity, as you suspected." Jonathan Price sighed. "We got lucky, I suppose. If she'd left the country straight away, we never would have caught her. She's quite some actress, though, fooling you and DC Medway like that."

"We didn't see her for very long," Paul protested. He groaned, as the exertion proved too much for him.

The nurse hurried over to check on Paul. "Two more minutes," she said firmly. "He needs his rest."

"It happens to us all," Jonathan said. "I could tell you some stories..." He smiled. "I just hope she doesn't ham it up too much in court and get a reduced sentence."

"How did Tammy get into our hotel room?" Paul asked.

Clarke squeezed his hand. "That's my fault. Tammy mugged me this morning. She took my car key, my phone, and my room pass."

"It's not your fault," Paul reassured her.

Clarke smiled. Paul was right. None of this was her fault. She finally believed that now.

"Of course it wasn't your fault," Jonathan said. He turned to Paul. "Clarke saved your life, from what I hear. You're a very lucky man."

"I know that," Paul said. He squeezed Clarke's hand. "I love you, Mrs Waterford."

Clarke beamed at him, knowing how much it took for Paul, who never liked to show any emotion, to admit that in front of his DCI. "I love you too, Mr Waterford." Today wasn't a disaster after all. It was the start of something wonderful.

THE THEFT

Find out what Clarke did in her previous career as a firefighter. This action-packed book is a prequel to The Clarke Pettis series. It's FREE to download when you sign up for my author newsletter.

This was twenty million pounds' worth of dangerous...
Firefighter Clarke Pettis' priority was saving lives, not possessions. But, when she discovers the painting that disappeared during the rescue of an injured man in a house fire was worth a fortune, Clarke couldn't leave things alone.
She puts herself in serious danger when she crosses paths with art thief, Antonio Balleri.
Can Clarke save herself from Balleri and find the stolen painting?

Be the first to find out about new releases, special offers, and other interesting stuff. Download the free book and sign up at https://dl.bookfunnel.com/hm3iserife.

A Letter to the Reader

Dear Reader,

Thank you so much for reading this book. Readers are by far the most important people in an author's world. Of all the millions of books you could have chosen to read, a massive THANK YOU for giving my book a chance. I really hope you enjoyed it.

I loved writing it. Tammy is my favourite character in this series, so I had to bring her back. Which character did you like best? I'd love to hear from you. You can contact me at christine@christinepattleauthor.com.

Finally, can I ask you a favour? Please would you review THE PAYBACK on Amazon. Reviews are so important to raise visibility and help other readers find my work.

Take Care

Christine

SECRETS NEVER DIE

Would you risk your life to save a baby?
Would you do anything you could to protect her from harm?
Even if that meant taking her and never giving her back?

Twenty-five years ago, Dan Peterson risked his life to rescue a baby from a dangerous cult, the Seventh Heavenites. That baby grew up to be the well-known model Pagan.

When Pagan gets the chance to be the face of a new perfume, she must spend a week working on the beautiful island of Jersey, the one place she will never be safe.

As Dan digs deeper into the past, he endangers both Pagan and her young daughter.

Can Dan protect Pagan from the Seventh Heavenites, and a secret that she knows nothing about?

SECRETS NEVER DIE is available on Amazon

About The Author

Christine Pattle writes mystery-thrillers with interesting characters and plenty of action. Her aim is always to write a good page-turning story that readers will love.

When she's not writing, she's busy scaring herself silly, riding big, feisty horses, or walking round the countryside dreaming up exciting new plots.

You can contact Christine at christine@christinepattleauthor
   Or visit her Facebook page ChristinePattleAuthor

Acknowledgments

A HUGE thank you:

To my brilliant editor, Emily at Laurence Editing.

Some of my readers have names some of my characters in this book. So, thank you to Ray, who chose *Kroft*'s name, Jan Tresize, who named *Janice,* Shaun, who picked *Shaun* for a character's name, and to Kevin Miles, who named *Bill*.

To my cover artist, Get Covers.

To all the authors who have ever inspired me.

To my parents for bringing me up to believe I could accomplish anything I wanted to in my life.

And to my fabulous friends who have encouraged me on my author journey.

Copyright

Copyright © Christine Pattle, 2023

Christine Pattle has asserted her right to be identified as the author of this work in accordance with the Copyright, Designs and Patents Act 1988.

All rights reserved. No part of this book may be reproduced, stored in any retrieval system, or transmitted, in any form or by any means, electronic, mechanical, photocopying, recording or otherwise, without the prior written permission of the author.

This book is a work of fiction. Names, characters, businesses, organisations, places and events other than those clearly in the public domain, are either the product of the author's imagination or are used fictitiously. Any resemblance to actual persons, living or dead, events or locales is entirely coincidental.

Printed in Great Britain
by Amazon